THE OBEDIENT WIFE

THE OBEDIENT WIFE

JULIA O'FAOLAIN

JAN 21 1986
CARROLL & GRAF PUBLISHERS, INC.
New York

First Carroll & Graf edition 1985

Carroll & Graf Publishers, Inc.
260 Fifth Avenue
New York, NY 10001

Library of Congress Cataloging in Publication Data

O'Faolain, Julia.
  The obedient wife.

  I. Title.
PR6065.F3026   1985   823'.914   85-17145
ISBN 0-88184-197-8

Manufactured in the United States of America

For Sean

THE
OBEDIENT WIFE

Chapter One

Weeks of rain had so distorted visibility that the Glen seemed to be under water and the mail van, nosing in, had the look of a bathyscaphe sent to probe its depths. The van paused at the Verdis' mail-box and the driver, shiny in a rain parka, poked in a bundle of papers. Assessing them through her front window, Carla guessed at bills and the presence of one or two airmail letters striped along the edges with the Italian national colours. These she would put off reading.

As the van moved off, she saw something scuttle past the drip of her bougainvillea. The rabbit! She ran out. Maurizio must have left the hutch open again. He cared as little for his old pet now as for the discarded toys she had finally sent to the Salvation Army. Lovelessness must have addled the creature's instincts. Something certainly had for it was running once again towards traffic instead of back to the safety of the hills. Carla could not have counted the times she'd found it cowering behind ashcans, dazed by trafficky decibels and smells.

'Got you!' It was guileless for all its urge to freedom.

'Freedom for what then, bunny?' Carefully she put the throbbing lump back in its hutch. Even in the hills there were rabbit-eating coyotes.

The rabbit nuzzled the wire. Twitch. Stare.

'*Tieni.*' She poked a lettuce leaf through and stood watching the busy flicker of the muzzle. Here, where furriness tapered to a point, was where its faculties were concentrated. Quiver. Sniff. It wasn't a visual beast at all, but an organism attuned to tactile progress in the dark. Turning, it struck her that lately, at a loss in her own life, she was a bit like that herself. 'Poor bunny,' she commiserated, '*poverino! Va!*' and left it nibbling at the ghost of a lettuce leaf.

The next time she saw it, it was dead. This was on a mild Saturday. The maximum temperature predicted for the Los Angeles area was the usual seventy degrees and she got home from shopping to see what looked like a wrung-out floor cloth hanging from her pomegranate tree. It was swollen with bulges which at first she took for knots. A closer look sent her rushing to the kitchen closet to grope for a shears, knife, anything to cut down the obscene thing whose innards had been pulled through a gash in its lower belly and hung – hell! She'd cut her finger on the blade. Grasping the handle, she climbed towards the tree, telling herself not to panic or be clumsy. The thing must be got rid of before Maurizio got home – not that he would be any more surprised than she was. There had been a rash of animal killings in the Glen. A cat had even been crucified on a cactus, its paws horridly splayed. Religious freaks, people guessed, or members of some Satanists' coven? There were a lot of oddballs living around. Panting, she turned her eyes from the mucus-covered red ones which were no longer luminous but sunken like small, leaky bags. Keeping her attention on the noose and off what she knew it to be supporting, she hacked. The carcass fell and she ran to the porch where she seized an old coat belonging to Maurizio – there was wear in it yet, but never mind – then back to throw it over the mangled remains of their pet. The next thing was to bury it. There was a spade but it was heavy. Her wrist trembled. *O piccola manina! Tosca.* Never meant for this. Indeed not. The spade cut downwards. Chip. It split a root and pith showed white like a limb disinterred. The Glen slopes were densely planted to prevent soil erosion. If the topsoil were to be washed away by winter rains this whole area could revert to the desert from whence it had come. Carla hacked and imagined

8

herself a pioneer woman: some early settler come in a waggon across the Mojave where some had been reduced to cannibalism. Had there, one wondered, been women among them as unsuited as herself to such a life?

When she'd finished, she felt both pleased and gloomy: the one because of having managed a man's job, the other because of having had to. She'd finally dug the hole deep enough, rolled the carcass in Maurizio's coat and tipped it in. Only then had it struck her that she ought to go through the pockets. Maurizio might have left something in them. At thirteen, he had moved from the stage of displaying possessions to one of intense secrecy. Pockets, drawers, locked boxes, secret hiding places were gorged with – well, with what one didn't know.

'I'm going through a phase,' was Maurizio's explanation. 'Don't worry, Mamma, everybody my age does.'

'Who told you that?'

'A boy in my school. He's been through dozens.'

She frisked the pockets. In an inner one, just as she had guessed, she found something: a notebook. Slipping it into her own pocket, she began tipping loose earth into the grave. When she'd finished, she tamped it flat and laid stones on it lest the softened ground be a temptation to burrowing dogs.

At one o'clock she tuned into a local news bulletin which was as minatory as an old-time rural gazette. The abnormal rainfall was to resume; slide areas were at risk and a major earthquake was thought likelier this year than in any of the previous hundred and twenty-three. On the front of the *LA Times*, which she had brought home from the market, a seismologist endorsed the message, showing a map of a cracked California.

Pessimism soothed her. Having a notion that private worries were somehow soluble in the acid misgivings streaming across public air, she had just the other day got up the nerve to do something she had been shirking since coming here. She had taken a driving test. The experience had been an ordeal, though not in the way she'd feared. For years she had been driving illegally with a licence obtained in Italy where her brother had sent the examiner a case of wine – not necessary, but she had felt bolstered. Here, how give a bribe? Coming from a woman might not a case of wine be misconstrued? And her husband was out

9

of town. ('Out of town,' was what she told anyone who rang. 'Sorry. No. Indefinitely. I can't really say.')

These conversations upset her. So did surrendering her old licence before the test. It wasn't that she thought herself stupid. No. She had an excellent law degree from the University of Florence – useless, to be sure, outside the purview of the Napoleonic Code; but forsaking one system for another seemed psychologically rash. As it happened, she passed the test easily, but her sense of it as ominous proved sound.

'Italian?' the examiner commented without interest. 'When dja come over?'

She lied: 'Three months ago.' You were allowed to drive for three months with an out-of-state licence.

'Says here how you've had this car two and a half years.'

'Not me. My husband's been driving it. I've been in Europe.'

'Separated?'

'What? *No!*'

She had never been separated from Marco. Never once in fifteen years of marriage. But now she was. The examiner's question – random, intrusive – had come on her sorest secret. As though a doctor, ausculting for some minor trouble, had found a cyst which might be malignant. Might. Might not. It was to be a trial separation and nobody need know.

Marco's firm had recalled all Italian employees to Milan. People there would be told that Carla had stayed on so as not to interrupt Maurizio's schooling.

The new licence had arrived yesterday. It was less impressive than the Italian one which had been solid: a little book with a crest and an assertive, gold-circled capital 'I' centred on the cover. Its replacement was a card with particulars clipped to fit computerized slots: Sex F, Hair blnd, Eyes gry, Height 5-5, Age 36, Carla Verdi.

She looked at the signature. Even that was precarious. Next year she might be divorced and signing with her maiden name.

As though to confirm her fears, a Christian psychologist now came on the air to discuss the Family, a social unit which had survived severe tribulations. From the start there had been trouble. Look at Adam and Eve. They had had a perfect environment; they had had no parents to blame for their warped

10

impulses; *and yet* they had fallen into sin – so what, asked the speaker, could the rest of us expect? We could expect the California divorce statistics. Quickly, before he could start quoting these, Carla turned him off.

Her feelings for Maurizio had two rhythms: a smooth flow when she wasn't with him, a choppy turbulence when she was. Right now he was in the kitchen. Eating. Between meals. Things meant for eating later and as part of something else. She told herself that it didn't matter. Try to remember. Oh dear – but her struggle to bind the ceremony of family life around him was for *his* sake. Surely you were meant to teach your children the rituals by which your kind preferred to live? Or had these too been discredited along with eggs, wine, butter and other ingredients traditionally associated with good living and now shown to be conducive to cancer or cholesterol? Carla, defying the new findings, cooked as she always had, though queasily, being assaulted from time to time with a qualm, as the Holy Inquisition must have been when denying the discoveries of Galileo. Maurizio actually enjoyed the old ways and clamoured for them when she let them lapse.

Today, however, he wanted to go to dinner with people she didn't know: the family of some boys he'd met at the YMCA pool.

'Gotta ask you sumpn, Mamma!' He sounded excruciatingly Californian when he'd been with local children. This happened on weekends only. All week he attended the French Lycée, wearing decent flannels and a blazer with a badge.

'Wow!' A caper had escaped from his mouth. He clapped a fist to his lips, giggled and lost another. The dark, falling things looked distressingly like rotten teeth. 'Their Pop's goin' to take us to a Kung Fu movie. We're to have a cook-out supper prior: barbecued spare ribs if the rain holds off.'

'What about your homework?'

Maurizio had a practised pout. It reminded his mother of a no-good uncle on his father's side and of the dangers of letting boys get away with things.

'Mamma,' he was now speaking Italian. 'You know how lonely I am without Babbo,' he wheedled. 'And these kids I met

are in the same boat because they too are a one-parent family.'
His blandishing smile was too sweet to be trustworthy.

'What do you mean "one-parent family"? Your father is on
an extended business trip. In Italy.'

'Yes, well, it's lasted three months and *you* can't take me on
cook-outs or camping or skiing on Mount Ranier or riding or
to Sequoia National Park and you haven't time to devote to me
because you're on your own, so ...'

Carla, looking with amazement on this caviller who was turning her own words against her, saw a true chip off the block of
his wicked uncle Dario: a bigamist who had been given two
years for peculation. Dario's charm, his relatives now agreed,
had been his undoing. His entire foolish family had worshipped
the ground he walked on until he grew up to drag its name in the
mud.

'Homework!' She cut through irrelevancies.

'American kids don't have to do lousy homework for hours
and hours.'

Stock answers to this pivoted on the risks of slipping from
your social class. ('Do you want to grow up to be a labourer? A
janitor or car-park attendant? Spend your life breaking stones
on the road?') Maurizio knew them as well as his mother. Un-
willing to trot them out now, she grabbed at his arm, missed and
knocked down something he had been concealing under his
leather jacket. An overturned can and scores of worms rolled
around their feet.

She screamed. 'What are those beastly things?'

'Worms.'

'What are you doing with them?'

'They're night-crawlers. I was going fishing with these kids I
met. Their Pop has a boat.'

'You *said* you were going to a movie!'

'What difference does it make? You wouldn't let me go anyway. I didn't want you worrying,' said Maurizio reasonably. 'I
was sparing your nerves.'

'Get up those stairs. Do your homework. I don't want to see
or hear from you until dinner time: eight o'clock.'

'I'm hungry. Americans eat at six.'

'*We are not Americans!*'

12

Minutes later she was bringing him up a plate of sandwiches.

'Ai,' she heard herself moan, falling into an ululation as unmeaning as the wind: 'Ayayai!' It had nothing to do with the self, individualism or the sound suggested in English, but seemed to hark back to some primal source of stress and fury – perhaps to the founding of the family or the sacrificial moment when the notion of order was first conceived.

Sitting down to rest and prime herself for preparing dinner, she felt something poke her in the stomach. There was a hard object in her apron pocket: the notebook she had found in Maurizio's coat. At another time she might have respected her son's right to privacy, but she wasn't going to now. She opened the notebook. It was a diary.

The first pages were reproachfully innocent. They contained the vital dimensions of a motorbike, an address of a mail-order firm, entries regarding homework! 'Got assignment done. Boring. Finished model. Went swimming. Mamma says ...' Whatever she said had not been noted. Boring, Carla guessed. Boredom stretched in desert pages across November and December. In January came entries about a school friend called Aladdin. Better times: 'Aladdin's father taught us to fire a gun. Aladdin waved a pistol and a bullet missed me by inches. Jerk!' Could that be true? Carla's heart stood still, then thumped. Aladdin's people had seemed so reliable! She flipped pages and read more entries: 'Went swimming with E. See E. tomorrow. E. and I all day.' What all day? 'E' must be Evie, the girl next door. 'Wrote away for prospectus.' Suddenly, a formally addressed letter to Mr Casimir Dobrinski:

Listen Mister,

You are committing unethical conduct which is making love to the wife of another. You are being watched, dumbell! So look out. You think nobody sees your game but you're wrong. We know you're planning to run away with her and take Evie. You could come to bodily harm! Evie is a MINOR and if you cross a state line with her you'll be in BAD TROUBLE! So, watch out, Mr Degenerate. Evie has rights. She does not want to go with you. You ran off with a girl before, so people have your number! What if the cops got an anonymous complaint? ('Anonymous' was correctly spelled. Maurizio must have looked it up.) *Adults should not kidnap girls,* the letter went on. *Keep your hands off, Mr Degenerate. You have been warned.*

The letter – a rough copy? A copy of a letter never or not yet sent? – was signed 'Anon.'. Like a poem in a school reader.

Was it a joke? Oh dear! Cazz Dobrinski, an acquaintance of the Verdis', was living next door with a woman called Wanda in a shack which violated a number of safety ordinances. Carla didn't want trouble with either of them.

Meanwhile, what was she to make of this letter?

Perhaps, intended for no eye but Maurizio's own, it had been written as a flushing out of rage or anxiety? He didn't like his father being away and might be fearful of his family breaking up as so many of his school mates' families had. Quite possibly, his mother guessed, his real doubts were about *her*.

Soothed, yet upset, she felt a surge of stricken affection for her son whom she had so unjustly accused of irresponsibility. How could she have forgotten what it was like to be thirteen? And how *could* she have read his private diary – though maybe it was just as well she had?

Feeling furtive and tearful, she crept up to Maurizio's room – he was doing his homework in his father's study – and slipped the notebook into a drawer where it looked perfectly at home among bits of a model Messerschmitt, a Flash Gordon comic, some stickers, cards with pictures of Italian soccer players, an outgrown tennis sock and an irremediably knotted Los Angeles Lycée tie.

At dinner she asked: 'You've been seeing a lot of the new girl next door. Why don't you bring her round?'

'I will some time.'

'What about tomorrow? She could come to tea.'

'Oh *Mamma*! Evie wouldn't come to *tea*!'

'For a coke then – just to get acquainted.'

'OK. Some time. Not tomorrow.'

'What about Cazz? Is *he* OK?'

'Sure.'

'You haven't had … trouble with him?'

'What kind of trouble?'

'I don't know. *Do* you get on with him?'

'Sure. He's helping us make a tree house in the pomegranate tree. He nailed down boards for the floor and made a rope-ladder. It's real neat.'

'*Really* neat.'

'Really neat.'

'Cazz did all that?'

'Sure.'

'Well, that's nice,' said Carla and scrutinized her son's face. It was as unrevealing as a clean plate. Sometimes Maurizio seemed naive for his age. He was a trilingual child and perhaps, spreading himself between three languages, had failed to burrow deeply into one. Fine points might elude him. Or was it that, like still waters, he ran deep and sly? To Carla, whose native city, Florence, was prickly with articulacy, talking to Maurizio was like playing a slot machine. His eyes were bright hazel; his features regular and his healthy, inexpressive good looks gave little away. Suddenly, unpredictably, he would spew out words.

'Know what's funny though?' He was burbling with laughter. 'Guess who cooks in that house?' Maurizio jerked his head in the direction of next door. 'That guy does. Cazz. Does all the buying too. He gets the queerest food: day-old bread, soy beans and today he had a pot of something really icky cooking. Evie and I went into their kitchen and there was this big pot boiling on the stove and *creaking* like doors do in a horror movie. Cazz said it was called "lights". Icky! Yech! It looked like old elephants' ears. Evie said she'd starve before she'd eat it. Last week he brought home two sheep's heads. Evie kept the skulls. We're going to put them in front of our tree house to scare off breakers-in.'

Carla heaved a prevaricating sigh. 'Maybe we'll be going home to Italy soon.'

'Gee, I hope not.'

'What? Don't you miss your father?'

'Sure I do. But I'd rather he came back here. When will we know, Mamma?'

'It depends on his work.'

The excuse was wearing thin, but Maurizio seemed content with it. Maybe fathers were normally absentees in his set?

Maurizio doubted that his mother and Evie would get along, but this was not why he didn't want to bring Evie around. His mother would be 'gracious' – that was a word of hers. Later, she might talk about making allowances for children who had not had Maurizio's opportunities and he and she might have a spat. That didn't matter. What did was that he wanted to keep Evie private. The girl's queerness – almost weirdness – was what he liked about her, and his mother's aim would be to make her seem like everyone else. That was the way she liked people to be. She always had to deny the newness of any thing or person and say it reminded her of something she'd known back in Italy. This led to her getting a lot of things wrong. Maurizio wasn't pretending that he didn't get things wrong himself, but his mother's way was sure-fire.

It surprised him that she should think there might be trouble with Cazz, because he had had doubts about the guy himself. Sometimes his doubts seemed silly and at other times dead on. His opinions swung from one position to the other. He hadn't enough hard information to decide anything for sure.

His trouble was that he was over-protected. All the Lycée kids were and people told them they were but went right on protecting them. They hardly ever rode on public buses – there was no route in the Glen anyway – but went everywhere in their parents' cars or the school bus: to each others' houses, the beach, the movies and the YMCA. From the world outside these places came reports of weird happenings which they never got to check on. That was why Evie was so different. Dauntless, in Maurizio's opinion foolishly so, she had laughed when he'd warned her against Cazz, and Maurizio hadn't been able to put his case properly because he wasn't sure whether the thing he suspected was possible at all and not some nutty story that people put out for a laugh.

Evie was the least protected kid Maurizio had ever run into. She was a half-wild girl with hair the colour of string and knees like knots and thin, snaky arms. She had intrigued and challenged him from the first time he'd got talking to her through their

16

chain-link fence. Seeing her there, it had struck him that she was the same colour as the scrub which grew on her side of it, needed very little water – it started just beyond the range of the Verdis' sprinklers – but sometimes got uprooted and blew down the hill in tangles as big as a sheep: tumble weed.

'Hey, know something? Your hair's the colour of tumble weed.'

She'd pretended to laugh, but later, coming round to his side of the fence, had tripped him up and managed to send him skidding down the slope, his heels slithering on the smooth, succulent ice plant.

'Who's a tumble weed now?'

He'd come back then and wrestled with her until he felt her limbs subdued beneath his. He'd pinned her down to prove his victory and, feeling her wriggle hotly under him, had had an odd sensation as if their bloodstreams were flowing into each other. She wasn't a bit like the Lycée girls but was a puzzling mix of ignorance and surprising knowledge. Sometimes she seemed foreign, which was nonsense, because she came from Kansas – and how American could you get?

Often she didn't even go to school, but spent the day in the tree house as if she were a woodland creature – not pretty, like pictures of elves or dryads in books, but more like some freckled relative of the squirrels or other brownish, blondish creatures who came by: coyotes, does. She could spend hours doing nothing, not even reading, just sitting still, like a hibernating animal. She wasn't like a dog or cat whom you could forget about. She was very strongly *there* and made the moment thrilling just as the sea does or the moon. You couldn't explain it. You felt it. That was all. Maurizio dreamed about her, and in his dreams they got as close as a seal or dolphin must to the wave that carries it. When he was awake and with her they seemed to lose each other and quarrel.

'Just sit quiet,' she'd tell him. 'Quit chattering.'

He was offended for a while but, watching her, saw that she hadn't meant to be rude. Words didn't interest her. She picked them carelessly. Lying along a branch of their tree, she seemed to be soaking in the surroundings, feeding on them as a plant might and, again like a plant, she seemed to give something

17

back, to exude it with her breath, to nourish the air. Her strong presence excited and excluded him. Again, he thought of the beckoning, live remoteness of winter sea.

Having phoned to say she was in the neighbourhood and would like to drop by, Sybil Steele came to visit Carla and began to beat about the bush.

'Coffee?' offered Carla.

'Oh please, yes. You make such good coffee. Espresso, isn't it?' Sybil, an old hand at soliciting, was clearly not doing it today for the Church or the Lycée playing fields. She'd have been forthright in a good cause. 'I'm sorry!' She had slopped coffee on the floor. Her hand trembled. 'Let me clean this up,' she offered. 'Where's a sponge?'

Unworthily, Carla felt cheered. Prone to weakness herself, she had thought Sybil a pillar of the foreign colony to which they both belonged. Now here was the pillar cracking and perhaps made of sub-standard substance like the ones in the Nash terraces which Carla had been taken to see on a tourist trip to Sybil's native London. The bus conductor had informed Carla's group that the colonnades were just fill and casing. 'Horse hair and old rubbish,' he had explained, 'was what the restorers found inside. Odd, innit?'

Spilled coffee oozed into pale carpet.

'Please,' Sybil begged, 'let me do something about that.'

Carla got a cloth and mopped at it. A stain remained. 'Never mind,' she absolved. 'It's rented. Everything in this house is. It makes it hard to be houseproud.'

'It's a splendid house though. Oh God!' Sybil groaned with excessive emphasis. 'I'm such a fool!'

Carla saw, too late, that mopping might have been good for Sybil who looked, in her best moments, like one of the Brontë sisters and, right now, like a Brontë back from a walk through a storm. Her hair seemed live and brittle like an electrified bush.

'I'm a bit on edge,' she confessed unnecessarily.

Carla put a match to the fire. It was cold. Outside, the rains which were scheduled to wash away houses in vulnerable parts of the city over the coming weeks had begun their slow, erosive labour. Sand and mud, pouring down the slopes of the Glen,

18

had begun to clog drains and gutters. Water, in low-lying areas, had risen to the hubcaps of parked cars.

Sybil asked whether Carla wasn't worried about her house's foundations. Building codes had been slackly enforced up to the 1940s. 'How old is this house?' she asked. 'Many are built on sand.'

Carla didn't know. 'I'm sure we're safe,' she said. 'Marco's careful about things like foundations.'

'He's been away for months, hasn't he?'

'We're not separated,' Carla denied, 'but he has, yes. It's ... it's to do with business.'

'I'm sorry.' Sybil blushed. Her spoon, rattling in its saucer, distracted Carla from wondering what gossip about herself might be going on. Had her visitor perhaps dropped round because misery likes company?

'Self-absorption is disgusting,' pronounced Sybil. 'It's what makes one make gaffes. So does inexperience in personal relations – I suppose that's some excuse? Anyway I'm sorry.'

Carla didn't know her well. Their husbands had played squash and their children – Maurizio and Sybil's five – went to the French Lycée, which meant that she and Sybil sometimes met in the parking lot and waved or managed to exchange quick greetings. The place was small and cars had to keep on the move in and out of its bottleneck if the job of collecting children was to take less than a quarter of an hour. Sybil was often obliged to pull out of the queue and lose her place while waiting for her full contingent. It was odd, Carla thought, that a family Catholic enough to have five children should send them to a lycée rather than to a parochial school. Sybil's husband, an anchor man on a local radio station called K-LUV supported every reactionary cause imaginable.

'Why do you send your children to the Lycée?' Carla asked. It seemed a safe topic.

'Terry insisted. He hates priests.'

'Terry?' Carla was too surprised for discretion. 'Isn't he a sort of lay priest himself?' She had tuned into K-LUV by mistake that very morning and heard Terry Steele promote the 'Right to Life' movement between plugs for a course teaching how to sell real estate and a call from a woman who couldn't sleep because

19

true American values were in jeopardy. Terry had got his job years ago on the strength of his English diction and, as this lost credibility, tried to compensate by keeping his sentiments wholesome and his manner concerned. He sounded nowadays like a priestly Polonius.

Sybil began to cry. Now it was Carla's turn to apologize.

'I'm sorry.'

'No, no, *I* am.'

This led to laughter.

'Oh Lord,' groaned Sybil, 'it's easily seen you and I went to old-fashioned schools anyway: *mea culpa, mea culpa!*' She beat her big, buoyant breasts and gave a hysterical hoot.

It seemed a case for desperate measures. Carla removed the coffee cups and produced a bottle of grappa.

'My mother-in-law sent it from Italy: Grappa di Bassano. It's good,' she warned, 'but strong.'

'Where's Maurizio?'

'At a neighbour's watching TV. Marco,' Carla admitted, 'disapproves of it so we don't own a set. He'll be back in an hour to do his homework.'

Pressed by this deadline, Sybil began to tell of her troubles. She was in love. The man was a priest. No, he didn't want to leave the Church and she didn't want him to.

'I know it's self-destructive. I know. I know. I can't help myself,' she said. 'I don't even know if he knows. We haven't talked about it.' Her foot began to tap excitedly then stopped as though held by an invisible clamp. Her glance, mobile as a trapped bee, flew in all directions except Carla's. She explained that she had worked as a volunteer in the parish and had felt that in doing this she was sharing his ministry – how ask him to give it up? She apologized if this sounded abysmally stupid. It did, didn't it?

'He was so dedicated,' she explained. 'So unselfish, that I never thought of him as a *man*, and so the situation never seemed threatening. I felt he was lifting me out of the petty meannesses of my own life. You can't imagine the squabbles when you have five children in a house: rivalries, egotism . . . Everyone grabbing what they can, especially now that the older ones are adolescents. All I hear from morning till night is "that's mine" and "I

20

want" and "don't touch my this or my that". Then, if I turn on the radio, there's Terry sounding off to all Southern California about the Christian Family while keeping carefully away from his own. Not that I blame him. I took up volunteer work to get away from it myself.'

Sybil slid a glance at Carla. 'You can guess the rest. Here I was with a man who wanted nothing for himself. Nothing. We were working on social projects and I felt as if I was contributing and at one with him; linked in a greedless love and then ...' She laughed, shrill with self-mockery, and stared through her glass of grappa at the sparks which the eucalyptus logs were throwing off along with an oily, medicinal scent. 'Flesh!' she said furiously, 'and the self began to make their demands. I became as greedy as any of my children. I want to go to bed with him. I can't stop thinking of it. I want him as a man ...'

'And you hate yourself?'

'Yes. Do you understand?'

'Well, in the terms you describe it, yes.'

'But they're not your terms?'

'How could they be, Sybil? I was never much of a Catholic. My father – a Socialist – let me stay one until my First Communion. That was a concession to my mother. She liked the white dresses. Then I gave it up.'

Carla felt unsympathetic. Sybil ought to have known better. The trap into which she had fallen was one of the oldest in the world. At the same time, her own anxieties – more serious – seemed to be dying down. It was as though her guest had magnetized the bad energies in the room, drawing them away from Carla. For a moment, this too annoyed. Sybil's story was too dramatic. Life, Carla felt, was not like that.

'Am I wrong?' Sybil's hair was, Carla now noticed, wet. She had been in the rain, of course, but the explanation didn't quite do away with the outlandish look of her. She was like some beast from the hills. Coyotes patrolled these and came down the Glen at dusk to frighten and sometimes kill domestic animals. Deer too came and snakes and raccoons which Carla had caught fumbling with black, glove-like paws in her garbage can. Sybil was like some more magical creature from still further away: from a myth-ridden past which people like her and her husband kept perversely alive in this technologically sophisticated but superstitious city. Sitting by Carla's fire, like a woman under a spell, she looked like one of those princesses in childhood stories who revert, at dusk, to animal form and grow tails or fins, fur or scales, which for the old tale-tellers figured pagan lusts and were best cured by a sprinkling on of holy water. Love and lechery, thought Carla with impatience, what trouble they caused.

'Of course, you're wrong!' she told Sybil. 'Look at the state you've got yourself into! Other people,' Carla was thinking of her husband, 'would be easier on themselves. They'd give themselves a safety-valve.'

'You mean go to bed with him?'

'Why not?' At least, Carla was thinking, Marco didn't make a big thing of sex.

'He'd hate me.'

'Can you be sure?'

'I'd be disappointed if he didn't.'

'Ah!' pounced Carla. 'Maybe, then, you're the one who's blown the thing out of proportion?' Standing up, she switched on a light in whose diffuse brilliance Sybil cringed and shrank. Her hair, just now blazing like faggots behind an immolated martyr's head, became a damp fuzz comparable to a crinkly pot-scourer. 'Pride!' accused the unkind Carla.

'Oh, I know. I know.'

'Pride *and* poetry.' Carla revenged herself on romance.

But she had gone too far. Sybil was provoked to argue. 'Don't you *see*,' she cried, concerned that Carla should, 'that so many have succumbed recently – priests,' she elaborated, her skin flushing for present possibilities, ' – and *then* rationalized this and pretended they were right and that the ones who have been able to resist the flesh's greeds were wrong. Isn't *that* a more destructive kind of pride?' If it was not, what were her scruples worth? She must have lain awake debating this, torn between inflammatory admiration for the priest's soul and a creeping tenderness for his flesh. It was his indifference which thrilled her. She was on the horns of a paradox. His weaker colleagues were contemptible. 'They'd pull down the whole structure as they

22

leave rather than admit blame! *That*,' she argued, 'is surely despicable?'

The ardour of old inquisitors burned in her. Like them, she saw the heresy's lure and raged at it the more. Within her, order, disorder and arguments for a new order were violent with abstract rage and carnal velleities.

'Oh Sybil!' Carla was suddenly all pity for this foolish victim. Such intricate folly could only be sincere.

'Am I a prig?'

'Well, yes,' Carla spoke gently, 'a bit of a one. Why does Terry hate priests, by the way?'

'He's had calls at the radio station. Accusing me. I suppose I've been indiscreet – as I wouldn't have been if there'd been anything to be discreet about.' Sybil's laughter came out in shy, immoderate spurts. 'Once the caller nearly got on the air and had to be bleeped out. Now the girls who screen incoming calls have been alerted to the thing. You can imagine how embarrassing that is for Terry. He doesn't believe it, but he can't be sure people in the studio don't.'

'How dreadful for you both!'

'It is. We never go out together any more. Terry is on the air at night. That's our excuse – but I think he took the evening work deliberately. We'd given up sex anyway because of not wanting more children.'

'Oh Sybil! But don't you *see*, you should really have the affair. You've paid for it. What about your priest? Does he want to go to bed with you?'

'We've never spoken of it. Anyway, there's nowhere we could do it. *Our* house is a public highway.'

'Did the person who rang Terry mention this priest's name?'
'No.'

'And am I the only person you've told?'
'Yes.'

'Why?'

'I'm not sure. Are you offended?'

'No, no, of course I'm not – only it says something about the way you see me. Forgive my self-concern, but ...'

'Forgive mine.'

This time the apologies didn't make them laugh.

'Have some more grappa.' Carla felt desolated. Even awful Terry Steele, she saw, deserved pity. How depressing such things were. And how unforeseen that she should be listening to such a story in swinging Beverly Glen. 'Beverly Glen,' someone had jokingly told Marco some years ago, 'is where it's at this year.' Marco had appeared to pay no attention but, later, after two divorced men he knew had set up house here with new, younger women and started growing organic vegetables, he had come home with news of an Italian who had found and bought a marvellous old house in the Glen, then had to return to Italy. 'I'm going to ask him to let it to us,' Marco said. 'It's very beautiful by LA standards, hand-finished with lots of natural wood, quite big.' Carla had agreed, doubtfully. Many of the acts on which Marco embarked were charged with a ritual significance. This one could be a substitute for the divorce he couldn't bring himself to demand of her.

Sybil put a hand on Carla's sleeve. 'I'm awkward,' she said, looking at the hand. 'Odd, isn't it? I could never play ball games. You asked why I came to you. I just think you're likely to understand odd things and accept them as odd. I wouldn't confide in a Californian.'

In the bleaching light, Sybil's face looked spiritual, but her body was the opposite: muscular, not fat, but very live. Flesh, moving like something in a trap, spoke a secondary language under her cotton T-shirt. She had started to sweat, and whiffs of body odour reached Carla. It was as if Sybil's body were rebelling at the way she was denying it and making its own acrid and insistent plea. Surely the priest must see what she needed? Carla imagined and disliked him: a youngish, balding man in jeans, flirting with worldliness, then bolting for celibate cover. He should have discouraged Sybil or else done something for her long before she got into the state she was in.

'I don't want to be told there's no problem,' Sybil was saying. 'I need to talk to someone who'll see that there *is*.'

'How long have you been wanting this man?'

'Two years. Well, I had a sort of disincarnate passion at first, or thought I had. He kissed me once – but I'm afraid it may have been brotherly. How childish one becomes! Being a child is bloody painful.'

24

'Go to bed with him, Sybil. He can't not disappoint a wait like yours. Nobody could. Then you'll be free.'

Sybil didn't believe her. Maybe she liked living like a salamander? Her face had a pursy, lickerish look. Women in old paintings had it too, Carla remembered: pale merchants' wives in Van Eyck and Georges de la Tour. Passive, like Sybil, waiting in the fusc of old canvases, they were withdrawn, concentrated, absorbed and undistractable.

'You wanted me to disapprove!'

'No.'

But Sybil must have. Who but Carla, she must have thought, would give her an argument to struggle with? Surely everyone else in this misnamed City of Angels would advise her to favour her body over her soul? Perversely, Carla too began to argue against self-denial. She had an illustrative story. It was about a neighbour.

'You don't know her,' she said, 'so I feel free to tell you.' Last spring, this neighbour, an actress in her thirties, had grown tired of her lover and given him notice to quit. He was living in her house, so it seemed fair to do this. 'He's a philanderer,' said Carla, 'but attractive and I'm leaving out the complications which were many. Anyway, in March, she gave him until June and then, which is my point, he began to pine. He had treated her abominably but once he got his walking papers he fell in love with her all over again. It knocked the stuffing out of him. *Then,* to illustrate my point further, the tables were turned. Unexpectedly, in late April, she was told she might have to have a breast removed: cancer. As you might expect, this shook her confidence and *she* became very dependent on *him,* begged him to stay, put off the operation and even considered not having it at all, though her doctor was warning her it might be urgent. "Will you feel the same way about me when I've lost my breast?" she kept asking her lover. His answer was: "I can't truly say I will. Your breasts," he told her, "are so lovely, they're so important to me that it would be a lie to say I won't miss one. I don't think I'll be able to bear sleeping with you once you've had the operation." It was his revenge,' said Carla, 'and she knew it was, but couldn't help exposing herself to it. Sex,' Carla drove her moral home, 'is only powerful

25

when it's denied or threatened. It's the *idea* of it that's poison. Go to bed with your priest.'

'Where?' moaned Sybil. 'Besides, I couldn't. Celibacy is his strength. I'd ruin him, don't you see? Virgins sacrifice fulfilment in this life so as to bear witness to the next. It's a charism of the spirit, a gift. I read about it in *Sacerdotalis Coelibatus*.'

'In what?'

'Pope Paul's encyclical on priestly celibacy: *Sacerdotalis Coelibatus*.'

'Oh.'

'I'm like people,' said Sybil, 'who admire flowers in parks and immediately want to pick them: vandals. Do you mind if I pour myself more grappa?' The colour in her cheeks had condensed into red, angry spots which looked as if they must burst into spitting blisters. 'I'm ashamed of being so self-centred.'

'Do you feel I owe you a confidence?'

'No,' Sybil admitted, 'if I come here to do a strip-tease, it doesn't mean *you* have to.'

'But it would be considerate? Like not going clothed to a nudists' camp?'

'Well, I do feel naked.'

'I'm sorry,' Carla said, 'it's not the same for me. I'm in an uncertain position. I don't want to talk about it.'

'Your friend who lost the breast – do you confide in her?'

'I let her advise me. She says that now she's odd-breasted she can't afford any more oddities in her life, even odd friends. She wants me to get into the mainstream and sleep around.'

'The advice you gave *me*!'

'No.'

'No, you didn't say that,' Sybil admitted. She was tipsy and agitated her hands, making points which eluded Carla who failed to understand words like 'incarnational reality' – unless Sybil's sharpening body smell was an emanation of it? Sybil said that *Humanae Vitae*, the encyclical on birth control, had ruined her marriage. She was a woman crucified by encyclicals. The word reminded Carla of 'bicycle' and she imagined Sybil strapped to a wheel or rack. Sybil's breath was coming in quick, nervous puffs. She told Carla that she was possessed by fantasies. 'No, I don't want to talk about them – Oh, I'm sorry, Carla, I'm getting silly with the drink.'

At six-thirty the door bell rang and it was Maurizio back from across the way with his hostess, Jane, the woman with the one breast. Her lop-sidedness was of course concealed and Sybil could not know that this was she. Jane was beautiful with green eyes, swags of coarse, possibly dyed but handsome, honey-pale hair and a wide, strong jaw. The only sign of her vacillating confidence was that she wore too much make-up. Her manner was theatrical and she and Maurizio bounced in exclaiming about the TV show they'd been watching and full of their own mood.

Carla introduced the two women and went with Maurizio into his room to get him started on his homework. When she got back Sybil, as though some of Jane's theatricality had rubbed off on her, was talking in a heightened manner about love. Carla tried to turn the talk to the less charged matter of mudslides. Jane's house was on a cliff. But this topic led straight back to the first one.

'There's a tree leaning directly over my roof,' said Jane. 'The earth has been washed from its roots. Casimir,' she named her lost lover, 'would know what to do. I'm damned if I'll ask him though. He moved in with an Okie slut,' she explained to Sybil, 'presumably to spite me. A creature called Wanda.'

Carla went to get Jane a glass. When she returned Sybil was again talking about love, this time of animals. She had been brought up in an English village. 'It was full of spinsters with cats. One used to suckle hers. She'd trained them. The postman told us she'd had their teeth removed so they could suckle her breasts. He'd heard about the teeth from the vet and then one day he saw her through a downstairs window painting her nipples with fish paste.'

It was a fatality, Carla saw. Breasts *would* be brought up. Jane's face flinched. Sybil stared, baffled, at Carla's head shakings then went inexorably on.

'Can you imagine pulling out a tit and offering it to some toothless cat? Nature I suppose. Maybe she knew the postman was there and wanted him to see it? Having treasure that nobody sees gets to a woman. It was said in the village that ...'

'Please, Sybil! Don't tell us.'

But already Jane had put down her grappa, clasped a hand to her prosthetic bra and raced, weeping, into the rain.

'What . . . ?' wondered Sybil.

'Breasts,' Carla mouthed at her with late and foolish caution. 'You went on about them. She's the one who lost one. *And* she has two cats.'

'Oh Lord! Oh Hell!' said Sybil. 'I'm cursed. I'm a bringer of woe.'

'No, no!'

'Yes.'

Carla was upset, felt that this was a moment for generosity and, with a misdirected splurge, bestowed hers not on the victim but on the offender.

'Listen,' she said, 'if you need somewhere to be alone with your priest, you may borrow this house for a night. Maurizio and I will be away for the weekend from Saturday week. Jane's invited us to her mountain cabin.'

Sybil accepted with such alacrity that Carla guessed she had been angling for the offer all along.

Over dinner – *tortelloni*, veal scallops, braised fennel, stewed plums – Maurizio reported, 'You know, Mamma, families here eat really yucky food.'

He had been out lately to houses where the mothers fixed meals by assembling such items as ready-grated cheese ('They don't *own* a grater!' he marvelled), tinned spaghetti ('Yech!'), or defrosted pizza followed by a store-bought pudding. 'It was meant to be a compliment to me because I'm an Italian. *Poverini!*' he commented with pity.

Carla was gratified. Good culinary standards were probably as significant to her as religious ones seemed to be to Sybil. What she liked in life was conviviality and a table full of people – preferably relatives – enjoying her food. Wine, jokes and an argument as to whether the *pesto* wasn't too garlicky drew people together. The solitary egotism of lovers was treated with defensive laughter. You put up with it as you'd put up with a low-spirited guest but wished away the contagion. Carla, domestic and gregarious, was as much out of her element living alone with Maurizio as the heroines of the great romantic novels had been among the restraints of family life. Even as a girl, reading law rather than literature, she had focused on the principles underlying these restraints and condoned them. She was suspicious of romantic feeling – though she enjoyed cultivated landscape, and Marco liked to argue that hers was a pre-Enlightenment sensibility. He could be right. When – to please him – she first read a few of his favourite novels, she had been horrified by the women in them who followed undomiciled loves only to end up throwing themselves under trains, being swept over rapids, or eating arsenic. Such people did arouse compassion and the law now provided remedies for their needs. Carla quite saw that it should. She was glad she had offered to help Sybil and would help Jane too should she be asked. Her own plight was less easily dealt with.

After dinner, she sent Maurizio back to his books, poured herself a vodka, closed her eyes, opened them and told herself that she should try writing to her husband. Marco was, after all, the head of the house and responsible for their son who was perhaps going through puberty and in need of a man's hand and some stability.

Stability was not Marco's strong point. To be sure, he claimed to be hyper-stable in a flexible and imaginative way. He was given to paradox. One wondered whether puberty needed paradox? Probably not. What it probably needed was a father right here in the house capable of working the barbecue and laying down the law. Instead of that, Marco had been in Italy for three months, issuing bulletins containing amendments to all and every understanding which had ever existed between himself and his wife. She had a shoe box full of them. Certain passages she knew by heart.

Look, Marco had written; he wrote frequently and fast: a business habit. Some letters were typed by his secretary. Others, Carla hoped, were not. *I know I'm not easy to live with. Who is? Think about that a minute. I know that you feel you have put a lot of effort into our marriage. My mother approves of you. But you are not married to my mother.*

You think I am unfair – but so are you. The fact that you can't see this drives me mad. Mi manda in bestia! *Sometimes I'd like to shake you the way my sister used to shake her dolls until their eyes fell out. When they did, those pretty blue-and-white china ornaments turned out to be backed with opaque lead. So I sometimes think are yours.*

I'm trying to spell out a problem. It's this: you have, as you were reared to do, 'conformed in every way to my temper'. Right? Right. Florentine girls of your generation were good at this and so were you – fifteen years ago. Eight years ago you were less good. Now you're hopeless! My temper, Carla, has changed.

I'm sorry but, you know, if you'd got a job fifteen years ago, you would have been expected to learn a few things over the years, to adapt!

Look, the conditions you were reared for are gone. The man I used to be is gone. I am not the same. You go on treating me as though I were and this – I have trouble believing you don't know it – is a form of torment. You go on giving me what I once wanted and now don't. 'Giving' is the key word. If you were even being yourself! But no! You must keep sacrificing yourself – and me, Carla! – to your idea of me! It's funny – though I don't expect you to see the humour. What it isn't is generous. It's an investment you were brought up to make. But I won't pay you dividends, Carla!

That one had come in December. A khaki aerogramme. She did not need to re-read or even unfold it. Her fingers, prehensile as a Braille reader's, extracted the message. It still stunned and hurt her. After she had glossed and pondered every syllable of it, what stayed with her was that she should never have let Marco return to Italy alone. If she had not had the thought herself, her mother-in-law would have had it for her: Paola! A stack of letters written on Pineider paper – handsome, rough-textured with bevelled edges and engraved address – showed the extent of Paola's concern. She worried about Maurizio – drugs, California – and about his parents' marriage. Why wasn't Carla in Milan with her husband? Who was to keep an eye on him? Paola hoped Carla wasn't relying on *her* because at her age with her health the way it was ... Her handwriting flew across the paper in loopy nooses. Her Fs and Ls ballooned like thought-bubbles and bore innuendoes. These had to do with the rashness of wives who left their husbands too free. Paola had done her duty valiantly by her own husband, 'poor Aeolo', whose mother had named him after the God of the Winds and whom his wife dubbed 'poor' because of the arthritis which had put paid to any velleity he might have had to storm or waft himself from beneath her benevolent thumb. Many healthier Italian husbands had recently managed to do just that. *Things have changed here*, Paola reminded, *since the divorce law*. This was her favourite topic and around it her narratives swirled in an indignant circuit, turning and returning like the water in Roman fountains which combine display with an ingenious and vital thrift.

There was now, she repeated, no security at all. None. Husbands, and even wives, were daily welshing on their debt. With the encouragement of Church and State! As though seized by senile folly, these rival institutions had begun to dismantle the ground on which they stood. Zany scrap-merchants, they had turned their wrecking-balls on the structures of the family. First the Italian state had legitimized divorce, then the Church had opened a bargain-basement in annulments. All you needed now to annul a Catholic marriage was to say you had entered on it with a mental reservation. *A mental reservation!* Paola's pen tore through her linen-weave paper. Who could not cook up one or indeed ten of those? At the drop of a hat! At the zip of a fly! It was Open Sesame to legitimized promiscuity. Open Season for turning decent wives into concubines and bastardizing their children ... Unlike divorce, annulment denied there had ever been a marriage. Husbands – since no longer husbands – had no obligations at all, financial or otherwise.

Carla went back to the shoe box.

Why, hectored a letter posted in January in Viareggio – what had Marco been doing there? – *must I be forced to feel responsible for you? As if you were some old ex-serf or slave who couldn't adjust to freedom? To growing up? Do I have to carry you on my back? All my life? All right. All right. I married a very young girl but I expected her to develop. You're thirty-six, Carla. Older than Christ and I'm damned if I'm going to go on letting you make me feel guilty. You're adept at that, aren't you? What I want to say, I will and it's this: if I want to have new experiences I will. I have a right to. Sexual experiences if I have to spell it out. Sexual! Yes. Esatto. Proprio cosi. I'm not ashamed to say it and I don't believe in the Double Standard either. I'm coherent. Modern. Fair. Go and have your own. That's why I left you in California. Seize your chance, Carla, I'm going to. You may count on that. We don't live in a fairy tale. Why should I be bound by your childish expectations? Give me one good reason.*

You point out that I used to be jealous. Yes. I used. I'm not now. Oh God. I can see your hurt vanity squirm. You'll twist this up. You'll say: he loves me less. Carla, do me a favour. Take what I say at face value. I'm not asking for a divorce, am I? If I were there would be no need for me to try and get you to understand me. I say 'get you to understand me' because you have deliberately turned yourself into an old-style Italian wife, i.e. a reflection of your husband. Thus for me to try and understand you would be like studying a distorting mirror of my former self. A bit pointless, you may agree!

Conceits, she thought bitterly. He could amuse himself making conceits! That was how pleased he was with himself! He was probably having some affair. Well, couldn't he just get on with it as he had with all the others? If he didn't want a divorce – or did he? No use asking Paola. *She* was already upset at the way her world was shifting around her. As she said herself, it was too bad at her age to have to put up with that. She liked to know where she was and now she didn't.

As I said to Monsignor Capponi ... The Roman rhythms of Paola's voice leapt from the page. It was a lively voice, the voice of a woman who had lived through Fascism, World War Two and the Historic Compromise. She knew what treachery was. *'I'm too old to mince words,' I told him, 'and what I say is that your Church has sacrificed principle to politics and little good may it do you.' I needn't tell you he had nothing to say,* she commented in gloomy triumph, *nothing but a lot of gabble about how decent people followed their own consciences and didn't seek to take advantage of loopholes in the law. 'That's Protestantism, Monsignor Capponi,' I told him and he looked at me open-mouthed like a caught fish. Like a fish,* wrote Paola sombrely, *hooked right through the mouth.*

Carla sighed for her mother-in-law. Paola worried about her old age. Marco, the active male in the family – for poor Aeolo was too ill to count – was, in his mother's scheme of things, the Atlas who held the heavens over all their heads. Unfortunately,

32

he was now an Atlas with an itch, one afflicted with a carnal impulse whose intemperate caperings risked bringing their firmament down on top of them. This was nothing new to either woman. Carla had seen her mother-in-law cope with her own husband when at the height of his powers. She knew too that Paola, at the age of twenty-four, had prevented her widowed father from contracting marriage with a working girl who was one third his age and pregnant by him. That had been a tough battle and Paola had fought ruthlessly, mobilizing her own and Aeolo's connections, begging, harrying and insisting, until at last she found someone who knew the girl's father's employers and could persuade them to bully him into forcing his daughter to break off the engagement, accept money for an abortion and leave the city. The jilted old widower never knew of his daughter's intrigues and when he died, leaving his money safely to his own family, it was she who nursed him at the end.

'After all, he was happier this way,' Paola had said, 'with his own.'

Carla could not contradict her. Only wondered did the old strategies still work? Might Marco, as Paola's son, be inoculated against them?

I wish, said a letter written only three weeks ago on February 1st, *I could remember one flaming row between us – all the flame coming of course from me – which didn't end with your cooking my 'favourite meal', wearing my 'favourite scent' and waiting with submissive face and false nonchalance for me to kiss and make up. I didn't want the damn meal. The scent nauseated me and so did the submission. In memory, what sickens me most is that I often did kiss and make up simply because I could see that you had no inkling of what was wrong, and how could I keep holding out on you when there was no hope of your guessing why? And yet you're not stupid, just caged up in a whole set of assumptions.*

On the back of the page came a paragraph on distrust. *It paralyses you*, he wrote. *It paralyses my mother. Neither of you knows how to live because you don't know how to trust. Not me. Not life. Not yourselves. And it shows in your mouth, Carla! The corners turn down. You look, you want to be, defeated. Can you imagine what it's like for me to have to live with that? To be constantly forced to summon up the will and drive for two?*

33

Angrily she threw the letter back in the box and did not pick up the more recent one lying underneath. She considered screaming like a peahen, relieving her annoyance in the long, nerve-freezing shriek of that dun-coloured bird which guards the nest while its pretty mate delights viewers with the iridescent brilliance of its tail. Distrust! Why wouldn't and shouldn't she distrust? There was every reason to. Reminded, she stood up and checked the side and back doors. Coming back into the drawing-room, she fancied she heard a knocking on the window-pane and jerked the curtain aside. A group of poinsettia heads bumped softly against the glass. Some were red, some a luminous albino in the outspill of light. Like life-sized Raggedy-Ann and Raggedy-Andy dolls, they shook their shaggy petals at her and swayed gently in what looked like a derisive dance. Further out, the light caught the fat, phallic shape of a banana flower coloured evilly like old vinegary blood.

Leaving the window, she paged through her address book, looking without hope, for someone to phone. The directive which had summoned Marco back to Milan had taken his Italian colleagues too. Their wives had gone with them and these had been her only close friends. They had been a band of couples who had given dinner parties for each other regularly, exchanging addresses of baby-sitters, Italian grocers and copies of Italian magazines. A few old copies they had left still lay on her coffee table: *L'Espresso, Oggi, Il Mondo.* She picked one up but the distant scandals did not hold her attention. Instead the scandal of Marco's most recent letter surfaced in her mind as a piece of refuse might bob from the mud into which it had been thrown. Resignedly, she picked it out of the shoe box.

What I would like, he had written, *is for someone ...*

She did not want to read this. She put it back and again picked up the useless address book. Could she phone Sybil? No. Jane? Certainly not. Her doctor? What could she say was wrong? That she felt isolated? A little insane? If she had been a Californian she would have had an analyst. They all seemed to.

What I would like, (she had fished the letter back out of the shoe box) *would be for some man to give you the pleasure we so obviously no longer get from each other. How could we? We've been married fifteen years. We were engaged when you were seventeen. I make this suggestion soberly, Carla. I've thought about it and mean it and am putting it forward out of concern for us both. But mostly for you, Carla. You have gone frigid. That's a sort of death. What I would like you to do while you're alone, Carla, is to get yourself laid. I know that you'll think this is in terrible taste, but I am convinced that it would do you good.* YOU. ME. US. *Look – if only to see, so that you may see, how unimportant it would be to our relationship and therefore how unimportant anything I may do or have done of the same sort was or is, you should do this, Carla ... And Carla, I want to tell you that you are an attractive woman still. Very. It's just that you and I ... Besides, you have never understood the erotic ... We are hybrids, Carla, living abroad as we have, we could hardly stay the same. Though you don't think you've changed, you have and I am asking you to change more ... You are alone in Southern California, one of the world's playgrounds ... I'm convinced it would bring us closer. It would make you more like me.*

She didn't know whether to laugh or cry. He's playing a role, she decided again. Another. He's like a child. An American child. Greedy, always playing. One life isn't enough for him. He has to imagine others.

She felt numbed, frightened, assaulted by these letters and resolved to read no more.

Chapter Two

Maurizio spent hours at a stretch in his room. Lurking, thought his mother and wondered whether this was puberty and whether she should worry about it.

'Why don't you go out in the air?' she asked, knowing she must be echoing every mother since Cain's.

'To do what?'

'Walk. It's stopped raining.'

'By myself?'

'What about the girl next door?'

'Evie? She's gone on a church outing. There's nothing to do here.'

This was true. The Glen slopes were good only for hide-and-seek and after a school mate had come down with a bad case of poison ivy from playing that, nobody in Maurizio's class would visit.

'It's not just the flora,' one mother had explained on the telephone. 'My dear Mrs Verdi, don't you know that the human fauna in those canyons is more dangerous still? Strangers can just walk up to you and stick a hypodermic needle in your arm!' This woman, an Iranian, was full of fears. She sighed. 'Maybe,' she offered on the tail of her sigh, 'you'd better bring

36

your son to play with my Aladdin. Here at any rate they'll be safe.'

That had been during the Christmas vacation. Maurizio, listening on the extension, had yelped with glee. What drew him was Aladdin's Olympic-sized swimming-pool which lay before the Iranian family's French-style château where a real château might have had a fountain or beds of topiaried box. The house was surrounded by a sugar-pink machicolated wall and had its own rifle range. Humming birds vibrated in the bottle-brush blossoms. Burglar alarms were strung through the bougainvillea and, outside the spiked, electrified gates, hired security guards toured regularly in patrol cars. Returning such hospitality was utterly beyond the Verdis.

'Maybe,' Carla offered, 'I could take the children one day to Marine Land? To see the whales?'

'Whales?' Aladdin's mother was alarmed. 'You would have to go by freeway! No, no! I think Mrs Verdi, there is no need for you to play "even-Stephen" with me. I am happy to have your son play with my Aladdin in the safety of his own home.'

After that, Carla didn't try to compete, but dropped Maurizio off at Aladdin's as uncompunctiously as if the family had been running a play group. Aladdin's father taught the boys to shoot and dive and although she disapproved of fire-arms, she said nothing, for it was good, surely, to have an interested father about. The friendship lasted until the day, three weeks ago now, when the two began to shoot their bullets into the pool. The bullets ended somehow – Carla did not quite grasp how – in the water filter. The water level sank and Aladdin, providentially alone at the time, dived in, concussed himself and had to be taken to hospital. Despite his family's precautions – in a way because of them – his own gun had got him. Carla was stunned. The freakish disaster defied forethought. And yet *she* might – should – have protested, she the only one concerned to disapprove of guns. Why *hadn't* she? What if the victim had been Maurizio? Unsteadily, she went to commiserate with Aladdin's mother but, hearing the woman tell and retell the story, found herself mentally exchanging Maurizio for Aladdin at every point. It was Maurizio she saw dive into a sparkling, sky-blue, half-empty pool. Maurizio who was knocked out cold and carried off a little later in a screaming ambulance. Effortfully, she substituted Aladdin's face for her son's and felt her body loosen in relief. Ashamed, she began to fear that Fate, a clever knife-thrower, might have aimed to the side of its chosen and eventual target. It could get her son yet.

Maybe it was getting him already? Slyly and by attrition. Maybe it was Maurizio's part in Aladdin's accident which kept him fretting in his room?

'Why don't ...'

'... I go out in the air?' Maurizio finished her sentence for her. Of course she'd said that already. 'Haven't you any friends, dear?' She recognized a parody of her own voice gently chivvying in a Tuscan accent. It was also a parody of her mother's which she remembered resenting twenty years ago. *Did* she sound like that now herself? Obviously, she did. '*You* go out a lot less than I do!' her mother-and-son baited her. 'If you took a nice little walk you might meet some nice new friends. Anything's better than staying cooped up all day growing old before your time like a little old woman! *Vecchietta!*' mocked a triumphant Maurizio, revelling in his game. 'The world won't come to you, you know. One must make an effort.'

Carla flinched at the truth of it. Her mother's and no doubt her grand- and great-grandmother's wisdom gushed from Maurizio's mimicry. It hit its mark, though Maurizio didn't notice this. He was intent on his act, clowning with that explosive adolescent humour which, his mother guessed, was literally a humour in the old-fashioned sense: a body fluid, some fermenting secretion which threw his moods out of kilter. Physical things were happening inside Maurizio. Pressures. Shifts. He guffawed.

'Hey fans, listen ...' He was hilarious, manic, ready to throw rabbit-punches, wheeze, mimic, burn away the excess energy feverish inside him. Up and down he jumped like a yo-yo, one of those luminous battery-lit yo-yos that touts sell to tourists on summer evenings in the dusky squares of Italian towns. Or had for a few seasons while the craze lasted. Carla, swept up by memory, saw hubs of electric colour pistoning into cupped palms. It would be the aperitif hour between six and eight. Gaggia espresso machines released steam in a hiss. Waiters wore

38

striped livery. Women stepped in gold-thonged sandals past privet hedges on sidewalk cafés. Youth, she thought and felt the word twist inside her with the dry little movement of a paper-knife. I had it. He's got it now.

'Hey, Mamma, listen, dja know this one ...?' Some joke. Maurizio's manic eyes were fixed on her, just like the intent, excited ones which used to stare in the corner of her own eye when she walked on scented evenings past the café tables. She remembered wearing pale, fitted linen and feeling her body inside it more alert than she'd ever feel it again, ever, feeling it over and over in the sharp, multiplied lust of those cool, unflickering stares. Some of the starers then were no older than Maurizio was now. They'd hang round the warm squares and *viali* in groups, nudging, sharing a cigarette, more often just staring with that intent, assessing, avid, finite stare. Sometimes one would say something, but rarely. That was not in the rules. She walked. They looked. A total transaction. That had been twenty years ago and now here was Maurizio. Thirteen. Lonely. Charged.

'Listen,' she offered, 'shall we go to a film?'

He picked a Kung Fu movie with violence, astonishing exploits, but no girls. His mother hated it, closed her eyes during the fights but was relieved to find he did not want to look at girls after all. It made her feel that, though changes must come, they could for a while longer be kept at bay.

Today was the day on which Carla had promised to lend Sybil her house, but she had forgotten all about this. Sybil's troubles had been overtaken by public ones, for the Glen had now been officially designated a disaster area. Bushels of mud had been dislodged and with them hundreds of thousands of dollars worth of property. TV vans had been here filming and sight-seers had been warned off. Disaster struck selectively. A house might collapse, as though made of cards or softening gelatine, while the one next door stood firm. Evacuees shown on the six o'clock news, looking like the inhabitants of some stricken village in Cambodia, could turn out to be your neighbours up the hill. Flat parts of the city were immune. Perhaps with the aim of alerting residents of these lucky areas to their neighbours' plight, newspapers now started printing stories with a bleak, discomforting thrust. One told of rattlesnakes being washed down the Santa Monica mountains into suburban backyards. Another featured a graveyard from whence a silt of cadavers and broken caskets had swept onto the highway along with the shallow-rooted shrubs unsuitable for checking soil erosion which had been planted between the graves.

Many incidences of improvidence were coming to light and their price held payable by people who couldn't have known of them. Jane was one of these. Her house turned out to have no proper foundations. It was a pretty house covered with balconies on which she kept basil and jade plants and, in fine weather, lacy, handwoven hammocks from the Yucatán. Trippers had been known to photograph it and even to climb to her door to ask for an autograph in memory of a successful movie in which her name had appeared among the major credits. The film was nine years old and Jane was flattered and depressed by each reminder. When asked what she was doing now, she would talk about irons in the fire and a projected trip to Stratford, Ontario.

'But what *will* you do?' Carla asked urgently when Jane rang to say that her front balcony had broken away and rolled into the road, off which it must, officials insisted, be removed forthwith and only partly at city expense. Jane had no money at all, not even unemployment compensation which she had gone through after a prolonged spell of what actors call 'resting'.

'The bits on the road are their responsibility,' Jane explained. 'The bits threatening to roll onto it are mine.'

'Give those a quick shove onto it then,' Carla advised, 'when nobody's about.'

Her advice was recently less in keeping with the standards by which she liked to think she lived. But how expect civic virtue from Jane whose house, to top everything else, had now been condemned? It was illegal as well as unsafe for her to spend another night in it.

'You're welcome to come here. So are the cats.'

'Bless you, Carla, but I'll go to my friend Mia's. The trouble is my things. There's mud pressing against the back wall. Can I leave some stuff with you? I don't know how we'll get it across the road. It's like a river.'

40

Jane had some elegant possessions left over from her hopeful days. She was only thirty-four – but hope in the theatre dies fast. Reasonable hope, that is. Jane continued to dream.

'We need a *man*.'

'I could call Casimir.'

'*Darling!*' Jane's theatrical screech. 'If that bastard were the last able-bodied male on this side of . . .'

Carla, knowing the Casimir saga, took the opportunity of disentangling the telephone flex from the legs of the stand. Threading the receiver with Jane's voice issuing from it in and out of knots, loops and kinks, she managed, having freed the whole length of flex, to walk with it to a window through which she could see Jane's violated house. A hole gaped in its coquettish façade and ropes of water bright as spun sugar fell from every protrusion.

'Darling, I'm in despair!' groaned Jane.

'Maurizio and I will help.'

'We need a *man*!' Jane moaned so repetitively that when Carla saw one she thought for a moment that she had imagined him.

He was standing on the other side of the window-pane: tall, well set-up and clad, she saw approvingly, in rubber boots and a sensible raincoat. He must have been out in the rain for some time for he was soaked. Water ran from him in rivulets and flashed like mercury in his hair. Laughing and shining, he threw out his hands in apology for his plight. Even if he had only come to read the meter, he could, Carla decided, be pressed into service. It must surely be part of the Western tradition for men to help out in times of such obvious need. Tapping the window, she gestured that she would come and open the door.

'Hang on,' she told Jane. 'No, hang up. I think I've got one. I'll ring back.'

He was Sybil's man, of course: the priest. Carla had forgotten about him and Sybil and that this was Saturday week. How embarrassing! She didn't know his name and was damned if she'd call this unfatherly-looking fellow 'Father'. There was no question now of his and Sybil's having the house to themselves.

'My name's Leo,' he said. 'I was told I was needed here.'

'Well, you are actually.' Carla supposed they must be at cross purposes. 'Do come in.'

'I'm a bit mucky. All right if I take my boots off?'

She was on the point of saying: 'Keep them on. There's work to be done,' but thought better of this.

'The road's next to impassable,' he was saying. 'Except by jeep. I had to walk the last mile.'

'How will Sybil get here then?'

'Sybil? Is she coming?'

He had the boots off now and was hanging his raincoat in the porch. Not one scrap of priestly garb was he wearing. On the other hand, he did genuinely seem to think he was here on an errand of mercy. What could Sybil have told him? Some coy riddle, no doubt.

'Did you know we were in this state?' If he hadn't been watching TV he mightn't have and neither would Sybil. Carla hoped *she* wasn't going to turn up next with a weekend bag packed with scent, toothbrush and so forth. 'Maybe we should phone her,' she suggested, 'and tell her not to come.'

'Right. Where's the phone?'

He was efficient. She thought of offering him coffee, but decided to let him earn it first.

They had it at Jane's after he had shovelled several loads of mud into a wheelbarrow and Maurizio had carted it off to a safe place. The two then shoved planks against the side of the hill to prevent further erosion and buttressed these with stones.

Watching through the drizzle on Jane's back window, Carla was put in mind of sermons and parables. Menace was being averted by prudent toil. The wet grille of Jane's window turned the priest's fawn raincoat into a lacy surplice.

Her gaze jumping, as drops shifted on the pane, she examined him for shadiness or prudishness. Why had he kept Sybil at bay? A man much desired is interesting and Sybil's passion enlarged and hung about him like a cope. Carla, raised on Boccaccio, had no belief in clerical scruple. Women, in her experience, took chastity seriously. Not men.

It was clear that he had a way with boys, for Maurizio, usually so difficult, was digging with a will. The two were racing to get the job finished by nightfall and showed off for each other and perhaps for Carla. Shovels slid masterfully into mud; then the stuff was trundled off to be tipped all over Jane's sloping garden. It would be too much to expect them to know the difference between bindweed and morning glory. Carla saw too late that a strawberry patch had been engulfed.

Jane joined her at the window. 'Do you think I can ask them to start moving my things when they finish that?'

Carla thought a coffee break should be provided.

Coming in for it, the two gave off a steam of energy and looked like relatives. Bangs of hair bounced damply on their foreheads. Jane's house no longer qualified as indoors, so they did not remove their coats. Cold air was pouring through the broken wall.

'We'll have to nail something over that. Got any tarp?'

'I'll look. Coffee in the kitchen,' said Jane, 'this way, um, Father.'

'We're to call him "Leo",' instructed Maurizio. 'He was called after a pope.'

'Well, you,' his mother told him, 'were called after a Byzantine emperor. We opted for temporal glory.'

'They're closer than they used to be, the temporal and the other kind,' Leo told them. He was pouring warm water over frozen hands at the kitchen sink. 'Theologians are frittering eternity to a metaphor. I'd imagined,' he added, sitting down to his cookies and coffee, 'that it was a spiritual rather than a corporal work of mercy I'd be called to perform here. Sybil Steele gave me that impression.'

Jane giggled. She'd had no religious education. 'Corporal!' she marvelled.

It was clear to Carla that he hadn't an inkling of Sybil's plans for him. She hoped that Sybil was all right.

Leo, an elbow on Jane's kitchen table, was letting Maurizio try to force down his fist. The two were swollen and intent, but the man must be holding back to give the boy a chance.

How old was he? Mid thirties? Tousle-haired, physical – priests often seemed to be that. The impression could be in the beholder's eye, but there was often a suggestion of something pent. In the Rome of Carla's childhood – she had spent part of every school vacation there with her maternal grandparents – processions of skirted clerics had been a common sight, mostly uniformed in acne, black and botched hair-cuts, though some – from, was it the German College? – dressed in a demonic, fiery red. She had a memory too of purple cassocks (a mirage?); in her mind's eye these bobbed like crocuses along shady cobbles. Her grandparents had lived in the Prati district, an ugly, boxy, residential tract of apartment buildings slap next to the Vatican. Priests were less interesting than, say, the *Bersaglieri*, who always went by at a jog and wore rooster feathers pressed with stylish gaiety to the upturned sides of their hats. Seminarists, though, were in greater supply and rated the stare Carla, as an adolescent, would spare for any street spectacle. Sometimes, astride the pillion of some boy's scooter, she would be whirled saucily past a tight formation of them. Implosive, in regimented files, they used to proceed, at a centipede's gait, across broad sunny squares then burrow into the dark of narrow, back streets: scarlet or black, articulated, physical.

Sybil was too: that smell, that bubble of muscle. Would those two ever get together now, or would Sybil decide that God had spoken in words of mud?

Maurizio shouted from the front room: 'There's someone on our terrace, ringing our doorbell.'

Carla, going to look, recognized Sybil's husband. She went back to the kitchen. 'Do you know Terry Steele?' she asked Leo. 'He's over at my place.'

Leo looked unperturbed.

'We could ignore him,' she offered. 'After all, we're out.'

But Leo said: 'He may be looking for me.'

'Oh?'

'Yes. Mrs Steele sometimes comes on parish calls with me and when she does she leaves the phone numbers of where we'll be at the rectory. If something came up, her family could have been ringing your place and got no answer.'

Leo began to button his raincoat.

But Jane, seeing her work force about to defect, cut in: 'Couldn't we *all* go and each carry something?' She had prepared a pile of packages. 'Here!' She shoved a load at each helper. 'Mind your footing on the slope. Some steps have been washed away.'

TV cameramen would have appreciated the wretched cor-

44

tège which now slithered down Jane's slope, forded the flooded road and climbed Carla's three flights of steps. Maurizio went first with two rolled Bokhara rugs. Carla had a box filled with breakable objects and was scolded by Jane when she stumbled in the gutter. Leo carried an unwieldy piece of African sculpture and Jane herself had a basket of cats. Terry Steele stared down at them from Carla's terrace like a ship's officer scrutinizing flotsam. He was a broad-boned man with wettish blue eyes and stood very straight as though he felt he were on show. He wore a trench-coat with flaps.

'Hullo, Terry,' shouted Leo, 'come to check up on the emergency? I didn't think you big muckymucks ever left the studio.'

'Is Sybil with you?'

Leo began to slip. 'Terry, come and give me a hand. This thing's resisting me.'

Terry couldn't very well refuse. There was much panting and heaving before they were all up in Carla's porch, scraping and removing their boots. Jane suggested another trip before the light went. 'I'm Jane,' she told Terry, since nobody had introduced them. 'Jane Carrington. My house has been condemned.'

'I'm looking for my wife.'

'She didn't come,' Leo told him. 'I rang and told her her car wouldn't make it up the hill. How did you get here?'

'She's not at home.'

'Well, maybe she's shopping or something. Most of the city's perfectly normal, you know. Everywhere except the canyons and slide areas.' Leo was panting from his efforts.

'I'll hold you responsible,' said Terry, 'if anything's happened.'

'What?' Leo sounded surprised. 'Why should anything happen?'

Terry threw a punch at the piece of sculpture which he had helped Leo carry up the last flight of steps. It had a mask with beads and teeth and swags of queer hair. These swayed and clicked when he did this.

'What are you doing?' Terry asked Leo. 'Toting African gods about? Ecumenicism my butt! I want my wife to stop being a clerical groupy.' His eyes looked like crazed china. He was,

45

Carla remembered, of Anglo-Irish origin. It was possible that he drank. 'I don't want her hanging round priests. Priests in the rectory, women in their husbands' beds is what I say. What the hell do guys like you know of marriage? I'd legislate obligatory matrimony for one and all of you if I were pope. You guys have it every way.'

'Can we talk somewhere private?'

'I'm not talking. I'm warning you off.'

'Let's go inside,' said Carla. 'We'll freeze here.'

They tramped in, then stood uncertainly.

'Look,' began Leo but Terry interrupted.

'My wife,' he raised a hand to show who had the floor, 'is confused.' He had a deep, authoritative voice which made you think of him as big and powerful when you heard it disembodied on the radio. Even sitting down, he would look big, for his shoulders were broad and he could have worn a jacket designed for a much taller man. Maybe his troubles with Sybil and his radio success came from the same thing: his striving to be a grand patriarchal figure which he could only sustain while his legs were out of sight?

'These celibates,' Terry Steele jerked an elbow at Leo, 'are about as grown-up as Maurizio – sorry, Maurizio, they're a lot less grown-up.'

'Terry,' shouted Leo. 'Listen, I don't know what . . .'

'Let me *talk*, goddamn it, Leo. I'm a quiet man. I'm not calling you out. I won't try to beat you up. All I want is to *talk*. It's what I do, right? So, for once, you listen and try to take in what you hear. It's the voice of the temporal world, Leo, a place you know a lot less well than you may think. All this social work and helping to save other people's furniture – do you know what it is? It's *playing house*. It's what kids of six do under the dining-room table. They pull chairs around and make themselves little cubby-holes and play until it's time to put the stuff away and forget about it. There's no responsibility involved. Of course *you* probably never played house when you were a kid. You probably played at being in a pulpit. Carla, can I have a drink?'

'Of course.' Carla was relieved at having a role to play. 'What will you have?' Her sympathies were in suspense, but an animal response had been roused in her. Her blood raced. Would it do

46

Maurizio more harm if she tried to send him away rather than letting him stay here? Probably. Anyway, he wouldn't go.

Leo tried again: 'I don't know what you think ...'

'Nothing. That's my point. I think you did nothing, saw nothing, knew nothing.'

'Then I don't think you've the right to come here and abuse me and insult your wife.'

'I'm not abusing or insulting anyone. I'm upset. My wife is upset. My life is in a shambles because of the capers your Church has been getting up to. I'll have vodka, Carla, please. Or Scotch. Whatever you've got. Straight. No rocks. First you land us with five kids. Five. We'd have fifteen if we hadn't given up sex. We took you literally, you see, Sybil and I, and it ruined our marriage, our feeling for each other, our future. We never meant to stay in America. *I* never meant to become the voice of Conservative California, but how can I stop? There are no jobs back in England. I'm forty-nine and who back there has heard of bloody, goddamned K - L U V? I've got seven mouths to feed. School bills. The mortgage. Mind if I sit down, Carla? Payments on the swimming-pool – I never wanted a swimming-pool but it's part of the life style. You can't look broke. You wouldn't know about this back in the rectory, to be sure. Holy Poverty is a comfortable option. You wouldn't know the odds either in Vatican roulette. I'm sorry, Carla. I'm sorry – sorry for coming into your house and laying all this on you. You've probably got your own troubles. Everyone has. Everyone except God's anointed who come sniffing round our marriages telling us how to run them. Cuckoos. First they smash up the relationship, then they steal the wife's admiration – has Sybil been confiding in you, Carla?'

'No.'

'Well, you wouldn't tell me. Why should you? Any more than *she'd* tell Marco if the shoe was on the other foot. You women are dislocated. I know it. The things bothering you are hard to put into words ...' This admission from 'Mr Golden Voice of the Southland' – Terry Steele had been awarded the title three times in succession – was disarming. Carla felt indignant but also sorry for him, her sympathies switching back and forth.

Leo, it struck her, was genuinely baffled. Well, more fool he, she decided, opting for the party of the married.

'Falling in love with a celibate is regressive behaviour,' said Terry Steele in a wise voice. It was his weapon, Carla saw. He'd vanquish the priest with it, game, set and match. 'It's the equivalent,' sneered the voice, 'of a return to adolescence when we were *all* celibate, masturbating madly in our beds.'

'I must ask you not to talk like that!' Leo's pulpit-trained organ was no match for the media-man's. 'There's a young boy here ... women ...'

'I'm in my friend, Carla's house. You throwing me out, Carla? She's not, see. We're on my ground. This is Familyland. Here we all know the score: it's measured in blood, sweat, semen and money. All real, Leo. Forgive me if I don't call you "Father". Somehow it doesn't come trippingly off the tongue. I guess that's because I'm five times the father you are in real terms. No fooling with mystic metaphors here.' Terry Steele finished his vodka. 'You've alienated my wife's affections,' he told Leo.

Carla couldn't bear to listen. What, she thought, feeling jittery, what can anyone do? That was a line from what? Oh – a nursery rhyme.

Leo was saying that Terry Steele's imagination was overwrought and that he, Leo, had things to do. Looters might attack the house across the road if he didn't nail up the tarpaulin. This conversation would be better put off to a soberer moment.

The word 'sober' annoyed Terry Steele who began to talk about Leo's collar. Either Leo was tied down by it or he wasn't, said Terry Steele, as though Leo had been a dog. Carla concentrated on remembering the rest of the rhyme which had come into her head. Superstitiously, she had to come up with it if disaster, hovering like the bat-black night, were not to strike nearer. Maybe it was a surrogate for prayer? No: prayer itself must be a surrogate for familiar words which consoled and kept out fear. How did it go? Maurizio would know. It had been in his kindergarten reader. But she couldn't ask him while Terry Steele was shouting and Leo's conscience was being churned up. Then, smooth as syrup, the nursery words assembled in her head:

James James Morrison's Mother put on a golden gown.
James James Morrison's Mother drove to the end of the
town...
James James Morrison's Mother hasn't been heard of since.
King John said he was sorry, so did the queen and prince.
King John (somebody told me) said to a man he knew:
'If people go down to the end of the town, well, what can
anyone do?'

In her mind's eye, Sybil stood in a golden gown on a lurid
sidewalk. Poor Sybil would never do any such thing.

The men were telling each other 'If you don't leave, I will'. As
though ready to take butting runs at each other, they lowered
their heads. There was a distinct feeling in the room that someone might do someone an injury. Carla put a hand on
Maurizio's shoulder but he ducked away. He looked shocked
and very excited.

'Why don't we all,' Carla spoke in a firm organizer's voice,
'finish helping Jane. It's getting dark and it'll be dangerous
crossing the road once it *is*.'

'Oh please,' Jane chimed in, 'I'd be *so* grateful if you would.'

Astonishingly, Jane got the men to collaborate on lugging
boxes down her front path – the steps had been swept away
leaving it slick like a gummy mouth – across two foaming
gutters, then up Carla's solid steps.

'I've got to throw myself on your better natures,' said Jane
with bossy, half-flirty assurance.

'I think I've pulled a muscle,' said Terry Steele. His voice had
softened. Perhaps he had come to think of Leo as a work mate?
His flannel trousers were muddy to the knee.

Leo and he talked with muted urgency on Carla's porch, then
Terry Steele said 'so long' and tramped off in the direction of
Sunset Boulevard and his car. Jane departed shortly afterwards
in her friend's husband's truck, which drove up to fetch herself,
her suitcase and her basket of cats. The three, left behind to
watch the tail-lights dither down the slick hill, felt drawn
together and domestic. They looked, if anyone had been there

49

to see, like a model nuclear family. Leo began to laugh about Jane.

'*She* gets her pound of flesh all right,' he said, 'her pint of sweat!'

But this must have reminded him of Terry's accusations, for he grew sober quickly. 'I'm sorry,' he said, 'about the Donnybrook. I hope it didn't upset Maurizio.'

'Didn't it upset *you*?' Carla was curious.

'Oh, I'm used to emotional hassles – in the line of duty.'

'You don't take seriously ... what he told you?'

'Should I?'

'Yes.'

'Oh!' Leo was clearly upset. 'I see.' Pause. '*You'd* know, I suppose?'

'Yes.'

He was silent for a while, frowning and avoiding her eye. Then: 'You must think I'm insensitive – a sort of outlaw? That's Steele's idea.'

'Well, priests always had their own laws didn't they?' She was fiercely on Sybil's and Terry's side: divided territory, but an abyss away from where this man stood. However, she felt sorry for him too. He had swung from assurance to a dejected bafflement. Did living alone so deprive people of nous? He's like a wolf-boy, she thought, astonished. Now he was trying to scuttle off – unless, he wondered, she'd like some help in disposing of those boxes of Jane's? They'd been lobbed in Carla's elegant drawing-room, making it look like a way station.

'Stay for dinner,' said Carla on impulse. 'And have a bath.'

'I don't want to butt in.' Shyly. 'You may be busy. I don't know.'

'We're not. And, goodness, you've earned a meal.'

But he had grown touchy. 'No,' he said. 'Thanks, but no. I'll just wash my hands if that's OK, then I'll be pushing off. I have to get back.'

He was, she saw, hopeless at human relations other than the very forthright. She imagined Maurizio being like this, some time, somewhere, away from home. Dinner at the rectory would surely be over by now. It was seven-thirty and Leo had a mile to walk to his car. He would have to poke through a refrigerator

50

and spoon stuff from jars onto a cold plate. What would a group of bachelors keep in their fridge? Ice-cream? Granola? Cranberry sauce? At best, eggs.

'Please!' She touched his sleeve. 'We'd *like* you to. Maurizio is counting on it. He's going to cook the meal to impress you: *tagliatelli alla cacciatora*. He has only two recipes, so you'll know half his repertoire. He does it well.'

'Are you sure?'

'Yes.'

'All right then. Thank you. I will.'

A minute later he was in the kitchen, asking Maurizio to wait until he was through with his shower to start cooking the *tagliatelli*. He wanted to know how it was done. He'd be leaving the parish soon, he explained, to live in a flat. He needed to learn a little cooking. He was going back to school.

'School!' Maurizio was boisterously amazed. 'How *old* are you?'

'Maurizio! Don't be rude!'

'That's all right. I'm thirty-six. I'll be a mature student. I'll be doing a doctorate in psychology.' Leo laughed shyly. 'Seems like I have a lot to learn.'

'Thirty-six! That's my Mom's age.'

'*Maurizio!* You're not supposed to say things like that outside the family!' But even this slight move to exclude their guest might hurt. 'Go have your bath,' she interrupted herself. 'I'll be getting us drinks. Do you like mulled wine?'

'*I* do,' said Maurizio. 'The cook gets to drink.'

'If he's Italian he does. If he's American and thirteen years old . . .'

'I thought we weren't to talk about ages. Anyway, I'm nearly fourteen and I'm Italian for this evening.' Maurizio began to sing *Fratelli d'Italia* in his raucous, breaking voice. He liked having a guest, a senior male whom he could impress.

Carla considered her kitchen with an outsider's eyes. The Mexican tiles on the floor were almost exactly like the ones you got in Tuscany: thick solid slabs the colour of ripe meat. Woodwork, basket-work, earthenware crocks and handmade pottery added up to a clever pretence at rustic carelessness. It was efficient and tasteful but, a doubt struck her – was it too full of

51

everything the greedy consumer might buy on whim? Why, she wondered for the first time, have three ovens? One was microwave and small but she felt that Sybil with her Brontëish face and scrupulous passion might disapprove. The priest too. It was absurd to mind, but an equation, dredged from songs or some other manifestation of the way the marginal and high-minded saw things, lumped consumerism with smugness, middle age and dryness of the heart.

'Don't put out the silver,' she told Maurizio quickly. 'We'll use the stainless steel.'

The meal was a success, the *tagliatelli* being caught at just the right point of firmness. The three drank wine from Piemonte and, under its influence, Maurizio asked his mother in Italian: 'Are you on his side? Do you think Mr Steele was unfair?'

'*Attenti!*' said Leo, surprising them by speaking Italian too. 'I had an Italian mother and I studied in Rome for a while before I was ordained.'

This was a bond. Carla guessed, however, that the mother must have been from the Italian south. There was an edge of dialect to his accent, corrected, she guessed, by the stay in Rome. She beat back a small surge of prejudice against clannish, backward southerners. Here he had nobody to be clannish with and his trouble seemed to come rather from progressiveness than the lack of it. Odd that he should have been obtuse about Sybil! But that blend of lust and virtue must have been hard to read. Even Sybil's husband wouldn't have known of it if it hadn't been for the anonymous calls. When Maurizio went to the kitchen, Carla mentioned these to Leo.

'It's a bit late to be discreet on Sybil's behalf,' she apologized, 'and the point is that you must have an enemy in the parish.'

He had no idea who this could be and was aghast at his own innocence. He supposed that he came on too warmly or not warmly enough with people? Set up the wrong expectations?

He seemed to be waiting for reassurance, but she said nothing.

'It's difficult,' he admitted, 'being marked off as a celibate. Some people in the parish – older ones, mostly – treat you as if you were a god because you don't need a woman. Others think you're a creep because you can't get one. There's a danger of trying too hard to come across as an ordinary nice guy: overdoing the human warmth, you know?'

Was he telling her that this was what he'd done with Sybil? A blush rose blotchily to the surface of his skin. Toughen up, she wanted to say, then guessed him to be already as tough as old boots. Like an adolescent, he would be a mixture of softnesses he couldn't cope with and a thorny, protective rind.

Worrying about how he came across was, she suggested, surely a waste of time?

'I suppose you're right.'

She liked his rocky, prominent bones.

'Perhaps you're not vain enough?' she wondered. 'You're very good-looking, you know.' Fearful of embarrassing him, she added. 'You needn't be afraid that *I*'ll become troublesome.'

Laughter.

She longed to tell him about Marco. He, a professional, must know how to listen and advise. She took a deep breath. For months, she had been wanting to spill her worries. But relief, like a too sudden thaw, was after all unbearable. Immediately, she felt she couldn't burden this man with what she could continue to carry herself. He'd had a hard day. Let him simmer down. Besides, thinking of Marco, she found her picture of him blemished by the contaminating self-pity of his squash-partner, Terry Steele. She preferred to put him from her mind.

And anyway, here was Maurizio carrying plum compote and pistachio ice-cream.

'Look,' he paused by the window. 'There's someone over at Jane's. Someone with a flashlight. Moving.'

'Let's ring the house. Maybe she came back for something she forgot?'

But there was no answer to their call. The light disappeared and they decided to ring the police. As there was no vehicle in sight, it seemed wise to give the alarm and for Leo to stay until the patrol car came.

'Aren't you afraid here alone?' he asked. 'Looters will converge on the abandoned houses. The police can't be everywhere. You should have a dog.' He knew about dogs, he told them; he had been brought up in Oregon where he used to go hunting with his father.

Carla went to make coffee and when she came back the other two had arranged a trade. Leo was to train a dog for Maurizio if Maurizio taught him to cook.

'*Will* you buy a dog, Mamma?' Maurizio was all excitement. Carla was doubtful.

'There are great dogs,' Leo told them, 'in the city pounds. They cost nothing and taking one rescues it from the vivisectors.'

'What were your people doing in Oregon?'

'My mother's family ran a delicatessen. My father taught school.'

In the long school holidays he and his father had tramped over miles of hill country. 'Half Swiss, half Scottish,' he said so that they might imagine the views over the Columbia and Willamette rivers. 'Think of old engravings: lots of blur, mist and bright water.' His earliest memories were of beating walls of sweet-corn with a stick. They had been maybe three times his own height and arched above him in scrolls and ogives as he patrolled their papery naves, scaring out pigs which had been eating the corn and occasionally an abrupt, vertical flurry of pheasants for his father to shoot. Dogs would then retrieve the shot birds whose necks had to be wrung ruthlessly and fast.

Like Sybil's hopes, thought Carla, recognizing this man's absorption in things and activities. Men like that didn't focus on you at all – or on themselves. Staring out the dark window, he was back in the mushroomy Oregon hills. He described silver damp, the pink pith of pine trees and the glee of spying, secret among browned, fallen needles, the just-visible dome of a brown boletus mushroom: the most succulent of edible fungi.

'Of course!' cried Carla and Maurizio who hadn't thought these even existed in America: '*I funghi porcini!*' Dark on top, yellow underneath as a bath sponge, you ate them grilled with catnip and all the aromas of the forest were in your mouth as you bit through charred crust to the inner softness. It was like eating the land.

Leo had learned of them from his mother's father, a stout, passionate old man mad about nineteenth-century poetry, opera, mushrooms and roasted blackbirds. These tastes had scandalized Leo's own father who was ashamed to be served

54

game illegally netted with lime and snares. How could a poetry-lover eat songbirds, the father used to ask and push away his plate.

'I could teach you to cook *them*,' offered Carla, ignoring the moral issue – if that was what it was. 'You'd have to catch them though – or Maurizio might. It's a great Tuscan dish. Larks, too, and thrushes. There must be some equivalent around here, surely? Shall we set up nets?' She felt elegiac for greedy memories of her own. Crunch, went the memories through crisp, spitted carcasses flavoured with rosemary. ' "The sweeter the flesh the nearer the bone",' she remembered, 'so you eat the bones too!'

'I think I disapprove,' said Leo. 'I side with my father.'

'What was his name – your name?'

'Hausermann.'

'German?'

'Yes.'

Aahuhaahuhaahu, wailed the police siren, striving up the Glen and, in no time, two patrol men were knocking at the Verdis' door. They had Casimir with them in what seemed to be semi-custody. He had been found inside Jane's house with a flashlight and a key to the front door. He had not broken in, nor, as far as could be ascertained, done damage, though this was hard to assess as the place was in a shambles. Casimir's blond locks were dripping rainwater onto his deerskin jacket. He looked romantic and unreliable, but only the second was true.

Could Mrs Verdi identify him?

'Of course,' said Carla. 'It's Casimir. I can tell you where the house-owner is if you want to phone her: Miss Carrington. I'm sure she won't want to press charges.'

She was far from sure. Jane might well feel that a night in the slammer would be good for Cazz who had, very likely, been planning to steal some choice thing. He was Polish, a refugee, claimed to come from an old feudal family and was as predatory as a hawk.

'I was looking for some possessions of mine that I'd left at Jane's,' he said with dignity. 'I'd heard the house was condemned, so I was worried for them. The lights have fused.'

Cazz, who could never refuse anything to a person's face, had probably been searching for a couple of trinkets he'd given Jane.

55

His attitude to gifts and ownership was haughtily contingent. His English was odd and was clearly not predisposing the patrol men in his favour. He had picked it up partly from the overseas service of the BBC and partly from the waitress who had agreed to marry him so that he could get to this country. A girl from Milwaukee, she'd had the misfortune to meet Cazz on a trip to Europe which she and her sister had won in a church raffle.

The policemen phoned Jane. Mild-faced youths, they reminded Carla of country nursemaids brought in from the Florentine *contado* to look after the children of city families whose priorities confused them. Jane, it seemed, was reassuring and so was the driver's licence which Casimir now located in the lining of his jacket.

'It's not a good idea to go out without ID,' said the nursemaid-policeman handing this back. He seemed shocked that Cazz should have no credit cards. But Cazz, a freelance script writer who rarely sold a script, had neither solid credentials nor salary and no store would give him credit. The policemen lectured him on the unwisdom of his behaviour in keeping Jane's key and intruding on her property. Carla, on the other hand, got marks for citizenship and keeping an eye out for her neighbours' interests.

'It's the only way,' the two policemen agreed, 'to check the antisocial elements active in the neighbourhood.' It seemed likely that they counted Cazz as one of these.

Maurizio listened with care and learned that a man who hadn't even got a credit card from Sears Roebuck cut very little ice with the Los Angeles Police Department. Cazz had an elaborate framed copy of his family tree which he had moved from Jane's house to Wanda's where it was prominently displayed. It had gilded and emblazoned beasts in the corners and showed remote connections with Grand Masters of Knightly Orders and with one minor Crowned Head. This, it was clear, would have been of no help if Jane had not chosen to vouch for him. She'd been pretty decent, in Maurizio's opinion, after the way old Cazz had walked out on her. Today had provided proof of something Maurizio had long suspected: authorities around here agreed on nothing – zilch.

Chapter Three

For days the Glen was impassable and Maurizio's mother couldn't take out the car. Leo rang and asked if he could take her shopping in a jeep belonging to the parish, but she said she had all she needed laid in. Then he offered to give Maurizio a lift to the Lycée. He'd be passing their house early, he said, on the way to a church where he had to say mass. Maurizio could come with him, then he'd drop him off. Since it was either this or walk a mile in the mud, then wait on Sunset for the school bus, Maurizio was grateful and, as it happened, enjoyed the mass. Leo looked well in his robes – ('Vestments,' he corrected when Maurizio said this) – and Maurizio wondered whether his parents hadn't deprived him of his birthright by not bringing him up a Catholic. He didn't think he'd have gone along with the religion but it would have been interesting to struggle with doubts, then give it up. He'd seen films about young guys doing this in small European towns and suspected that life was easier to manage in places like that. If you were worried about something, you asked the priest. You needn't do what he said, but just asking might be a help. Maybe he should feel Leo out on the subject of Cazz?

However, when Leo came back to the front of the church in

shirt and pants, he didn't look like a priest any more and Maurizio didn't feel like confiding in him. He asked Leo if he wouldn't have preferred to wear black skirts like priests did in the movies Maurizio had seen in the Lycée. The Lycée showed scads of old French movies so that the kids should keep up their memories of home. Some were so old that the memories kept up were likely to be their grandparents'. Still, old or not, priests' costumes seemed a good idea.

'Like the Hare Krishnas,' Maurizio argued. 'They wear theirs out in the street so as to get attention. *And* they sing. People notice them.'

'Yes,' Leo said, 'but people also think they're odd. Our idea is to go *to* people, not to separate ourselves off from them.'

'We're not Catholics,' Maurizio thought it fair to explain. 'Not like the Steeles.'

'I didn't think you were.'

'Why not? We might have been.'

'The signs are easy to read. I'm an expert, remember?'

'When you talk of "going to the people", do you mean people like us or Catholics?'

'Both.'

'Which do you concentrate on?'

'Well, there are two ways to look at that,' Leo told him. 'Some say preaching to the converted is a waste of time. On the other hand, it's a bit mean to neglect the converted altogether, don't you think?'

'When are you coming to *us* again?'

'I'll be out of circulation for a couple of weeks,' said Leo. 'I'm going on a retreat – so as to get back in touch with the ground I stand on before I leave the parish. I'll be starting at UCLA in the spring term. I'll get in touch then. Is this the way in?'

They had reached the Lycée gate.

'It's a bit small,' said Maurizio apologetically, remembering that Catholic schools were big for sports. 'The French have no sporting tradition,' he explained. 'Italians are good at soccer though.'

Leo said he might be able to get tickets for a soccer game.

'I think I'd rather basket-ball or ice hockey.'

'Basket-ball then. Does your mother like sports?'

58

'No, she hates them,' said Maurizio, nipping that notion before it got going. Terry Steele's accusation was fresh in his ears and he'd seen several movies in which guys got around younger guys' mothers by taking the younger guys to sports events. It was annoying to have to rely so much on the cinema, but, on the other hand, if you had no experience of your own, it would be silly to discount it – especially when your father had been away for three months. He wondered if he wasn't getting a bit crazy? Was it normal to suspect every man you met of having the hots for someone? Cazz had them for Wanda. He'd had them before that for Jane. Maurizio's worry was that he might have them next for Evie – and now maybe Leo had them for Maurizio's mother. Who could he ask? If he wasn't crazy then everyone was. Even in the movies, sex was more restrained than this. It was glamorous there too and in life seemed to Maurizio icky and unmanageable. Maybe he'd end up as a monk? Maybe *that* was why Leo had gone into the Church? Ask – no, he couldn't ask Leo. Maurizio suddenly felt on the point of breaking out in sobs. He stuck his nails into his palms, hurting himself as much as he could to prevent such an appalling outcome.

'Actually, neither my mother nor I likes sports at all,' he told Leo ridiculously. 'I'll get off here. Thanks for the ride. Just follow the Way Out signs.' He jumped from the jeep, waved at the surprised Leo and rushed into the Lycée, telling himself that he was getting more unbalanced by the day and might end up in the booby-hatch. *That* was silly. The truth was that he was normal and dead average and nothing interesting would probably ever happen to him, not sex nor madness nor even being taken to a basket-ball game if he was rude to people who offered tickets. Maybe religion would be good for him? It might calm him down. Come to think of it, maybe he should be offended that Leo *hadn't* tried to convert him – or was the offer of soccer tickets a sly move? If it was, it was *too* sly. The Hare Krishnas ran after you in the street, gave you big, brotherly smiles and handed you their folders. No wonder they were getting to be so well known that there were notices in the airport saying that you could have them arrested for bothering you. At least they *worked* at their job. Maurizio wondered whether guys like Leo could compete with them. Still, now that he'd more or less decided that what Leo was after was his soul and not his mother's body, he felt he liked the guy and hoped he hadn't put him off.

Carla was climbing the hill behind her house. If the landlord did not return and Marco did, the plan was that the Verdis should buy the property. Meanwhile, she was supposed to be looking out for their joint interests and should have seen to it that the scruffy frame-house overlooking the slope on which she now stood was not re-let; while it stood vacant, she could easily have obtained an order to have it torn down. She hadn't moved fast enough and was embarrassed to take any action now that Cazz had moved in with the new tenant.

Turning her back on the eyesore, she looked out over the Glen which was green and steaming in the morning sun and overhung by air of an impure yellow like camomile tea. In the nose, this had a mineral quality with a taste like spa water. Breathing it in, she watched a squirrel ripple along a branch, turning drops silver then black. A bloated insect bobbed against the sky. Its wings were discernible only as a vibrancy and its frame was squat as a wine cork. Dipping in front of a screen of foliage, it revealed itself to be a humming bird, its bright-plumaged body suddenly in perfect proportion to the now visible wings and beak. Amused by the metamorphosis, Carla turned to follow its flight and found herself staring in the window of the next-door shack. Casimir, naked as a worm, stood not nine yards from her. Beside him, with her back to Carla, was Wanda wearing a mumu with a design of large, cut water-melons. With a swift movement, Cazz crouched, caught the hem of this and drew it over Wanda's head. Before Carla could look away, he had folded Wanda in two and begun making vigorous love to her.

Carla turned and moved quickly down the hill. She was upset. There had been a cold violence about his assault which she felt sure was aimed at herself. It was excessive and seemed to ricochet off its immediate object as a ball will do in croquet to reach one less accessibly placed. Worse: in the moment before Cazz stepped in front of Wanda's body, Carla had seen that it was covered with painful-looking bruises.

'Okies,' the Glen grocer had said knowingly of Wanda and her family when they first moved in. 'They're on Welfare,' he'd added with a sense of injury. 'Come in here wanting to pay with food stamps. First time we've had *that* around here. I thought I'd heard that that shack was to be pulled down?'

The new residents had come in a truck which they'd unloaded themselves.

'Those are transients if ever I saw transients,' said the grocer. His was the only shop in the Glen and he liked to know what was happening. 'The man left, you know. Right after unloading. Just turned round and left. I thought he was a driver they'd hired, but the little girl told me he was her Dad. The women are her mother and aunty. He's gone back to Kansas. To work, she says.'

Someone must have warned them against Carla. They scarcely returned her greetings and didn't take advantage of her offer to lend them anything they might need. Sitting on her balcony, she heard them talk as they pegged out clothes with one hand and held cigarettes at the ready in the other. They struck her as familiar: women of a pattern she had seen in her Florentine childhood. Joking with nervy vigour, they had the art of milking a laugh from the drabbest moment and hoping against all odds that some unearnable luck might transform their lives. They were sitting ducks for someone like Cazz and reminded her of girls she'd known who had come to bad ends, and because they did she had taken it upon herself to warn Wanda against him.

'Mrs Briggs,' she had said – that being Wanda's name – 'I hope you will not take this amiss. I feel it only fair to warn you, since you're new here and I, since I introduced you, am in a way responsible, that Mr Dobrinski – Cazz – is not reliable. He does not ... treat women in a good way. Forgive me.' She had felt acutely embarrassed.

'That so?' Wanda had stared back unruffled.

Cazz was already the woman's lover. Entrenched. Carla should have known that by the time *she* noticed something, it would be a fact consecrated by the knowledge of half the Glen. Now Wanda would have told Cazz of Carla's warning. She imagined them laughing together and attributing coarse motives to her.

It was Marco who had brought Cazz to the house. Restless, half cautious, yet curious about ways of life he hadn't the time nor perhaps the urge to try himself, Marco, like an armchair anthropologist, enjoyed hearing about other people's experiments with Californian fads. And Cazz was a one-man research team. When the Verdis first met him he was studying Zen Buddhism with a Japanese *roshi* in a convent somewhere up state. Later, he took up various forms of therapy, Rolfing, the Synanon game and had spent time with members of the Jonestown cult. Restlessly sipping at odd doctrines, he committed himself to none. Sexually, he was more decided. His preference was for very young girls. He had lived with one two years ago and brought her unexpectedly to the Verdis' one afternoon.

The girl had been small and silent: a child cultivating a childish air, she wore clothes too big for her, looked like a waif and was in fact a runaway. She might have been fourteen. Silently, she had sat on the Verdis' sofa, balancing a plate on her knees, eating food Carla had offered her. Cazz and she were staying in a mansion he had been lent by a Polish friend who was away in Europe. It was palatial, but neither of them could cook. They lived, Cazz explained, on packaged raisins. He had found her in some guy's bed.

'"Take her buddy," this guy said. Well, wow, I didn't wait to be asked twice.'

The child ate and said nothing. Marco wouldn't hear of Carla's going to the police.

The girl stayed several months with Cazz in apparent bliss. Cazz, at any rate, was blissful and Carla couldn't remember *her* ever speaking at all. Her parents, Cazz explained, were impossible people, old-time Germans who bullied and browbeat her. 'There was no communication!' he explained. 'Anything was better than living with them. Even me!' He laughed with an odd humility and Carla guessed that the girl's appeal for him was that she was even more protean and more of a refugee than he was – and maybe Cazz himself, like a clever child, had never had time to grow up? Anyway, they seemed content in their borrowed, unswept mansion where they never mended anything so that the owner, when he returned months later, had to get in a team of cleaners, plumbers and electricians.

Before that happened, however, the girl telephoned her mother who (this was reported by a rabidly angry and frenzied Cazz) had sobbed into the phone, sworn to let bygones be bygones, made promises and begged her daughter to come over to the house, 'just for a moment, honey, just to let me see you and get yourself some clothes! Come in the day-time when your father's not here.' The mother swore not to betray her to him. 'I love you, honey. I'm your Mommy, trust me!'

Cazz laughed with sour fury at this point of the story: 'Yeah, well, she fell for it.'

The girl had gone home as arranged and when she got there found two policewomen waiting who whisked her off to a reform school.

'There and then. Can you beat that? Her mother committed her. She's locked up. In a place in the Valley.'

Cazz had been desperate and in tears. 'I really love that girl,' he explained to Marco. He had come round to ask for help.

'I've been wondering,' his eyes flicked from Carla to Marco, 'could you guys help me out? I've been to talk to the mother, see, posing as a concerned and responsible friend, a sort of welfare figure. Naturally, she doesn't know ...'

'What you ... were to each other?'

'Right.' Cazz's slow, despondent little smile. He had managed to persuade the mother that her daughter could not live with her after what had happened and that a reform school was no good educational experience either.

'I really laid it on her, told her how she's lost her daughter's trust, needs a breathing time, a sort of moratorium. Anyway she's agreed to let her out if I can come up with a suitable pair of adoptive parents – you know: straight, acceptable ...' Cazz grinned anxiously. 'I was wondering, would you ...?'

'Cover for you,' said Marco, 'while you go on screwing her and feeding her dope?'

'Yes.'

No apology. No softening the request. Well, that was fair, wasn't it? He was their wild man, they his straight couple. Each to his role. They could surely be outspoken.

Or could Marco? He had a half-grin on his lips as he stared at Cazz, his angelic, corrupting alter ego. Carla knew what was expected of her.

'No,' she told Cazz quietly.

Cazz waited but Marco made no move. He was smiling still

63

as though the scene had not concerned him. Anarchy had to be put down but it pained Marco to see this happen.

'I'm afraid that's the way it is,' Carla concluded.

Cazz shrugged. 'Just thought I'd ask. Never be afraid to ask. That's my motto.' Laughing weakly – he was, Carla had been surprised to note, taking this loss hard – he hurried off to canvass the rest of his respectable or near-respectable acquaintances.

'Were you going to agree?' she fired the question so suddenly at Marco that he recoiled.

'Do you think I'm raving mad? What kind of a man do you think I am, Carla? My God, we've been married fifteen years.'

Yes, but now he was admitting – proclaiming that he had changed. 'My temper, Carla, has changed!' By how much?

When they next saw Cazz – months later; he had been staying with his *roshi* in between – Marco asked what had happened to the girl. Cazz laughed. Yeah, he agreed, that was a kinda funny story. What had happened was that he had managed to find adoptive parents and the girl's mother had duly handed her over to them. They were the required straight couple. Too straight. Truly straight, they had cleaned her up, dressed her in proper clothes and expected Cazz – Cazz! – to respect the teenage dating etiquette when he came to call.

'They expected me to come in and meet them and chat and call them Mr and Mrs, the whole bit.' Cazz's voice was dispassionate and unmodulated. 'It turned me right off. I quit seeing her.'

'Poor child!' Carla wondered what this second betrayal had done to the girl. Though, might it not have been the other way round? Perhaps it was *she* who had, knowingly, betrayed Cazz by stepping out of the game they had going together and signing up for a fresh season with altered costumes and a different role? Someone, after all, had to be left dangling when the music stopped.

For several months, after that, Cazz had buried himself in the penitential rituals of a new therapy group which he described to the Verdis afterwards with a mixture of triumph and self-mockery.

Later, he met Jane at their house and moved in with her, then out, then back and out again. Probably, he would return to her eventually. Poor shiftless Wanda could hardly hope to hold him.

He had met *her* at the Verdis too on a day, two months ago, when he'd come round to borrow sugar. He'd been still nominally living at Jane's, but Jane was in hospital for her operation and grocery-buying was not something he considered part of his role.

'Don't you get lonely?' he'd wondered while Carla poured sugar into a plastic bag. When, he asked, was Marco expected back? Carla had hedged painfully, since it no longer seemed to be a question of Marco's returning or not returning but of his deciding who he was. She steered Cazz out the door and pushed the sugar at him.

'Here. Take this.'

'Sugar?' Laughing. His other hand landed on her neck. 'Loosen up, Carla,' he advised. 'Life's a river. Flow with it. Let things happen.'

He was massaging her neck muscles and for a moment she closed her eyes and let herself imagine that it was Marco's hand doing this. It was a drugged moment: expanded and undercut by the simultaneous awareness and refusal of the fact that this was not Marco. These feelings reached ebullition when Cazz put his face next to hers, and fizzed over into a fever of fury when, among his alien smells, she recognized the very toilet water that Marco always used. Rage vented itself. She pushed him down the slope. The act was dual: Cazz and Marco fell. Had they planned this together? Cazz's terror of mutilation and the knife which Jane was undergoing had made him flee the house across the way. Had memory of some sly, pimping joke of Marco's sent him to *her*? Bastards both, she felt, pleased to see Cazz, caught off balance, fall heavily into a bush of prickly pear.

'Are you all right?' she asked hypocritically.

'Jesus ... Carla!' His arms and legs were flailing. 'I'm full of ... Jesus Christ.'

Seeing the Okie women's faces stare with interest over the fence, Carla found herself introducing Cazz in a hostessy voice. 'This is our neighbour, Mr Dobrinski ...' Her voice wove on, producing untimely bits of chat while Cazz failed to extricate himself from the chubby cactus which held him prisoner in its bear-shaped paws. Carla made half-hearted gestures in his direction but was afraid of his assaulting her this time in wrath,

65

and besides it was clear that to pull him out was simply not possible since the thing had caught him like a trap.

'Give him a hand,' instructed Wanda the Okie. 'But gently because ... No. Better wait a sec. I'll come in and help. Wait. Stay put till I come. Pulling will break the thorns off. Then they're kinda hard to get out of the flesh.' As she spoke, she was climbing the fence. Intrepidly, she threw one pink-clad leg over and in no time at all was helping to deliver Cazz from his plight. The burden of conversation fell entirely on her but she proved quite equal to it.

'No bones broken, I guess,' she said cheerily, 'though your clothes are sure in some state! How'd you ever get yourself so mussed up? Those pants sure are a sight. If you come round to my place I can mend them for you. I guess you'll have to take them off first though. Hope you're not bashful.'

That was how Carla came to introduce the two.

Terry Steele on K-LUV was talking about security. 'It doesn't exist,' he told his audience. 'Security is hype. Why should you expect to have it? Security would mean that the Dow Jones average would never fall, your kids never grow up, inflation would disappear and so would old age, death, breakdowns and sickness. Does this seem likely? No. So forget security and learn to take charge of what you can be responsible for: yourself.'

His voice on the radio sounded full of authority, but Maurizio remembered his row with Leo and how Terry Steele's whole aim had seemed to be to spread his own discomfort – not to get rid of it, just to spread it around.

'Dr Sunmaker,' said Terry Steele, 'is here with me, live, in the studio ready to answer any questions you may have about how to do this. Also, you might like to share a success story. Maybe you managed a tough life-experience head-on? Or maybe you're faced with one? Maybe your mate stepped out on you,' suggested Terry Steele. 'Share that with us. We're here to help.'

Maurizio turned him off. Terry Steele was a really uncool guy. Maurizio knew his wife, a big, boney, friendly woman with messy make-up. It amazed him that she should be thinking of love. Leo had said that Terry Steele had imagined the whole

66

thing and Maurizio thought this likely. He had tuned into the
Terry Steele programme a couple of times since then and it
seemed to him that the guy was losing his marbles.

He had a point about security though. Believing in *that*, in
Maurizio's opinion, was like believing in Santa Claus.

Jane had come round some days after the mudslides, looking
nervous and very excited. Her eyes were sunk and shiny; there
was a bubble of spit on her lip and while she was waiting for his
mother to come downstairs, Maurizio had begun to worry that
she might get hysterics and have to have cold water thrown on
her.

'Well,' she'd said, smoking a cigarette in a twitchy way, 'I
gather the drama went on after I'd left? Cazz? The police? Burg-
lary by one's formerly nearest and dearest! My house is too
destroyed for me to know what he took, if anything – other than
my heart.'

Maurizio could tell that she'd been unable to resist the joke
and that it was rebounding on her because her voice began to
crack as she made it.

'Old Terry Steele, the Moral Watchdog is right,' she'd said,
'this place is going downhill in more ways than one.' She'd
laughed because her house, or bits of it, *had* gone downhill and
her hand began to shake; then he saw her turn the shake into a
gesture and clasp it to her breast. He couldn't remember which
side she'd had removed.

Luckily, his mother had come into the room then and he'd
beat it. He left the door open, however, and heard Jane's voice
calling his mother 'darling' and getting back to the subject of
Cazz. She kept wondering what he could possibly be doing with
Wanda. Like Maurizio, she wondered if his interest wasn't Evie.

'After all, that girl he was with before was the same age,
wasn't she? I don't blame him. It's a compulsion that goes back
to his childhood – he never had one, you see. He was out on the
streets of Warsaw, scavenging, when he was six years old.
Naturally, he's trying to have it now – but society won't let him.
He should marry *me* and have children of his own.'

Parking outside the local grocer's, Carla saw a page stapled
to a telegraph pole:

WARNING
SUSPECTED RAPIST
LOOK OUT FOR DRIVER OF WHITE TOYOTA COROLLA
FIRST TWO LETTERS OF LICENCE PLATE GO
DRIVER OF MEDIUM HEIGHT, BROWN HAIR,
BROWN CHINOS
HANGS AROUND THIS NEIGHBOURHOOD
TRIES TO GET TALKING TO LONE WOMEN.

The leaflet had been put out by a local women's group. Carla tried to dissipate the bad feeling it gave her by buying truffles and macaroons. There was no pretending she didn't hate being a lone woman and living in the Glen.

A man standing by the meat counter asked her how hot he should make his oven for a centreloin pork roast and her mind fluttered with the effort of trying to match him with the description and a subsidiary worry as to whether his request had erotic connotations. Pork, she worried. Heat? Oven? What were chinos? The man's hair was brown.

'Slow,' she told him in a discouraging voice. 'Cook it twenty minutes to the pound in a slow oven.' Deciding against meat, she turned away. A badge on his shoulder saying Los Angeles Fire Department did nothing to douse her fears.

The next morning when Maurizio was in school, she set out to look for a dog. One of the marginal ills – or pluses – of this city was the number of thoroughbred dogs abandoned by its transient population and left in the city's pounds. Knowledge that any dog *she* saved from the vivisectors might be back here in a couple of months made her feel irresponsible. Marco would never stand for her bringing a dog back to Italy. Still, perhaps she might find a good home for it if the dog was attractive enough in the first place? And right now she needed the security.

She visited four pounds, was depressed and came to no decision. They were like prisons – or as she imagined prisons to be. Cages lined the aisles and, as in prisons, there were special security quarters. A Great Dane was in solitary confinement in the dark because it bit. A saluki seemed to have gone out of its mind. Cards pinned to the wire bore such information as 'house-trained', sometimes a name: Pooch, Bingo, Sarge. Plebeian, loveless names. Carla did not return for days. At night she dreamed of the dogs. It was clear that some had been maltreated. Some were fierce, some mad. Most betrayed of all, it seemed to her, were the shiny-coated pets with coquettish collars and fetching ways which nothing had prepared for such rejection. In one dream she herself was in a cage while Marco walked past. She did not want to go back to the pounds and, when Maurizio asked about the new dog she had rashly promised, said maybe it might be better to buy a puppy in a pet shop. But a puppy would be no protection. Besides, should she not, if she could do so, rescue at least one victim from its plight? She thought of the graceful Great Dane kept in solitary darkness, withdrawing into a bewilderment unmitigated by any understanding of the how or why. She saw its crazed, almond-set eyes blink into hope in the gleam of the opening doorway. But how could she manage such a dog? She was a small woman and abandonment had made it fierce.

The mailman brought three letters from Marco. The mail did that – bunched things up so that you went for days with nothing, worrying and trying to keep from cabling, then suddenly produced a harvest of three.

She stood them, unopened and in the order indicated by their postmarks, on her chimney-piece.

Walking to the grocery store, she passed a young man in black leather gloves and, on her way back, passed him again. What was he doing, walking up and down the Glen where nobody walked except herself and there was not even a sidewalk? Was he checking out the empty houses? Prowling? Did he perhaps have a skin-disease on the glove-masked hands or were they a thief's or a strangler's hands whose fingers, twitching for action, had to be covered as hawks' heads must to keep them dormant between hunts?

She wanted to answer her husband's letters which were unfair, cogent and selfish – cogent because selfish. He put his case squarely. How could *she*? 'You owe me ... I am weak ...' No, she wouldn't write. And she wouldn't read any more of his letters either.

She went back to one of the pounds. The keeper greeted her. 'I'm glad you came back, Ma'am! There's a real nice pooch

I want to show you. This is his second time in. A lady took him but she works all day and he was lonely all alone and took to howling. The neighbours complained so she had to bring him back. Seems a shame ...'

He was a golden labrador. Light cream with a dark nose and dark rims to his eyes, big but with the buoyant pliancy of a puppy. And he was thumping his tail. Banging and reverberating against the wooden floor, the sound drowned out all others with that repetitive movement which is supposed to mean good humour in a dog but in this one was clearly a nervous, almost hysterical affirmation. Caramel eyes looked blankly out of the foam-pale, delicately marked face and the thick otter-tail thumped. This sad tattoo was the dog's only means of conjuring away inconceivable, doggish anxieties. It kept it up when Carla – she didn't want to raise, then dash its hopes – walked on to another cage.

'Labs are friendly,' the keeper pleaded, 'good with kids.'

'I couldn't manage him.'

'He'll go to the ...' Appalled or squeamish, the man did not say where.

The thudding continued behind her. Sad? Hopeless? Persistent anyway. Persistent but inarticulate: he reminded her of her.

'I'll take him,' she said before she knew she had decided.

'OK, lady. You got yourself a dog.'

The keeper opened the cage door, fastened a lead to the dog's collar and handed it to her. A man standing by the door grabbed and held the animal while she signed papers, paid a small fee and braced herself to deal with fifty pounds of frenzy. The dog trembled like an appliance plugged into a current too strong for its voltage. The short, dense hairs of its coat were on end.

'Ready?' asked the man who was holding him. He was laughing.

'I think so.'

'OK, Ma'am, all yours. Hey,' he shouted after her, 'you look good together. Two blondes!'

She heard the fragments of some joke about who was taking whom for a walk but was by then halfway down the parking lot. The dog had bolted under a low-growing, horizontal bush and appeared to liquify, pouring its bulk flat to the ground like

70

spilled honey. This tactic made him impossible to move. Terror trembled up the leash and registered in her palm.

'So why were you wagging your tail then,' she whispered. 'Silly creature, silly. Take it easy, boy, easy now!'

By half garotting him, she managed to jerk the dog out and then out again, edging him a few yards closer to her car with each manoeuvre. When she had finally tricked him into bolting into the back seat instead of under a bush, she was shaking as violently as the dog himself. Her blouse was sticking to her shoulder-blades. She sat a few minutes in the driver's seat, catching her breath while the animal crouched and panted on the floor behind. The car enclosed their anxiety in its warm, streamlined shell, enlarging and blurring Carla's sense of her own confines so that the thud behind sounded persuasively like her own pulse.

There were now five unopened letters from Marco on Carla's chimney-piece. It occurred to her that he might have asked some question – about money, Maurizio or the house, who knew? – which required an answer. She picked up the one with the most recent postmark and tried to slit it with her fingernail. It was a flimsy, tightly stuck aerogramme and she couldn't get a purchase. As she struggled, she began to feel nausea, then fear.

'I can't,' she said out loud, 'cope with him now. I don't want to.'

She put the letter back.

The blond dog was watching her. He watched her constantly. He had chosen the lowest landing – just a few steps up the stairs – as his place. He refused to go higher and only moved when he needed to relieve himself in the garden. The rest of the time he stayed indoors, couchant, paws bent at the wrist, keeping an eye both on her and on the front door. He did not bark at delivery men, had no sense that this house was his, but whimpered if Carla went out and soon raised the whimper to a howl which he kept up – Cazz had phoned to complain – until she got back. He did not approach her when she was there or respond much when patted but his anxiety increased when he saw her make for the door. Taming him was going to be slow. She stared back at him now.

He was more beautiful than she had seen at first: pale with warmer shadings on ears and underparts, a dark nose, an invisible moustache with a darkish dot where each translucent bristle emerged from his cheeks so that these were delicately mottled like a thrush's breast, eyes whose darkness spilled onto the surrounding fur, a strong jaw and fluid, dancing movements. What he didn't have was self-confidence and this ruined his looks. When the cleaning-woman plugged in the vacuum cleaner, the dog's stance would crumble in clownish terror as he tried to scramble under a sofa. He seemed unable to gauge his own bulk and would cram his haunches under a protective coffee table which he would then look astounded to find riding on his back.

According to pound records he was six months old and must have been doubling his size since birth. Now he was as big as a baby calf. Perhaps the shocks dealt him – loss of at least two owners, two recorded spells in the pound – had prevented his noticing this? When he finally responded to Carla's attempts at affection it was by trying to sit on her lap. The effort was ludicrous. Clambering on the sofa, he turned round and round in a spin of perplexity, paws slipping, toenails tearing against her skirt, large head colliding with her chin. It was a grotesque effort to recover a sensation remembered perhaps from when he was a small puppy coddled by the owners who had later cast him off.

'You're too old! Too big!' Carla told him. 'When are you going to start barking? That's your job. There are freaks out there, cops, rapists, bad statistics ... Bark!'

'Mamma, you remember that girl Cazz was with that time?'

'Mmm?' His mother had a cookbook in front of her and was wrinkling up her lips as though it needed all her attention.

'Cazz and the girl he was with. *Remember*, Mamma!'

She pretended not to know what he was talking about.

'*Ma si*, Mamma! You told Jane she was a runaway and that that made Cazz into a sort of kidnapper. I heard you. What does he do to girls that age?'

'Do?'

'Yes. Cazz. What does he *do* to the girls?'

'Oh Maurizio, don't bother me now. I'm busy.'

'You're not busy. Listen, how old was she?'

'Who?'

'The girl. Was she Evie's age?'

'Perhaps. I don't really know. What does it matter now anyway. Sweety, you look a mess. Is that your new blazer?'

'Did they make love? Don't ask "who". You know who: Cazz and the girl Evie's age. Did they?'

His mother looked him in the eye. 'Yes,' she said. 'That's what they did.'

Terry Steele and a guest speaker called Dr Gold had had a programme on child-molesting. They said that the children never recovered deep down but had to go to therapy sessions with people like Dr Gold. They might *seem* all right for years, said Dr Gold, but in the end their sickness came to the surface and they had to go to these sessions. What *kind* of sickness? Maurizio doubted if his mother would know about such things. They probably didn't happen in Italy.

He thought of phoning the Terry Steele programme and asking a question. He would say he was eighteen. Nobody under eighteen was let on the air. He tried talking through a cardboard tube to deepen his voice and practised saying: 'I'm Jim from Anaheim,' in a cheerful, clean-cut, American, eighteen-year-old way. He taped himself on his tape-recorder and was satisfied by his performance. He didn't ring the show though. It was impossible to think up a question that would force the two adults to make a really enlightening reply.

Maybe when Leo came back from his retreat, he'd get something out of *him*?

Looking for something in Marco's desk, she came on a copy of *Singles Register* which he had bought from a newspaper dispenser and talked of taking back to amuse friends in Italy. Instead, he had left it behind and Carla imagined him teleguiding her into contacting the Oriental Gentleman who weighed 200 pounds and was young in all ways at forty-three. Or the Caucasian from Pakistan who frankly needed to marry to stay in this country or the Capricorn looking for an eternal mate. That would rid Marco of his guilts and scruples, wouldn't it? Where had he got those scruples? she wondered. They were not part of

73

his heritage and she preferred him without them. She had known where she was with him before, whereas now ... She turned to the lead article in *Singles Register*. It was by a psychiatrist who said we were all living in a high-paranoid, low-trust society.

She took her dog on the beach, preferring to run him by twilight when fishing-lines had been drawn in and the beach abandoned, for he was hopelessly untrained and she didn't dare let him off the leash.

'Who's taking who for a walk?'

The stale joke crackled predictably behind her. It was always behind by the time she heard it, for she let herself be swept out of the parking lot, saving her strength for the traffic crossing where she must arrest the wheat-coloured element snuffling and tugging in front of her with a tail mobile as a dislocated rudder, a foam of teeth, and a white-edged eye. On the corner, if a car was coming, she could stop the dog with a mean, human wile: a sideways and sudden jerk to his collar which fastened cruelly like a noose. Past that one danger, she let him speed her along the beach, catching her breath only when he paused to make use of a post or parking-meter in the beach car parks or to sniff in surprise at the corpse of a pelican, a piece of fish, once a freshly dead, perfectly intact seal. On reaching the shoreline, their passage scattered the fishing birds whose gait – legs scissoring so fast they looked like spokes of invisible wheels – must surely be not unlike her own. Three miles each day was the dog's ration: a compromise. She couldn't stand more; he wouldn't slow down for less. As they raced, the water blackened, the sky went from pink to lemon to lime green as the sun dipped into the ocean and the dog reflected all the colours in the prisms of his spray-wet fur. 'Champagne', she thought of calling him because of this bubbly effect. The sound suggested 'Charlemagne' which was nobler. Finally, she chose 'Carlomagno', the Italian form whose firm, guttural plosive dithered in her throat as the air knifed her, a stitch stabbed her side and she was ready to weep from exhaustion.

'C-c-carlomagno, *mascalzone! Ferma!* Stop, you devil. God-dam you, Carlomagno!'

But these runs on the beach had for the first time made her aware of the country which underlay this city's cheap, impermanent architecture. The shoreline, despite blobs of coagulated oil and other refuse, was alive with a visibly moving mud-life which provided fodder for the fishing birds. The smells were primal; the colours shifted like the sheen on a fish scale. Luminous, indifferent and vast, they enveloped and temporarily wiped her mind clean as the sea sucks fibres from an abandoned shell. She imagined this happening: a tide of pallor scouring anxieties from the whorled matter of her brain. It would scour out little storage containers, units difficult to visualize but which held fears, formulae and all the ingredients of niceness, self-abnegation, good-mother-and-wifehood which, she knew, she knew, were what Marco had now turned against. Maybe it would rid her of concern for Marco? Would it? Could it? Could anything? Was she programmed for life? And should she mind a firm identity bracing her? Wasn't your programming *you* and the thin substance of American personalities due to their quick-change dexterity: actors all and so fit survivors on a changing stage? She was too tired to think, too drunk: drunk with the salty tonguings of this darkening air. So was her dog who had collapsed in a wet, seaweedy heap of plenitude by her feet. Roused, he lunged forward and she trundled after him despite the stitch in her side. This was not the way to deal with animals. Marco would have screamed with fury!

'Take him to obedience school! Pay someone to train him! It's a vice with you. Being a victim! A bloody female vice. You have to sacrifice yourself. You were brought up to it – the fucking female dialectic: "Kick me and I become your superior! Nail me to a cross!" That stuff starts as tactics and ends as vice. You get to like it, goddam it, you need it so much now that you'll sacrifice yourself to anything in sight, *porca madonna!* A dog, a poor, buggering, unconscious shit of a dog!'

'But Marco ...'

She gave up trying to imagine an answer. He was so chameleon in his accusations, so unhappy, she supposed. Why else did he carry on so? And why was he? But she abandoned even this anxiety, for her faculties were dulled by an embrace of damp light, sensations of kelp crackling under her instep, sand oozing upwards to take the imprint of her bare feet and in her hand, the dog's nose smooth beneath a bristle of fur.

Living with a child, you become one, Carla worried, and at times the house next door seemed a place of evil. At others, she scoffed at her fears. Cazz, after all, had been introduced to the Glen by Marco, and Wanda's values, judging by those of her sister Joanie, must once have been rock-solid. Joanie, a hairdresser, spent a lot of her time in a church off Sunset Boulevard which Wanda too had attended when the pair came first. It was small, pastel-coloured and had rounded corners like a sucked and spat-out piece of candy. Neither Wanda nor Evie went near it now. Los Angeles was like an acid bath. It ate your certainties.

Maybe that was a good thing? Certainty was a trap. Look what had happened to Aladdin in his careful parents' pool. Whatever else about Maurizio's new friend, the thing in her favour was that she lived and played in full view of Carla's kitchen window. An eye could be kept on her.

Actually, however, Evie lived largely in her head. As she explained to Maurizio (who was embarrassed), she had been able, for as long as she could remember, to doubt that she existed. She had stumbled on the trick when she was four. How did she know how old? By the room where it happened. It was a room you couldn't confuse with any other: kind of dark and full of pine-needles. These came off a tree which leant against the window and dropped in earwigs too.

'I used to be afraid to go to sleep for fear they'd get in my ear. They don't but *I* didn't know that.'

She mimicked the noise the tree made on windy days where two branches had got crossed and scoured each other to the pith. Strips of bark used to fall off: brown and flaky like flaky-chocolate bars.

'I asked my Mom how old I was when we lived in the house with the pine tree and she said I was four.'

Evie's family had moved about a lot but she was sure it had been in that house that she had first started wondering whether she was really there. They – her Mom and Pop – used to lock her in and drive away, putting her to bed so early that she couldn't get to sleep for the longest time nor stay asleep when she did but

76

kept waking up to find the sky-colour changed and to listen to forest noises outside.

'My Mom says we was living in Washington then, bein' my Pop was working in the lumber yards.'

'How about me getting us two cokes from the fridge?'

Maurizio felt jumpy. He had to get up, had to say something. Listening to Evie excited him terribly. She was very cool and not bothered by the, well, funny sorts of things she kept coming out with. It was interesting but people didn't talk about things like that. They were too afraid that other people would think they were nuts. It *interested* Maurizio. It was just that he couldn't think of anything to say and you felt you should say something. It seemed only fair to trade one embarrassing thing of your own. But he was too shy and when he came back with the cokes the things Evie started saying showed that he needn't have worried. That girl probably didn't know what the word 'embarrassment' meant.

She went on talking about the room in Washington. There had been wood-pigeons nesting in a pear tree climbing up the wall outside her window. 'Who? Who?' they called. Sometimes, if she leaned out she could reach a pear. But this was risky and there was a ditch below into which most of the fruit finally fell. Some pine-bark fell into it too and it occurred to Evie that the falling strips looked more like shit than chocolate. The tree, she decided, was shitting and this interested her because at the time it wasn't so long since she had learned to control herself and not shit in her pants the way babies did. Maurizio wished she'd get off the subject. She did, but the next one was only a slight improvement. It was pee. Evie could remember peeing in her sleep. She didn't know she was doing it. She described what it felt like to get out of bed and walk across the floor on bare feet, lifting them fearfully in case she'd tread on an earwig which would squash open and smear its insides on her bare soles.

'They made a sort of crackly sound when that happened.'

She had to walk down a corridor to the closet where the john had a big wooden seat which seemed awfully high. She described how she would clamber onto it and the relief of finally being able to let go. Sometimes the strain of waiting would have given her a pain and that always got worse just before the moment of relief. Maurizio had to admit that she described that well. He could almost feel the ease she got when she felt the flood escape into the safety of the bowl. But the safety, it turned out, wasn't real. It was a trick of sleep. She'd been dreaming the whole trip to the john and would wake up to feel the warm flood around her in the bed turning cold.

'I couldn't help it,' she screamed when her father beat her. 'I thought I'd got to the toilet. Really, Pop, I did. I did. I dreamed it.'

Only of course that dumb woodcutter or whatever he was didn't stop to listen. He went right on beating the little four-year-old kid. With a belt. What a bastard!

'Dirty beast,' he yelled at her. Evie described it all. Even mimicked his dumb, redneck voice. 'Liar!' the mean old bastard hollered. 'A big girl like you! Four years old! What a smell! We'll hang the sheets out the window and disgrace you. Dirty, lazy little thing! I should stuff a wad of the wet stuff down your throat!'

Maurizio was choking with anger when she told him this. The unfairness of it. He really hated that pig of a father.

But Evie went on with her story calmly. She hadn't reached the important part yet. This was only explaining what happened later. Maurizio got too excited about things. He knew it. His mother said he got that from his father. He settled down to listen.

Evie's terror, it seemed, was that one night she might shit in her sleep the way babies did because then the father would do something terrible. One night she went to sleep with a piece of chocolate under her pillow. She must have moved it during the night, pulling it out, then rolling on it so that it melted. When she woke up she found brown smears all over the sheets and was sure her worst fears had come true. 'Shit!' she thought with horror and began to scratch it off with her nail and then, finding that it was chocolate, to eat it.

Maurizio giggled a bit at this but Evie didn't crack a smile, so he shut up. He was beginning to understand that the embarrassing stuff was made all right by the fact that it was explaining something else. And of course it went back to when Evie was

78

four. Still, it was a private sort of memory. He supposed he ought to feel honoured at her telling him.

Well, Evie's heart was pounding when she tasted the chocolate and her mind was jumping with excitement. 'Shit,' she kept saying to herself. 'Crap!' She had really been frightened and kept thinking of the threat she'd escaped and then got to thinking how strange it was that great chunks of stuff should escape her body without her deciding – because she *could* have done it in her sleep after all – and stuff that had been part of her not be part of her any more. This chocolate she was eating could turn into Evie – blood and so forth – or it could turn into shit and drift down the john. She thought of it drifting down the sewer into the septic tank at the bottom of the yard. First it would be in her and then it wouldn't be. If she cut off a finger or a slice off her butt – because, she explained, that was the place you could best spare a slice supposing you really had to – she would still be she and those cut-off bits wouldn't. Maurizio agreed that it was puzzling. It was like the tree, Evie said, shedding its bark. How much of me, Evie got to wondering, is me? Someone had read her a story of a king who chopped off people's tongues. The tongue! *That* seemed very near, Evie thought, very close to the part you couldn't lose and still be you. At night she used to lie awake in the room strewn with pine-needles and wonder about her own edges. Where did Evie stop and the rest of the world begin? When she lay in a hot bath, she felt edgeless, diluted by the warm water. Later, when she pulled the plug out and the water flowed away, she shrank into her own parcel of skin and hair. But hair was disposable. So was skin. When she got to thinking this way, it occurred to her that as she didn't seem able to control herself maybe she didn't exist at all? Any part of her? Maybe someone else controlled her? Maybe she was part of someone else's dream.

'That's in *Alice*,' Maurizio told her. '*Alice in Wonderland*, I think. Or else *Alice Through the Looking Glass*.'

Evie hadn't read them. 'What do they decide?' she asked.

Maurizio didn't remember.

At one time Evie had decided that she might be in her parents' dream. Or maybe they were the ones who didn't exist and she had imagined them? This was a satisfying notion, Maurizio could see, but not convincing as they were so clearly in a position to beat and lock her up. It seemed that that was what they mostly did. They drove off in their old jalopy, locking her in the house or even into the room, then came back and, finding she'd done something she couldn't help, beat her. They were big and they smelled.

'Do you remember,' Evie asked Maurizio, 'that when you were small all big people smelled bad?'

He couldn't remember. He would have liked to say he could but he couldn't and hoped she hadn't had the thought he had that maybe *his* parents washed more than hers.

Well, Evie's parents, it seemed, had had a number of smells when she was small. All strong and mostly bad. Sweat smells, breath smells, feet and underarm smells. Even their boots and hair smelled. There was no doubting their existence, she decided. They were very obviously there and made bigger by noises and smells the way a lamp is made bigger by its glow and a king by his robes. There was a statue of a child king, she explained, 'the little king', wearing a stiff golden dress which spread out around him. It hung on the kitchen wall and had a small glass bowl, like an eye-bath, in front of it. 'Jesus,' her mother called it. 'That's a statue,' the mother told Evie. 'That's a statue of him but the real Jesus is up in the sky.'

Her father said: 'Jesus doesn't exist. Stop filling the kid's head with crap.'

'Your mother musta been a Catholic,' Maurizio told her.

But that wasn't Evie's interest.

'You don't exist,' she had screamed at her father once when he was coming at her with a belt. For a moment the poor kid had hoped the bastard would disappear like genies and suchlike did in fairy tales. Maurizio didn't know whether to laugh or cry for her.

'You thought you'd found a magic word!' he nodded.

But of course the big bully had kept coming and walloped the daylights out of her.

Another time she had decided: 'I don't exist! I'm not here, I'm invisible.' She was becoming smarter – less crazy, thought Maurizio – and didn't try to put the notion to the test, only used it to soothe herself when things got bad.

'Like, I could make myself go numb,' she explained. 'I'd say to myself: "Nothing's real. I'm not. I could die this minute if I wanted to." Then things would *feel* less real. Like when my Pop left my Mom the first time and she kept picking on me for nothing and hitting me. I'd make myself all numb and hardly feel it.' Evie giggled. 'When she came all sweet and sorry afterwards wanting to kiss and make up I'd go numb again. *That* made her mad.'

'I'll bet.' Maurizio recognized that. Adults were that way. Always wanting you to be in *their* mood.

'My Mom's a dumb sow,' said Evie shockingly. 'She knows it too. She says I'm tough and that she's glad I am because no man will make a fool of me the way they do with her.'

'Do you talk this way to everyone?'

'What way?'

'Telling about your family.'

Evie considered. 'Well, I guess I don't know too many people I could talk to,' she said. 'See, we always seem to be on the move. Pop don't hold jobs too good.'

'Where's your Mom now?'

'On the beach with my Aunty Joanie. They lie there for hours covering themselves with grease and frying. I hate the beach,' Evie said. 'I hate all that fat, floppy flesh. All those naked corpses.'

'What corpses?'

'They all look like corpses. All the people on the beach – lying there like dead things.'

She sounded angry. Her manners and language were terrible. Maurizio didn't see how he could introduce her to his mother. Not to start with. Maybe he could prepare them for each other? The funny thing was that what he liked in Evie was partly the terribleness of her manners. He meant that people didn't normally talk the way she did and embarrass you all the time but in the end the embarrassment worked like glue. It made you feel related to the person you'd been embarrassed with. He felt very close to Evie now. But it wouldn't be possible to explain that to his mother. Being discreet about family business was a big rule at the Verdis'.

Later, thinking of the way Evie had run off at the mouth, he

81

decided not to worry any more about Cazz. If the guy got fresh with her, Evie would probably shout the news out over the roof tops. She'd probably phone in and tell it to the Terry Steele Show.

Chapter Four

Sybil in her car looked like the old woman who lived in a shoe. The car itself could have been a fertility emblem. It was big, rabbit-brown and always cluttered with a spill of Kleenex boxes, book bags, children's possessions and children themselves. It was impossible to drive past pretending you hadn't seen it and now Sybil, waylaying Carla at the Lycée, had drawn her into a plan whereby their children should swim at the UCLA pool, leaving Carla and herself free to take in a coffee and a lecture by someone who had, said Sybil, been compared to Martin Luther.

'Not Luther King, Luther period.' Sybil bit into a doughnut.

She and Carla were in the North Campus Eating Facility and Sybil was visibly priming herself for more talk about her heart. She had only just dropped her children and had not quite sloughed off her motherly role. The speaker's name was Küng, she clarified, and he had been compared to Martin Luther *not* King, all right? 'Have a juice or something? I can't *believe* you haven't heard of him,' she marvelled. 'Don't you read the papers?'

'Not the religious page.'

'I gather you had a rotten time with Terry,' Sybil apologized.

'I'd have rung you but heard you were coping with mudslides. I'm glad Leo helped.'

'He was very kind.'

'He always is.'

Sybil was as feverish as ever but today it was a social feverishness as though she expected at any moment to be solicited by jammy hands, untied shoelaces or some other childish claim on her attention. Drinking coffee from a paper cup, she seemed to be slowly recovering her private self. Carla, she promised, would be interested in the lecture. Hans Küng had been fired by order of the Vatican from his Chair at the University of Tübingen. A major scandal. He'd challenged the infallibility of the Pope and run afoul of the Office of the Holy Inquisition. 'They're not called that now, but it's the same office.' Sybil, a rebel for lust, burned with approval. Carla hadn't remembered her being a rebel. Her passion must be entering a new phase. Hair fell across her face so that she seemed to have regressed to her teens. Around them, real young people looked strangely placid. Sybil apologized again for Terry's behaviour, but there was a swell of pride to the apology. She drained her coffee and leaning close to Carla put her in mind of teenage colloquies almost twenty years ago with virgin girl friends. They'd invariably needed bolstering in their resolution to give or not give their fiancés 'the final proof' of love. Sybil's topic was almost the same.

'I've been thinking,' she said at last, 'of your expression "safety-valve".' Sex-as-safety-valve must, she hoped, make it easier for the lonely cleric to continue in his solitude. It would be a deviation from the rule in order to preserve the rule; a way to give these isolated men a little human warmth. '*That*'s all they need,' she claimed, 'sex is only the sign ...'

'A secular sacrament?'

Sybil, unsure whether she was being mocked, threw back her head defiantly. 'Why not?'

Carla groped back to their earlier conversation. 'Wouldn't it be a cheat?' she wondered. 'I think your Leo is gorgeous-looking and very nice. That seems reason enough to just go ahead. But *you* seem to want to turn the thing into a sort of inoculation against worse. Do you really want to think of yourself as a serum or safety-valve?'

84

'It was your word.'

'Was it? I must have meant it would be for *you*.'

'But I'm concerned for *him*.'

'Surely he must decide what he wants?'

'But his situation, his celibacy . . .'

'Well, either you do or you don't want to violate that. I don't see how you can have it both ways. I mean if celibacy is, as you said, a divine gift, surely one shouldn't pretend to have it if one hasn't? Doesn't that turn the priestly witness into a liar?'

'But he wouldn't be a liar *all the time*. Hypocrisy isn't a bad thing, Carla. It's a yearning to be better than we are. You pretend to be better so as to encourage other people to achieve what *you* only manage to mimic. It can be a form of humility.'

Carla said nothing.

Sybil collapsed. 'Oh, I'm a double hypocrite!' she groaned. 'I should be whipped at the tail of a cart.' Indeed, she looked like a woman from the centuries when that might have happened. Her hair hung in sad, shadowy tresses like the hair in a woodcut of a witch or doxy.

'Religion,' burst out Carla to her own surprise, 'is a dangerous damn thing. It seems to stop people seeing the obvious.'

'Don't judge it by me,' said Sybil miserably. 'You're right though. I'm a hypocrite.'

'I didn't say *you* were.'

'Well I am. I don't want to admit that the lust may be all on my side – or even that it *is* lust. It's lust for his purity which I can't touch without destroying it. I'm caught in a paradox like a rat in a trap. Funny, I suppose, though I want to cry rather than laugh. I've no idea if *he's* interested – nothing to go on. No sign. You led me on, though, You promised . . .'

'Me? What? How could I?'

'Nothing. I'm mad. Let's go to the lecture.'

It was in a ballroom.

'You see,' said Sybil of the visiting speaker. 'He's famous, scandalous. Most lectures are held in class rooms, small places. They knew they'd get a big turn-out for this.'

She seemed to be scrutinizing the audience, and indeed knew a lot of people. Several, she whispered to Carla, were priests. One or two waved and Carla remembered Terry Steele's saying of his wife that she was a 'clerical groupy'. The priests were healthy-looking youngish men wearing open-necked check shirts. They were shiny-eyed, boyish, hyper-active and, on second thought, not healthy-looking after all. They reminded Carla of descriptions her mother's generation had given of TB victims: manic, flushed. Sybil insisted on changing seats twice, moving Carla from one side of the ballroom to the other, and kept craning her neck to watch the door.

'A pity,' said Carla, 'that Leo's on retreat. I imagine he'd have enjoyed this.'

Sybil's face registered, then tried to conceal, surprise. She muttered something about having forgotten about the retreat.

'Don't you go to the parish any more?'

Sybil didn't. Terry had laid down the law. No more volunteer work. So that was why she was here then! To look for Leo. But why had she wanted Carla along? Oh, of course: the house. Did she want Carla to repeat her offer, this time in front of Leo? That *would* bring things to a head, one way or the other.

'He's leaving the parish too, you know.'

'Who is?' This time Sybil couldn't even keep up a pretence of being in the know.

'Leo. He's to take courses for a doctorate here at UCLA.'

'Leo?'

'That's what he told Maurizio. They got quite pally while digging the mud.'

Sybil's facial muscles seemed to have congealed. She was apparently unable to make the slightest social effort.

Luckily, the lecturer had arrived and everyone began clapping. He was introduced by a professor who had gauged the temper of the audience and tried to defuse it. He joked and his jokes drew barks of hilarity from the tartan-shirted priests and canonically-aged ladies (Mothers? Housekeepers?) who made up the bulk of the audience. A number of students, probably campus drifters who went, unselectively, to whatever was on, were writing diaries and letters, unaffected by the expectancy around them.

Carla sat worrying about Sybil. Had she been dealt a crippling blow just now? That Leo should casually tell strangers more about his plans than he had told her was fairly conclusive proof of his indifference. Wasn't it? Would Sybil see that it was? Her face was like that of some fierce stone image. Carla hoped she wouldn't do anything embarrassing.

To distract herself from this possibility, she started listening to the pin-striped lecturer who looked more like a diplomat than a new Martin Luther. He wasn't saying anything scandalous at all and must be disappointing his audience, who could hardly have come in such numbers to hear what they were hearing, which was an apologia for belief in God in the 1980s. Carla tried to catch Sybil's eye but couldn't. God-in-the-Eighties, as far as she could grasp, was hedged about by negatives. He was not anthropomorphic, nor an absolute ruler, and his existence could be neither proven nor disproven. He was outside the realm of rationality and couldn't, she judged, be of much help or hindrance to Sybil. Carla didn't see the point of such a God at all – but then she'd never seen the point of the old God either. She was not God-prone. Sybil was. Listening more carefully, Carla noted some of Sybil's words turning up: 'yearning' for instance. 'Yearnings,' said the speaker, 'neither validate nor invalidate their object.' In emotional matters, this, thought Carla, was untrue. Yearning for God mightn't prove he was there, but Sybil's yearning for Leo certainly magnified him – though Leo, a bit like God, wasn't quite there either. He wasn't a man – or was he? That was Sybil's quandary. Perhaps she hoped to find God in Leo? Yes, clearly, she did. This meant that there was more to him than to, say, Terry Steele, her husband. It made him unfair competition, as Zeus would have been to human suitors of Danae or Pasiphae. Religious people did manage to colour up the world for themselves.

The speaker now sat down and the check shirts began to bounce from their seats like beach balls. They were vying to catch the introducer's eye so as to ask questions about mystic experiences or about God as the infinite in the finite or as a primal ground beyond perceivable reality. These sounded to Carla like definitions of love. Sybil should be got right away from this heady place.

'I've got to pick up Maurizio,' Carla whispered to her. 'What about you?'

Sybil followed her out. She seemed shrunken, but had clearly not given up all hope for, just as they reached the Recreation Centre and their children, she asked: 'Is the offer still good? The offer of your house? Or,' her face sharpened self-mockingly, 'has it been cancelled? I speak as one who has nothing to lose.'

'Sybil, you look fierce – like Medea or someone.'

'Don't worry. I'm not about to kill my children – not that the thought hasn't crossed my mind from time to time. My pediatrician tells me that I wouldn't be normal if it hadn't.'

'*Is* that what Medea did? I'd forgotten.' Carla felt herself blush.

'You hadn't. In your mind – oh, maybe only in your *subconscious* mind, a mother intent on adultery has killed her love for her children in her heart. You're actually quite priggish, Carla, like all rationalists.'

'Am I?'

'No. I'm probably thinking about myself. Forget. Forgive.' Sybil's lower lip wobbled.

'The offer stands,' said Carla irritably, 'if ...'

'If I can hook my man?'

'Well, no, I meant if I can find somewhere for Maurizio and me to be. Jane's invitation to her mountain cabin won't be repeated for a while. She ...'

'A few hours would do me,' said Sybil. 'You could take Maurizio to the cinema – I'll pay for you to see a double bill. I'm sorry. Do I sound awful?'

'Yes. But I understand.'

'Do you?'

'Yes.'

'Thanks.' Sybil hugged her. 'Let's get the children.'

Maurizio, having rid himself of worries about Cazz, had returned to one which had been bugging him until he'd got distracted – and maybe the distraction had been half deliberate? Anyway, now the worry was back, clamped round his head, pressing in on him the way it had been, off and on, since Aladdin had knocked *his* head on the floor of his pool and maybe turned himself into a vegetable.

'He may be a vegetable all his life,' kids in the Lycée kept saying, 'a vegetable.'

Aladdin had been lying in bed for weeks now and Maurizio kept worrying whether the accident had been his fault. Why his? Well, *he'd* helped fire the bullets into the pool and maybe had the idea in the first place. Had he? He couldn't be sure. It was his kind of idea. He often had screwy notions like that and – in a sort of way – would rather feel the thing *was* his responsibility, something that could have been prevented. Blame fenced off the weird chanciness of the event – but he couldn't bear to take the blame either. Not for something like this. Open-ended. It hadn't ended yet. Nobody knew how bad it might be. He had racked his brains and not come up with any consolation at all. But then why should *he* be consoled? He wasn't the one lying in a coma. A perfectly ordinary game had turned sour and now poor dummo might die because of it. Die or be an idiot for the rest of his life. That would be worse. Maurizio would grow up and old and maybe return to Italy and become a soccer-star or marry and all the time there would be this zombie lying somewhere with a bandage round his head: a vegetable.

Different Aladdins flashed before him: a turnip Aladdin with hair like leaves, a human potato, an Aladdin with an apple face and a bruise on top of it. The foolish images – like something from a nursery-book for small kids – made him feel sick. He felt as if his brain had been rigged out with goofy, trick equipment that couldn't take hold of the thoughts he wanted.

He didn't see how the few bullets *he* had shot into the water could have screwed up the inlet and draining system. Aladdin must have gone on shooting for *hours* after Maurizio had gone home. It was the sort of thing that that spoilt rich kid *would* do: stand in front of his own big, beautiful, crystal-clear pool and shoot at it. Maurizio could just see him doing it.

And now he was trying to shift the blame and dump it back on poor Aladdin. Mean, Maurizio, mean! What he wished he could do was help. He really did. He would have liked to be able to pray or throw a spell or rend his garments – anything that might work. Not that anything would. Maybe the thing about growing up was that you knew you couldn't easily change things around? You were stuck with what you'd done and made: a turnip-head. Jeez, though, what a turnip-head not to have tested the depth before diving! He expected other people to do his thinking for him. Maids. Security guards. Even Maurizio. *Watch* it, Maurizio, you're shifting again.

He told Evie about Aladdin and telling the story made it seem like something that had happened to someone else. He began to think about it less and was maybe taking a leaf out of her book, for though she had plenty of troubles she didn't let them get to her nor waste time wondering if things were her fault. The way she talked of her parents took his breath away. 'That fat sow!' she'd say. 'That sonofabitch!'

'When I'm sixteen,' she said, 'I'll take off like a big-assed bird.'

Maurizio was amazed. *His* father had lived with *his* parents until he was twenty-six. Then he'd moved into his own place and started a family. Maurizio had uncles who had stayed with their mother until they were forty and aunts who never left at all. Their own families, they said, were good enough for them. They worked in offices but rushed across their traffic-jammed cities – Rome and Florence – to be together for lunch. Younger people, they complained, had stopped doing that and look where it had got them! Italy, they stated with flat acceptance, was going down the drain. Family life was the glue that kept the state together. When that went everything went. Boys grew up to be terrorists. Girls ... There were no girls any more, said the aunts. They thought *they* hadn't changed but, returning every summer to find them buying more and more canned sauces which his mother, faithful in her exile to purer standards, would never do, Maurizio wondered whether the network of habit which the aunts claimed held the country together was not being pulled apart by themselves.

When he'd said this the aunts had been astonished. 'Little worrywart!' they'd said, laughing, 'he's worried about *us*!' They were flattered too, for maybe nobody had worried about them in a long time. He could tell they were by the way they kept coming back to his remark. It was true, though, that he was a worrier. He knew it. Seriously.

Evie's assurance was one of the things that worried him. He wondered if she knew the score. She did no homework. How was she going to earn her living? She seemed to him like a tightrope-walker without a net. Did she think you could live like

Huck Finn on berries and wild produce? The dream turned up in all the games she invented and had perhaps invaded her life plans.

Carla, less at home in her own house, kept changing bath-room towels, threw newspapers prematurely into garbage cans and was on constant alert lest Sybil and Leo appear un-announced on her doorstep expecting her to take Maurizio to the cinema then and there. Passion knew neither discretion nor foresight and religion was not a stabilizing factor. It was *not* like opium. With Sybil it seemed to work like angel dust whose effects, warned an ubiquitous public-service announcement, were insufficiently understood. In a case much in the public eye, a man high on this drug had rushed naked into the street where members of the Los Angeles Police Department promptly gunned him down. Civil Rights lawyers had argued that this was over-reacting. Where, after all, could a naked man have been concealing a gun? The indicted cop swore, however, that the man had looked so alien and furious that he, the cop, had felt threatened. A jury accepted his plea and so did Carla. Naked folly had an unsettling contagion. The policeman too must have been briefly out of his mind.

Feeling righteous as a Roman *matrona*, she rang the rectory and asked to speak to Leo. Hans Küng's extra-rational forces – call them God's – should not, she was convinced, have been let out of the catacombs. Reason should have defended itself better from the start. Here now was Sybil, born into a sensible race, succumbing to an ancient, fermented and disruptive folly.

'He's not here,' she was told.

'Have I got the right number?' She doubted the sluttish voice at the other end of the line. 'Is this the Catholic rectory?' Then – for were there not Old, Anglican and Greek Catholics too? – 'The *Roman* Catholic one?'

'What other sort is there?' demanded the fury at the other end and slammed down the receiver. One of those grey-haired vixens Carla had seen at the lecture?

She rang back and demanded to know how to trace him.

'Who's that speaking?' interrogated the vixen.

Carla approved of suspicion and knew how to circumvent it.

'I'm phoning from the University Admissions Office,' she lied. 'It's about his enrolment.'

She got the number.

'Ah,' said Leo in a cheerful voice before she could get to the point. 'I'd been planning to ring you. Did you get that dog?'

'Yes.' She'd forgotten that it was he who had given her the idea. Perhaps, after all, it would be easier to talk face to face?

They agreed to meet at sunset when she would be giving her dog his run on the Santa Monica beach.

He hailed her from a distance, emerging from a glimmer of spume. It was twilight. The sun was dousing its last blaze in the sea, and reflections smeared pink and amber streaks on high-rise, cliff-top buildings along Ocean Avenue. Some, looking like lanterns, might have been hollowed out by fire. The dog, bounding towards Leo, dragged her, but her own greeting was cold. Preparing to tell him off for his blindness about Sybil, she waited for him to ask what was on her mind.

He, however, accepted her tone without question – failing perhaps to notice it – and it became harder then to bring the matter up. He was barefoot, frisky, his trousers rolled to his knees and black hairs, wet as seaweed, streaked his shins.

The dog leapt on him so that all three nearly fell in a heap.

'I'm sorry,' she admitted. 'I can't control him.'

He held Carlomagno's snout in his palm. 'Good boy, quiet now. OK, OK, gently, old fellow, gently, puppy. He's only a few months old,' he told her.

'I know.' She told him the dog's history: the two spells in the pound and that it had no idea how to retrieve or even run after sticks or frisbees. 'I'm afraid he's not too bright.'

Carlomagno, buoyant and unmanageable, was straining to be off. She jerked at his throat.

'Aren't you letting him loose?'

'He's untrained and doesn't know his name. I changed it, you see. I mightn't be able to get him back if I let him go.' She was frightened of the dog-catcher whose van patrolled the beach.

'But he needs to run free, to really run. Not on a leash. It's unfair to you both. Look. If he runs off I'll be responsible. I'll get him back. OK?'

'Are you sure you can?'

'Yes.'

'All right then.' She loosed the dog who streaked off then, stopping as though amazed, bounded back to Carla, sniffed her, then took off again.

Leo laughed. 'See.'

Taking off her shoes, she walked with him through the edge of the surf. The packed sand here was the colour of mussel-flesh. Ochre and navy shadows ruffled off towards slide-area cliffs and the Pacific Coast Highway where pale headlights pricked the dusk. Idly, she asked about his retreat and he said he'd been turning a lot of things over in his mind. Wondering whether Sybil was one of the things, she said she'd seen her but he didn't take this up. How was Maurizio? he asked. Oh, the same, she said. 'He needs some math tutoring.' She wondered how to bring Sybil up without seeming meddlesome. Watching the dog, even her own heart wasn't in the matter. 'Can you come to dinner after this?'

'I can't keep eating your food. Let me buy something? Wine? Groceries?'

'If you like.'

The dog raced back and forth, a shuttle of blond silk weaving further with each run. He looked, in the middle distance, like a detached panel of sand. Returning, he chased a seabird into the water, splashed in its roil, raced out, a ruff of drops leaping from his neck. For a moment he paused as though astonished, then plunged in once more. This time a wave caught him and suddenly he had been swept out beyond its cresting point.

Carla screamed. 'He'll drown!'

'No, he's swimming. They're water-dogs.'

'But he's never been in the water before. Not since I've had him! I doubt if he'd ever been.'

'Instinct. Nature. You see. He's not stupid. Frisbees don't turn him on. Birds do!'

Carlomagno had struggled out of the water. The gull rose. He barked and began racing it up the beach with such exuberance, raising his snout and vaulting through foam, that two Japanese fishermen who had been tidying away their tackle turned round to stare. Leo laughed.

'This is his trip.'

'Yes.' She was still worried. 'Let's hope we don't lose him. He's a good two miles up that beach.'

But they got him back.

'He's as afraid of losing you as you are of losing him.'

'Fear's a good thing.'

'You don't believe that.'

'I certainly do.'

When the dog gave himself up he was exhausted. His eyes were unfocused, glassy as the sea. He crept between them to the parking lot, loping, flat to the ground as a lizard, then lay inert on the old groundsheet which Carla had installed for him in the back of the car. When they reached the house he turned over on his back in the middle of the hall, his spine buckling so that it carried him across the floor. It was as though a child's wind-up toy had got turned upside-down and was unwinding in a single, swift, anarchic spin.

'What's happening?'

Maurizio had come to greet Carla and Leo.

'Is the dog mad?' he wondered.

'He's having some sort of fit.'

For maybe a minute, the dog rolled on its haunches, paws beating the air like upturned electric egg-beaters, body whirled by the impetus of some discharge of feeling, he let his head flop backwards, throat uppermost, skidding on his spine as though on a keel or skate. Then, abruptly, as if some quite alien spirit had vacated his body, he turned over, rose, shook himself and sank quietly down with his nose resting on his paws like any well-behaved domestic dog. A mild tremor rippled down his back. Another. He fell asleep.

'What is it, Mamma, is he sick?'

Carla touched his head warily. The dog raised a lid, showed the white of an eye, dropped it in fatigue. Lazily, he bared his teeth, gave a little snore. She laughed.

'I think,' she guessed, 'he's just happy. That's all. It was a fit of happiness. He's discovered the thing he enjoys.'

'He's a water-dog,' Leo confirmed. 'His first swim must have been quite an experience.'

94

'Leo's having dinner with us,' Carla told Maurizio. 'I'll call you when it's ready.'

'We're to trade cooking lessons for dog-training.' Maurizio was all elation at this chance to get away from his books. 'Remember?'

'No, no. You've got homework to do. I'd better do the cooking.'

Maurizio climbed sadly to his study. Eight more years of this lay ahead. He had been sentenced to a middle-class childhood.

'Drink?' Carla proposed to Leo.

'Thanks.'

There was embarrassment now. She was summoning her forces to speak. What had she meant to say? Doubts anchored themselves on the prostrate body of the dog. She imagined small demons pouring out of it as they did from the anuses of vanquished wolves in frescoes of St Francis. Carlomagno groaned. His belly heaved. A fart escaped like a full stop: pup! Concave and sodden, he lay like a stook of wet wheat knocked over by a cloudburst. The demons seemed to have abandoned him, moved on. She could feel them in the room though, palpable, brushing the bare skin of her arms. She must get this over with.

'Leo, I wish you'd get in touch with Sybil Steele.'

'Why?'

'She's in love with you.'

'Isn't that – if true, which I can't believe – a reason to keep away?' He rocked the drink in his glass, stared at it, avoided her eye.

'Believe it,' ordered Carla severely. 'She is.'

'Well then, I *must* keep away.'

'Is that what you want?'

'Yes.'

'But Leo, it's gone way beyond something that will die from lack of encouragement. This has been going on for a year – years. She's all wound up: taut, brittle. I'm sorry, but she's taken to confiding in me and I'm worried.'

'Aren't you exaggerating? Sybil's a bit bored. Perhaps she play-acts to distract herself from the lop-sided marriage she's got – marriage to a media-star.' Leo sipped at his drink. 'Women

95

do hang round celibates,' he remarked. 'It's a hazard we get used to.'

'God, you're smug.'

'No, no, it's not *me*, not any of us they see, only the challenge – like men with virgins I suppose? Scalp-hunting? With some. For others it's a safe game.'

'You saw a lot of her. You must have led her on.'

'It all seemed brotherly and sisterly to me.'

'Well, she's festering and, oh, extreme. Really, I think you should have an explanation with her.'

'How can I? What possible dialogue can you imagine between us? There's Sybil being a pillar of the parish and I have to say: "By the way, Sybil, you're not in love with me by any chance?" Have a heart, Carla, she'd probably slap my face.'

'She wants to borrow this house for a night so that you can consummate your love.'

Leo, Carla was pleased to see, looked shaken. The complacency he wore wrapped around him, with the bland protectiveness of a Roman collar, did invite attack. Perhaps she too, as he had said of Sybil, was after a scalp or some lesser mutilation. A scratch would do her, a wincing, some sign that he could feel. 'Her husband,' she reminded him, 'tried to tell you. Look, I find this conversation difficult. Imagine what it must have been like for *him*.' Leo's carelessness about ordinary people's feelings maddened. 'Do you enjoy your innocence so much?' she asked. 'It's paid for dearly – but not by you.'

His face had flushed a raw red. Carla had expected him to defend himself or perhaps leave, banging the door. Instead, he put his drink down, looked her in the eye and said quietly, 'You're right. I've been insensitive. Tell me what to do.'

His surrender – a brisk turning of tables – challenged her to venture into a morass from which she had hoped to extract herself. She temporized: 'You've taken the wind out of my sails.'

His smile was gloomy. 'A trick from the clerical arsenal: we're passive, falsely humble, secretly proud.'

She believed him. Under cover of irony, he told the truth. She said, 'You sound like women.'

'That's why we get on with them.'

'And make fools of them,' she thought. He had almost

deflected her. 'Look,' she mustered assertiveness, 'you'll say this isn't my business but why *don't* you do what she wants? What will it cost you? If she were ill and you had a cure, you'd help, wouldn't you? Say she needed a pint of your blood – is your purity that much more precious?'

He turned his back on her. 'Yes,' he told the far side of the room where a painting hung, a handsome one by Nicholas de Staël. Over his shoulder, pigment turned figurative suggested a bobbing of boats at anchor, then retreated to abstraction. 'And,' he continued, 'it's not your business nor Sybil's either. I don't have to defend myself.'

'True.' She thought he might do so, however, and waited. 'Monastic rules,' she reminded him, 'don't prevail among the rest of us. We have our own.'

He turned and, again, surprised her by a sudden submission. 'What – short of that – do you want me to do?'

'See her. Make things clear. At least then she'll know what she has to adjust to.'

'If I do, will you come with me?'

'Leo, she'd hate that. She'd hate *me*.'

'Is that important? Aren't we thinking of her peace of mind rather than yours or mine? You must see that it will be more final and ... tidier with a witness.'

She had to admit that this was true. 'All right. I'll come.'

'So it's settled?'

'Yes.' Carla shivered. 'I feel I've been finessed – also as if I'd killed something. Have I?'

'There was nothing to kill. Are you going to give me a cooking lesson?'

Sybil, at the Lycée, waited as usual for her tribe. 'Hot weather, eh?' she yelled and waved cheerfully at Carla.

Irritable with shame, Carla felt that Sybil could have worn more clothes. Not that people did. In the mornings, mothers drove into this parking lot wearing see-through nightgowns. Now it was afternoon and eighty degrees in the open. Cars were like toasters. Sybil's coming calvary seemed, however, to Carla, its engineer, to be what was burning and dehydrating her. Wrinkles wriggled from her armpit like cracks on a parched river bed. The sun struck a dwarf palm which blazed like a heap of surgical instruments. There was a liturgical ferocity to Southern Californian vegetation: palms, agave, cactus and bird-of-paradise blossoms with probing beaks.

School wasn't out yet. Commands shot, like glass sherds, through an open window: '*Silence! Ça suffit!*' A ruler cracked a desk. A facsimile of old-time discipline was one of the luxuries which parents paid for in a private school. A bell rang and children erupted through a door. One of Sybil's, making for his mother at a sprint, bounded against her legs so that she dropped her handbag. Its contents scattered, then were centrifugally propelled under wheels and feet. Carla felt that Sybil was being trampled in effigy, quartered.

'This yours?'

'Here you go.'

Tightly trousered youths in blue denim fielded the objects. Gaily they romped up to Sybil, handing them over with a flourish.

'Thanks.'

The women smiled at these absurdly youthful fathers. They knew they must be fathers. Lycée seniors wore flannels and blazers with Latin emblems on their pockets, as their own grandfathers might have done. Each generation mimed another as though the families were playing charades.

'Let's drop the kids at the Rec Centre again and have a coffee in Westwood. Leo's there.'

'Leo?'

'Yes, he's helping Maurizio with his math after school now. He has no car at the moment, so I'm to pick him up.'

Sybil's face blazed with what? Hope?

Leo, hidden in a booth in the artificial dusk of the Hamburger Hamlet, stood up when the women came in. Carla, ready to renege on her promise, suggested: 'Maybe you don't want me to stay? I could do some shopping.'

'No,' said Leo, visibly disappointing Sybil. 'I've got something I want you both to hear. Shall I order first?'

He chose for Sybil and Carla since neither could bring herself to decide what she wanted. There was a moment of asking about

98

the parish and the Steele family while they waited for their orders to arrive.

'What is it you want us to hear?' Sybil was tremulous and coquettish, her vivacity wound a notch too tight for ease. 'Give us a hint,' she begged.

He wouldn't speak until the soft drinks and ice-cream had come. Sybil might cry, Carla guessed him to be calculating. Better if the waitress was out of the way. She wished she too could leave. Maybe she *should*? Once alone, might not Sybil prevail over his indifference? Carla, however, was now wedged in the middle of the booth between the other two.

'Here we are,' announced the waitress and hedged them in even more efficiently behind an array of lavish, brightly coloured junk food.

'Sybil,' said Leo in a low voice, 'Carla has told me how you feel about me. She did it out of friendship for you.'

Sybil went very quiet. 'I see.'

'She feels,' the discretion of his voice – it was hardly more than a whisper – lent an odd intimacy to the occasion, 'she feels that I'm not facing up to my responsibilities to you.'

'I never said you had any.'

'I know you didn't, but Carla ...'

'Carla ...?'

'Carla feels that I ...'

'Oh God!' Sybil interrupted, 'how humiliating this is! You've brought me here to say "lay off" and you felt the need of a chaperone. Were you afraid I'd jump you, Leo? Throw a scene? Is that your opinion of me? Have I ever done the least thing to embarrass you?' It was clear she never would. Even now she spoke pianissimo. 'Ever?' she breathed.

'No, never, Sybil, I ...'

'And you, Carla, how *could* you blab my secret to Leo? Oh, I feel so ridiculous, so undressed. Naturally, that's how I look to you both now. I'd hoped – Oh *God*! – to have the same chance as any woman wants to bring the matter up delicately – deviously – on neutral ground. I suppose I'd hoped to ... seduce you, Leo, yes, but *gently*, giving you a chance to back away, while saving both our faces if that was what you wanted. Carla, I'll never forgive you for this.'

'Sybil, Carla didn't mean ... Look, it wasn't like that – isn't like that *now*. We're *friends* of yours. We just wanted the thing clarified so that ...'

'Of course it was. Of course it is. I'm a fool, a fool, a naked fool. You've both made me be one.' Her lowered, even furtive voice turned the booth into a confessional. She gulped for air. Shame and fury stifled and were muffled. The other two might have been applying the garotte. Ashamed of themselves, they denied their conspiracy – or Leo did. Carla couldn't bring herself to speak.

'Sybil, it was *Terry* who told me first on the day of the mud-slides. It wasn't a secret after that. How could it be?'

'Terry? What could *he* have told you? There was nothing to tell then. There's still nothing to tell. Carla, you're a meddlesome bitch! I was a fool to trust you. No, Leo, stop *defending* her, can you, for one moment and give *me* a chance to put my case. I'm not trying to seduce you now. How could I? I only want you to know that – as she knows – I was beset by scruples. I didn't *want* to upset you. I respected your special position. I believed in it. I still do. But she – Carla, you've been the evil demon in this case, you really have. Will you deny that it was *you* who said I should embrace sex so as to defuse it, that it would be an inoculation against worse: a small dose to preserve both of us from a greater malady.'

'But Sybil, she told me that too! Nobody's deceiving anybody. Carla's a pagan, Sybil. We can't blame her for seeing things her way. You and I don't. That's the difference. She asked me to sleep with you.'

Sybil gave a snort which became a sob: 'Christ!' she groaned, then, like a child, added: 'Sorry, Leo.'

'Sybil!' He put a hand on hers. 'You're not ridiculous. Carla didn't betray you and I don't think less of you. I *admire* you, but I must abide by the rules of the institution I represent. Carla feels I've been playing fast and loose with it, that the way we behave now leads women to believe we feel casually towards our com-mitment. But it's not like that. I'm sorry if I've misled you. I depend on friendship as much as anyone – *more* perhaps. It can be lonely being a priest. It's not always easy to explain that it's

100

only friendship we want. Maybe we ought to avoid women altogether?'

There was a pause. Leo now seemed to be the one in need of pity.

'Is nobody going to say "no"?' he asked with nervous jocosity. 'Do I have to leave? I *like* women,' he went on more soberly. 'I miss them. It's just ... Look, can we take this as read or do I have to go on accusing myself? I think embarrassment has been spread pretty evenly between us three – enough to cancel it out. Even Carla deserves her share as a giver of bad advice and a bit of a snoop. Listen – would you rather I left? Seriously?'

'No.' Sybil's voice was a husky whisper.

Carla, backing her up, tried for humour. 'You *can't* go,' she scolded vivaciously. 'The ice-cream's your treat – cold sweet comfort, eh, Leo?' Religiosity did seem to provoke quips from the non-religious. Like a passenger sitting next to an emotional driver, you found your foot reaching around for a brake. Or you got out. She planned to do so as soon as was decent. The air felt tainted to her. 'Conspiracy' had once meant 'breathing together' and that was what the three of them had been doing: exchanging and breathing in each other's contaminated air.

Maurizio and Evie were sucking pomegranates. She had shown him the neat way to do this: you pressed the fruit evenly all over so as to crush the seeds inside, then you pricked it with one tooth, closed your lips on the hole and sucked out the juice. It felt like sucking out a small, leathery breast.

'Ever wonder what it'd feel like to be a small baby?' Evie asked after a long suck. 'Cazz says he has drugs can make your memory work so you remember what happened when you were tiny – even before you were born. He told my Mom. She won't take the stuff though. It can turn you into a real dingbat and she says she hasn't much sense and is holding onto what she's got.'

'Cazz could go to jail.'

'I know.'

'He could turn dangerous. Isn't your Mom scared?'

'She says as my Pop never killed her she reckons she can manage Cazz.' Evie tore open a pomegranate rind and rubbed the red insides to her cheeks, leaving two clownish spots. 'My Pop's real mean. He hasn't the excuse of being crazy. Just mean.'

Maurizio still felt shy when she said things like that.

'Don't any of you miss him?' *He* had to write a letter a week to *his* father starting: *Dear Babbo, we both miss you very much* ... As a matter of fact, that was true.

'Nope,' said Evie. 'We don't.' She thought for a bit or anyway sucked a few uncrushed seeds she'd found sticking to the torn rind. 'Yeah, well, the reason we move around so much,' she spat them out, 'the reason is, see, that he gets into fights. When he's drunk there's no holding him. He split a man's skull one time and was in court. He got off though. On grounds,' said Evie grandly, 'of self-defence. He got some guys to back him up but I don't know if they were telling the truth. He has a real mean temper when he's roused and it don't take much to rouse him.'

'I wouldn't trust Cazz too much either,' Maurizio warned. 'He ran off with a girl one time. He wanted my parents to adopt her.' The dangers of Evie's life excited him. For all her tough talk, she looked weak to him. Her skin was transparent and you could see the blue veins through it on her wrist and up the side of her arm. He stared at these now and she caught him staring.

She laughed: 'The day I try to cut my veins I'll know where to look for them. Not like my Mom. She made a mess even of that. She was bleedin' and hollerin' and gave us all a bad fright but she couldn't find the artery. Well, better luck next time. They say if you try once you try again. Poor Mom's had some bad breaks. I hope Cazz sticks round a while.'

'Did she really ...?'

'Sure. It's not the dumbest thing she's done. I might do it myself one day.'

She might too. Maurizio was sure she might even if she *was* trying to impress him. You could be doing that and telling the truth as well. The thought of Evie's mother trying to kill herself wasn't frightening. Wanda's smoker's voice and fat, brightly dressed body made it seem unlikely she would die. But Evie was too frail to have to put up with the sort of family she had. She told him about it as though she were spitting out poison. Then, suddenly bored, would suggest that they play some game. A favourite was to pretend that there'd been a nuclear holocaust

102

and everyone wiped off the earth except for one boy and one girl: Maurizio and herself. They had to start from scratch, making new laws and building shelter: the house in the pomegranate tree. Maurizio recognized this as a version of playing house, a girl's game for which he didn't much care, but he fell in with Evie's fancies and was half pleased to find that she was in some ways so childish. No, not some: *lots* of ways. She was a Red Riding Hood dawdling in the forests of childhood and so was her mother. That dumb jerk had started dressing herself out of the Beverly Hills thrift shops. She wore lacy nightgowns and ball-dresses to please Cazz and at ten in the morning could be seen preening in bare feet and some torn bit of grandeur. She was retarded, in Maurizio's opinion. Incompetent. There wasn't one proper adult in that house. For a while he'd had hopes of the aunt but Evie said *she* had a screw loose.

Evie didn't like being treated as a girl – even in the nicest way.

One time he'd made some half-sexy remark: nothing off-colour, just a bit of flattery of the sort girls in the Lycée liked. Evie didn't. She didn't like it one bit and she let him know. OK. OK. He only did it because other guys did. Just to be agreeable.

'Well, knock it off then.'

Nervously (tell the truth, he'd been choking with shyness) he'd said: 'Well, I just wanted to be sure we're friends.'

'Well, *of course* we're friends, jerk.'

Afterwards it hit him that she might be afraid of growing up to be like her mother and that *that* was what it had been about. The sad thing was that she really might end up like Wanda if she didn't get her act together. One thing that bothered him about the way she wanted to play the holocaust game was the way she insisted they get their food. They were to steal it from stores instead of getting it from their mothers.

'We have to be independent,' she argued, 'as though only we existed. Everyone else has been wiped out, see? No mothers.'

'But if they *had* there'd be no food to steal.'

Was it the wiping out she enjoyed or the surviving? She was a weird girl: sad.

'I think you're scared,' she'd jibed.

He was, but not only. He disapproved.

'It's like my Mom says of your Mom,' she switched suddenly to family clannishness, 'your family is real square.'

'It's time I went to do my homework.'

'Are you mad?'

'No. It's just time I went in.'

Later, when he looked out his window and saw her straddling the pomegranate tree branch, dangling long, bare legs and rather dirty feet, he felt too angry to be able to apply himself to his geography assignment. It was to learn the names of all the bays of Brittany and struck him as a peculiarly pointless occupation for an Italian boy who was sitting in Southern California, staring out a window at a slightly crazy, thieving, bare-legged Okie girl. The fact that she too would think it idiotic made him furious. '*Idiote*,' he abused her through the closed window and, to remind himself of his superiority, repeated it like a kind of litany in the three languages he knew: '*bécasse, cretina, sciocca,* dumb shit!' He was beginning to mouth this last insult at her through the glass when he saw that she had left the tree. Where was she? Cautiously, he sidled towards the window, concealing himself behind a curtain for fear she might catch him watching her. But when he saw her he knew there was no fear of that. She had clearly forgotten all about him for she was playing on her own side of the fence with Cazz who had taken hold of her by one bony wrist and one ankle and was swinging her round and round. Face down, free leg and arm outstretched, Evie spun with the mechanical abandon of a wheel, a weathercock, a piece of browned meat on a barbecue spit. Her skirt had flown upwards and her tight, flowered panties didn't cover her nearly enough.

Chapter Five

The sun was filtered by smog and the Santa Monica Mountains which, only last week, had been opaque and inky seemed to have drawn closer. Tawny with minuscule tufts of dark vegetation, they looked like the hide of a large, lethargic animal stretched in dehydrated folds along the horizon.

Sybil, passing Carla on the Lycée drive, acknowledged her with a tight-lipped nod. Her children looked like jailers: five to one prisoner.

Leo hadn't started his course but was fixing up the apartment he was to share with another priest who hadn't yet arrived. Would Carla help? He was training the dog every second day now and coaching Maurizio in mathematics. He had agreed to accept payment for the lessons but needed drapes for his windows and had to buy them on the cheap. He was allowed only so much money for living expenses. Could Carla advise?

She suggested that he consult Sybil. Surely the point of that painful confessional scene had been to make it possible for the two to meet? But Leo thought a little time should pass.

'Well, she'd be good about drapes,' said Carla. 'I'm not the one who's a clerical groupy.'

He didn't pretend not to be hurt. Carla had rarely met an

adult with so thin a skin. Apologizing, she explained that she had her own worries. The *directrice* of the Lycée had called her in to talk about Maurizio whom nobody in the school could handle. Carla had wondered whether in that case she should send him to a school which could handle him, but the *directrice* hadn't, it seemed, meant that. Maurizio was a good-hearted boy, she claimed, but wasn't there a lack of stability just now in the home environment? The boy's father seemed to have been away a long time, hm? *No* school, said the *directrice*, looking hard at Carla, could supply the security and discipline which it was up to families to provide. Since Carla agreed with her, there wasn't much she could reply.

'His grades have gone off too.' The Aladdin incident might have unsettled him, said the *directrice*, adding: 'If you were Americans I might say take him to an analyst, but, *entre nous*, I think that just does the parents good. They like to think they've left no stone unturned. But what, my poor *Madame*, does one find when one turns stones?'

Carla's mother-in-law could have told her. Paola, a ruthless stone-turner, had written again. Her letter, riotous with gossip about a social fabric under attack by the termites of reform, had first amused Carla then, as it was intended to do, upset her. Paola's relish for her theme and the sustained energy of her letters made one think of some skilled creature building or mending a cocoon. A wasps' nest had hung from the eaves of a house which the Verdis rented one summer near Siena. It had been easy to watch from a dormer window but hard to reach and so had not been destroyed for a long time. It was a grey papery cone which the wasps spun painstakingly out of some substance too small to be seen, something within themselves perhaps which they wrapped in delicate layers around and around so that the cone grew from the size of a spool of thread until it was as large as a man's head. Around and around wound Paola too, obeying an iron instinct, committing doubts and convictions to thin, grey aerogrammes which she folded, licked, addressed and mailed with the unremitting diligence of a cocooning insect.

Leo asked Carla to share her anxieties with him but she refused.

Sybil was the one with whom she might usefully have shared

her mother-in-law's wisdom. Though old, it was shrewd when it came to female adultery. The trouble with women, in Paola's view, was that they were apt to mix long-term objectives with short. Men were less likely to lose their heads and hearts and what they did with their other parts was consequently of less account. Woman, however, was a ductile and a vacant thing quickened only by the male spirit. She – Aristotle and Paola held – was wax to his form. Woe then to the child whose mother was shaping herself to the form of a new male. She would neglect and forget it and what maternal wings would cover the poor thing then? Those of the anti-drug squad? The orphanage? The State Penitentiary?

These considerations made it easier to face Sybil when met in the custody of her five children on the Lycée drive.

Evie's mother let her hitch-hike and the dumb girl stood at Freeway entrances with a nail-bitten thumb aimed waveringly at all points of the compass, while trucks driven by rapists, nuts and guys rotten with drug-immune VD – Maurizio had heard about this on the Terry Steele Show – whooshed past or, worse, stopped. Skinny and quickly grown – her dresses couldn't hold her – she was like a bundle of coat-hangers and maybe the motorists wouldn't stop for her. Maurizio hoped they wouldn't but didn't say this for fear she'd take it as a challenge.

'Square!' she'd have said if *he'd* said anything and slitted her green cat's eyes at him and grinned.

It was an insult. But if not being a square meant having a father who was a sort of murderer and a mother who was half a suicide, well he couldn't see what was so great about that.

The Lycée was giving a concert for the parents and Maurizio expected that it would be the usual phony effort with camera buffs nearly knocking down your mother as they backed, ass foremost, into her chair, angling to get the perfect shot of their kid playing *Frère Jacques* on the piano. Big deal! Later, to be sure, there'd be nothing in the family album to show the kid wasn't playing Mozart. Maurizio would be stuck in the back as usual. In all Lycée photos, the children of film-stars, consuls and big donors were out front and the rest stuck on the edge like parsley round a roast.

He'd had a row with his mother who was all set to take Evie to the school concert.

'No,' said Maurizio. 'I don't want her to come.'

'But why, Maurizio? She might like it.'

'She'd be bored. The Lycée is a dump.'

'You may think that. It would be interesting for *her* – so different from her own school.'

'That's why.'

'Which are you ashamed of?' his mother had asked. 'Evie or the Lycée? Are you being a snob, Maurizio? Because if you are...'

He had walked off banging the door. He got burned up over people accusing him that way. Parents especially. They went on about your not being a snob, then got you into situations where you had to start thinking of the snobbery of everyone else. Evie would probably feel awful at the pissy old Lycée with all the girls gussied up and talking French to show off. Then the guys would take the piss out of him for bringing her. And *she'd* think he was dumb for going to a school full of kids who couldn't even talk English right. No. It was impossible. He didn't want her there and he bet his mother knew why, only she could afford to pretend she didn't because it wasn't her friend or her school. His mother was a snob about not being a snob. She thought she was so great that she had to feel sorry for other people and it never crossed her mind that other people looked down on *her* because she wasn't an American but talked with a foreign accent. Maurizio got it from all sides.

Leo, who had not yet bought himself a car, rang to ask if Carla could arrange for someone in her car pool to give him a ride.

'Is someone tapping your phone?' he wondered. 'I keep hearing clicks.'

'It's Maurizio on the extension. He sometimes listens in.'

'Why?'

'Who knows? Suspicion perhaps?'

'Of what?'

'Of the adult world, wouldn't you think? Didn't you feel that in your teens? He may want to check up on the horrid fate awaiting him – find out what we're like when he's not around.' She laughed, encouraging Leo to dismiss the matter, but had underrated his terrier qualities or training perhaps. Something.

'Do you want me to ask him why he does it?'

No. Definitely not. So why had she mentioned the thing *on the phone*? To tip Leo off? Of course not. He was saying nothing private and anyway didn't take hints. To tip Maurizio off? More likely. Yes. Just as well to let him know that his observing was observed. She didn't *mind* his listening. There was a touch of the Machiavel to any good Florentine and deviousness was survival strategy – but you'd better be good at it and not make clicks. *That* was probably all she'd hoped to convey to Maurizio who, of course, had been keeping tabs *on her*. His apprentice moves as her protector brought back feelings she'd had a dozen years ago when he'd made his first baby steps followed by his first words pronounced in a husky, funny Florentine accent – they'd hired a nurse for him from the oltr'Arno district. '*Hasa*' he'd said instead of '*casa*', she recalled with revived amusement, and '*haha*' instead of '*cacca*'.

But meanwhile Leo had been unleashed.

'Why do you listen when your mother and I are on the phone?' she heard him ask the following afternoon. 'Is there something you want to know? I'll tell you anything you like. Ask me. Ask your mother.'

Maurizio's answering murmur was inaudible: a verbal shuffle. As though a tape had been activated in her head, she heard his baby voice protesting in that long-lost Florentine lilt: '*Mamma, c'ho la bua!*' '*La bua*' was a baby word for soreness or discomfort and his present murmur was full of that.

'*Tell me*,' Leo harried foolishly. 'Let's be honest with each other.'

Maurizio handled him gently. 'Adults say that,' he skirmished, 'but they're never honest with kids.'

'Come on. That's' Sixties talk. "Never trust anyone over thirty," they used to say. Do you know how *old* people who first said that are now? They're my age.'

'And can you be trusted?'

'Some of us can. I hope.'

'Do you trust people? I mean all the way?'

'Sure.'

'I don't mean when you're being a priest in the confessional and that. I guess there,' said Maurizio, 'you're just a hot line to God.'

'Well, people trust hot lines.'

'I trust you,' said Maurizio, 'as much as I do anyone.' And laughed. He'd be a Machiavel all right, his mother saw and felt a shiver of relinquishing sadness. He'd manage.

But Leo, innocent of the fact that authority's representative here was not himself but Maurizio, seemed unable to leave well enough alone. '*Is* there anything you want me to tell you?' he asked again.

'I'll take a rain check on that. O K?'

'OK,' said Leo who hadn't an ounce nor even a grain in him of the Machiavel .

'If my Pop turns up,' Evie remarked. 'He'll beat the daylights out of Cazz.'

That was something Maurizio would have liked to see.

'Why doesn't your mother ask him for a divorce?' *That* would bring her Pop here, Maurizio figured. Bring him on the double, axe in hand.

'What for?' Evie asked. 'Cazz wouldn't marry her. Anyway, I think she kinda likes my Pop. They've split up and gone back together lots of times.'

'Then he can't be as bad as you said.'

Evie laughed. 'He's bad. Don't worry. He's real bad!'

'A villainous woodcutter?'

'Right.'

'A rough-neck and a bully?'

'Correct.'

Maurizio had a rubber tomahawk. A painted, kid's thing which he'd had around for years. He didn't play with it any more but had brought it up to the tree house to hang next to the sheep's skulls. Now he grabbed hold of it and, tightening his face, hissed: 'You said he once split some guy's head with an axe?'

110

'I did. He did.'

Maurizio waved the tomahawk with deliberation. Lifting it as though it were heavy, he tried to look like bad guys he'd seen in the movies. Irony wobbled into excitement. Surely, he couldn't be playing this for real like a small kid? Hunched up, knotting his shoulders, he willed a slow, bullish strength to flow into him.

'Like this?'

'I wasn't there. I didn't see.' She was leaving this story to him.

Funny story? Serious? 'It was like this,' he told her. 'He was drunk, see. He was feeling sort of slowed down by the drink and angry with himself. Maybe he'd had a fight with your mother and was sorry?' Maurizio felt an uncertain itch inside himself. This game wasn't going right. He had the feeling *it* was controlling *him*.

'He's never sorry,' Evie told him, 'just mean.'

'There has to be a reason.'

'Some folk are just mean.'

'Maybe he's fed up with – his work?'

'Him? He *likes* his work. He's strong and that's all he cares about and he can make a lot when he wants.'

'OK, then. He's just angry. He likes to get mad, right?'

'Ahuh.'

'He picks on guys who have something weak in them, guys he knows won't fight back. Then he turns nasty. Mean.' Maurizio was warming to this. 'Maybe someone like Cazz, huh? Some half-assed guy who thinks he can just move in on someone like your mother because for him anything goes. Guys like Cazz don't think anyone is going to challenge them ever.'

'What are you talking about?'

'Cazz and your Pop.' Maurizio realized he had been shouting.

'Cazz will run away,' Evie told him. 'He won't wait around to be caught.'

'That's what he thinks he'll do but your father will have thought of that, see. He'll be cunning and he'll creep up on the house when nobody's expecting him. He'll park his truck round the corner somewhere, then creep along the sidewalk on the opposite side of the street, watching the windows. Then he'll stand in the shadow of a tree. Maybe that one there, see it? Biding his time. He'll wait for the lights to go on. Cazz never

111

draws the blinds. What he sees will put him in a rage.' Rage
washed around Maurizio.

'You don't like Cazz, do you?'

'Do you?'

'Sure I do.'

Maurizio smiled craftily. 'Well, your father won't,' he told her
with satisfaction. 'I'll bet your father has a key to your front
door.'

'Could be.'

'Sure he has. So he can wait until everyone is asleep and creep
up the stairs in the dark. Then he'll take off his shoes and walk
very softly. He'll open the bedroom door and walk over to the
bed and *Boing!* he'll lower the axe.' Maurizio was dashing the
tomahawk against a limb of the pomegranate tree. The rubber
blade of it buckled and he slashed again This time the rubber
split. '*Boing!* on his head,' he yelled. 'Cazz's head will be
smashed like . . . a pomegranate.'

Evie was disgusted.

'You're talking about a friend of mine and my Mom's,' she
said with sudden propriety. 'And what about my Mom lying
next to him in the bed?'

Maurizio lashed the tree trunk.

'Stoppit!' She gave him a push.

He lost his footing, grabbed her to steady himself, turned the
grab into a hug and, before she could dodge him, got in a kiss.
It wasn't much of a one but the most he'd managed yet despite
several tries so clumsy they'd never hit target. Evie seemed to
know what he was after before he did himself – once or twice it
had been her backing off which let him know he'd been coming.
She was an expert dodger. Cool. He got the feeling she'd had a
lot of practice? Who'd been trying it on with her? Who?

'Cut it out willya, Mah-uh-reetzio. I'm not going to be like
her.'

'Her' was Wanda. Had Cazz tried? Sure he must have!

'You like him?' Maurizio yelled in a flash of inspired rage.
'You really like that bastard? *That's* why you're jealous of your
mother!'

It was a shot in the dark. He didn't even believe it. But it sure
maddened Evie. She pushed him off the edge of the tree house

112

floor: an unbelievable thing. He might have split his skull falling. Only he didn't fall. While thought of the danger was blasting his brain he had escaped it. He had a foothold in the rope-ladder, had caught her with one arm as he swung wide of the tree and held the top of the ladder with the other. Together they hung then fell, tumbling into a mound of pampas grass which broke their fall. It had been flattened by rain then dried out so that the long, broken grass blades were as dry as whips. The two rolled painfully across it while Carlomagno appeared from nowhere to bark and leap heavily athwart the pair of them.

'Maurizio, are you crazy in the head or what? I'm torn to bits. It cuts. Get that goddamned dog off us. Is he loony like yourself?'

She screamed. Carlomagno barked and Maurizio got his hand over her mouth. She bit it. He pulled it away and suddenly she was up and Casimir was standing over him.

'Well,' he looked ironically at Maurizio. 'What are you up to, sonnyboy? Trying to rape my ward here? Funny sorts of goings-on anyway. You in pain, Evie? Better come with me. I'll rub some balm on those rosy limbs. C'mon.'

He led her back to her own house.

Later, Maurizio, who couldn't sleep all night, imagined him holding her in a bath, smoothing some sort of lotion over her bare skin. The image jumped like a home movie and he couldn't get to see the whole. He was just as glad and didn't dare ask Evie what had happened or make more than a gruff mention of the matter when they next met.

'Sorry about yesterday. I got, well, you know, sorry. I mean it. Really. OK?'

'OK,' she said. Her thighs were streaked a hot, angry pink.

If she'd had a proper family, he figured they'd have banned him from playing with her and they'd have been right. He couldn't stand to remember his own behaviour or understand what had got into him. But then, when you thought about it, there were more dangers in her own house than she'd ever meet out of it.

'I'd be careful of him,' he warned her about Cazz. 'That guy'll get into trouble sooner or later.' What had fountained up in Maurizio must surely – he'd have laid any bet on this – lie in

113

more sinister reservoirs inside Cazz. 'He'll get what's coming to him,' he said, though with less assurance about this.

Later, when Cazz began to tease Maurizio, as he had got into the habit of doing, Maurizio found it hard to keep his temper.

'Hey Maurizio,' Cazz yelled across the fence, 'how's your sex-starved dog? How's your pampas grass, huh?' Cazz laughed a loud, dumb laugh.

Maurizio could feel the anger in his throat. His lower lip was quivering. Jesus! He hoped he wasn't going to *cry*! That'd about put the lid on it. Tightening his fists and digging his elbows into his sides as though to hold himself together, he asked through his teeth: 'Cazz, what would the cops do if they knew you were a pusher? What if someone told them?'

There was a silence.

An ooze of cold knowledge flowed into Maurizio and he knew he'd overstepped. He was in adult territory here, dangerous territory where he didn't know the score. Suddenly panicky, he tried to find something childish to do – something to establish his harmlessness. He'd have been ready to even cry. But now that he wanted them, the tears wouldn't come.

Cazz's mouth tightened. He stared at Maurizio for a sobering moment, then walked away.

Evie waited until he was out of earshot, then whispered, 'That was a dumb thing to say, Maurizio.'

Leo, ill for a week, had holed up in his apartment. He guessed he must have gotten sick from eating some old tuna.

'You should have rung me,' Carla said. 'I'd have brought over some food.'

'The place is too awful.' He hadn't got a cleaning-woman yet, he explained, and was intimidated by her drawing-room. It was looking particularly pretty just now with bunches of tall, branching home-grown orchids which Jane had brought over. 'I didn't want you to see my squalor.'

'Unworldly squalor?'

'Just squalor.' His candid grin flicked like a bulb on the blink. 'Coming *here*,' he said, 'is like returning to harbour. It's like going home.'

'Home?'

114

It had been a vision, he said, on that first day of the mudslides. Her house, in that chaos, had glowed like an ikon. Later, he'd found his mind returning to it. It was years since he'd had a home to go to . His mother had died while he was in the seminary and his father was a bit of a recluse. 'Like me maybe?' the grin flicked on briefly. 'Should have been a monk – maybe it's genetic? He's a great guy in lots of ways but lives like a bear.' Leo himself in recent years had been spending most of his time in slums and ghettos, doing missionary work and starving his eye.

'It has its excitement. I don't regret it. I did good work. I'm sure I was useful.' He laughed. 'Sensory deprivation is known to procure a high. Then there's politics, polemics . . . *They* send you so high you're in orbit. You become committed, compulsive, can't give an inch, think the fate of the world is on your shoulders – and then, quite suddenly, from one day to the next, your assurance can collapse. Just like that. Like a house in a mudslide. It's not that the problems change. What falters is belief in one's indispensable rightness about how to deal with them. I began to wonder whether I wasn't trying to empty an ocean with a thimble, rushing back and forth, moving faster and more efficiently all the time – but still there was this ocean. Am I boring you?'

'Of course not.'

'I can see it must sound vague. I could make it concrete but you can imagine the sort of thing: good works and, in the end, I began to see that it was good works without faith because if I thought myself so indispensable then what about God? Why wasn't I a politician anyway? Which was I opting for? God or Mammon? I thought I was fighting Mammon, but when you concentrate on that you think of nothing else . . .'

He talked on. Carla found his eagerness contagious in much the way she did the energy of people talking about games whose rules she didn't know. Earlier in the evening there had been a basket-ball game on the radio and Leo and Maurizio had sat listening and rooting noisily for the home team. Their yells and the commentator's spiel had come hurtling and bounding into her kitchen, interrupting any thoughts she might have had with the same, unstoppable zest as a salesman who's managed to get a toe in the door. Carla understood very little but *not* understanding gave the proceedings impact. Purified, universalized, the sound became a vehicle for one's own emotions. Leo's account of his job – job? – worked the same way.

'It's an old pratfall,' he was shrugging. 'You're warned against it in the seminary ...'

She wondered whether his persuasive enthusiasm was quite healthy? Might it be unwise to let him spend time with Maurizio, an impressionable boy?

'Prayer ...' he said, talking of it as 'a resource'.

She switched her mind back to the basket-ball commentary. One of the players was called 'Magic'. 'Magic,' the commentator had yelled breathlessly, 'Magic takes the rebound; Magic down the court; passes; over to Wilkes; back to Magic under the hoop; Magic up and in ...' The player could have been called 'Prayer' or 'Mammon'. It was the focused energy which ignited, the skilled taste for contest. And *that* was how they recruited you as a fan. They? Who? You know who, Carla. Always distinguish between the pleasant individual now flagellating himself on your sofa and the institution to which he belongs. You were brought up – rightly – to distrust it just as you – also rightly – distrust the Communist Party. Both organizations have high ideals and low tactics.

'You don't like my world,' said Leo, reading something on her face. 'A pity, for I like yours.'

'Domestic life?'

'Small things beautifully cared for: flowers,' he waved at the orchids, 'order, the day-to-day, dog-training, child-tutoring ...'

'Perhaps you should have married?'

'Now you're making Sybil's mistake. It's not ...'

'Sex. All right. You've made that clear.'

'But it's *true*. There's a whole dimension which women create – *some* women – which is so much more than ... It's not any of the *things* you do but the precision, the ease with which you do them. I could buy flowers myself, learn a recipe. It's not that.'

'Maybe it's that very old-fashioned art: bourgeois living. Mammon harnessed. Perhaps you're missing it?' Laughing, needling him. She found it embarrassing and, remembering Marco's feelings about her proficiency in the lesser domestic

116

arts, *sad* to be celebrated as Our Lady of Flowers, Children Dogs and Fine Food.

'No,' he said, 'it's grace.'

The flat sweetness of this made a hole in the conversation. There was nothing to say to it. Not that he'd mind. His ease with silence came, he had explained, from long nights with incompatible companions in rectories, sleepy old pastors; dull pauses after arguments had been beaten to death. It wasn't only his eagerness which was contagious. There was a sadness about him too – elusive, fugitive – which connected comfortably with her own. Now, however, he was smiling, his face alight like a young child's – younger than Maurizio's for *he* was learning guile. He talked of his childhood – had perhaps summoned his childhood grin? He'd *loved* home life, he explained, and talked of his mother, Christmas gatherings, the names of long-dead dogs. In that Oregon wilderness, the Italian family closeness had been all the more precious. She'd understand that, surely? He'd given it up – the chance of a family of his own precisely because he loved it so much. That was what celibacy was about. It wasn't imposed as not marrying was imposed on air hostesses for the duration of their job. No, you gave up one love for a greater one – of which you couldn't have conceived without knowing human love first.

'Leo, you're being pious.'

'Does it bother you?'

'A bit.'

'Sorry, it was only to explain how much I do appreciate aspects of the world which I've been – I think erroneously – denying myself.'

'Flowers, women, dogs?'

'Did I sound offensive just now? Silly?'

'No, but you take a roundabout path to something very simple. You sound all tied up in knots.'

'But I unknot myself here. Here I'm a delivered Houdini. I relax, straighten out, expand. I feel I'd be lost if I couldn't come here – yet, I wouldn't want you to misunderstand.'

'Like Sybil?'

'I suppose.'

'For a dark-complexioned man you blush like mad.'

117

'I don't mean,' he said carefully, 'that I'd lose my whole self if I couldn't come here – one self maybe, as we say a cat has nine lives. Yes, I'm sure I'd lose a self I value if I couldn't come here.'

'No need to lose it then.'

'Look,' he said, 'I feel you're holding me off – and why shouldn't you? Maybe I embarrass you? Say if I do. I know I can sound a bit ... leaden. I'm not a total fool but I do have a ball and chain on my foot. I hate saying this but I am tied, handicapped and I'm not sure you allow for this. Sometimes, I'm flattered that you don't – then panicked that the situation can seem false. There's a real paradox here because what I love about this house is that there are no crucifixes and bits of dried palm stuck on your walls and no feeling that I'm a bit dried up myself and to be kept apart. Only then *I* start to worry that that leaves me ... unprotected. What I want from you is a pact of friendship, of trust. Then we can relax and I'll stop annoying you with my pieties.'

'I haven't gotten any wrong ideas about you, Leo, OK? I'd be a bit dim if I did, wouldn't I? After all, who clarified the thing with Sybil – and was called a snoop for her pains?'

He walked to the window and looked out. Maybe years in the confessional made him more at ease talking to people he couldn't see?

'It's like rowing upstream,' he told the darkness outside. 'I keep trying to get closer to you and every move seems to take me further off. Maybe *I've* gotten wrong ideas. Do I bore you? Would you rather I didn't come round?'

'Leo, it's hard to know what you want. A declaration of friendship? OK I enjoy your company. I wouldn't have you here if I didn't. So does Maurizio and so does the dog. I can't answer for the orchids.'

His back faced her with the blankness of a sandwichman's board – more blankly for this had nothing written on it. Countering blankness with silence, she said nothing. Eventually he came and sat on the sofa, looking gloomy.

'I'd offer you a drink,' she said, 'but if it was food poisoning you had it would be bad for you.'

'Like everything else.'

'Leo, your signals are confusing.'

118

'I'm angling – begging maybe for an open, honest and special friendship . . .'

'I know it has to be special.'

'I don't mean disinfected, safe – or yes I do too, but *also* I also mean *strong* – something more than your dog might feel for anyone who stops to give him a pat or scratch his head. Is that possible?'

'But, Leo, you already have that.'

'Have I?'

'Yes.'

Two men in white karate uniforms stood under the pomegranate tree. They were looking for Cazz. Evie told them he'd gone out with her Mom.

One of the two wore his hair in a pony-tail. 'Ahuh,' he said, 'that'll be Wanda. And you're Evie and this,' he paused briefly, 'this'll be Maurizio, am I right?'

Evie agreed that he was.

'We're buddies of Cazz's,' said the man. 'Friends.' He gave the word a light emphasis. Everything he said seemed studied, even pedantic. 'Yeah,' he added, 'hi Maurizio.'

'Hi,' said Maurizio.

'We'd like to be your friends too,' said the other man who was pale, square-faced, fair-haired and maybe twenty-five years old. 'We're Poles,' he said. 'Like Cazz. We Europeans ought to stick together, don't you think?' He waited for an answer. 'Mmm? What do you say, Maurizio?'

Maurizio mumbled something. He felt uncomfortable.

'What's that?' asked the man with the pony-tail. 'Whatchasay?'

'I said "sure",' Maurizio told him.

'Well that's OK then,' said the man. 'That's fine, just as long as you're Cazz's friend too. We came to take him to do some training. You interested in the martial arts?'

'Why not?' said Evie perkily.

The men ignored her. 'We could give you a lesson.' The pony-tailed man addressed this to Maurizio. 'Know how many murders were committed in LA County in the last calendar year? Over one thousand! There's a crime wave on and the cops can't

119

handle it. It's no use going to *them*, you know. Every male has to learn to defend himself. Self-defence is a natural human right. You'll agree with that?' The man paused the way teachers did in class. 'Huh?' he insisted.

'Mmm,' said Maurizio.

'The young,' said the man in his schoolteacher's voice, 'are especially at risk. I'd be worried if I was a kid today and didn't know how to defend myself. Wouldn't you?' he asked his friend.

'Sure thing,' said the pale-haired man. 'There's lots of accidents happen to juveniles right in the vicinity of their own homes.'

'Yeah.'

'Yeah.' The pony-tailed man shook his head and his hair waggled like a whip. 'My buddy and me got into a fight last night which is one thing we both hate to do. Guy made a remark we couldn't tolerate. Didn't know how to keep his mouth shut, see? So we had to fight. And once you do you don't pussyfoot. It stands to reason. When we'd finished with him that guy couldn't get off the floor.'

Suddenly Pony Tail caught Pale Hair's sleeve, crouched away from him and brought his foot up in a swift, circular kick to the midriff. 'Round House kick,' he said pedagogically. 'That was light: only a demonstration. You could follow up with this,' he aimed an elbow at Pale Hair's throat. 'Or a knife-hand blow to the side of the neck. Very tender that spot. Or two fingers in the eye-sockets. Like so. Or this.' He laid a spread finger and thumb against the side of his partner's neck, then made as if to catch his head and jerk it towards the buttressing hand. 'This'll break a guy's neck in a split second. I'll bet we could teach you a lot, Maurizio.'

'Be thinking about that,' said the other man.

The two did some more lunges at the air, twirled around, then, slithering down the steps to a red pick-up truck which they'd left parked on the road, climbed in and drove off. The after-image left in the empty Glen was of two giant white moths.

*

Dear Babbo,
How are you? I am O K – but only just. Like I told you, I
120

am friends with Evie but I have no defence against Casimir who has turned into an antisocial element. He pushes drugs and sleeps with other people's wives and may be a child-molester. I think he thinks I will snitch on him. I told him what I thought and that may not have been too wise. Evie thinks it wasn't. I don't stand a chance if he decides to turn against me. I wish you had let me learn karate. I haven't time now. All the guys around here like girls. It is a very immoral place. All perverts. If I told the cops about Cazz they might not believe me because I am only a boy and they are busy with a crime wave. I don't want you to worry too much. Anyway, you can't help while you are in Italy. I hope you are happy. When are you coming back? Mamma is no use so I don't even tell her. She gets nervous. So do I. If my school report is not good that is why. You should think about that. When you and Mamma get nervous you make mistakes too. Sorry if this letter is not well written or interesting. I am nervous like I said. I will write a better one next time.

Love and kisses,
Maurizio

Dear Mr Briggs,

Do not be surprised to get a letter from a secret friend.

I am a friend of Wanda and Evie. They are in bad company which is something I think you should know. The bad company is a drug-pusher who is living in the house with them. He belongs to the Church of Satan and studies karate. He also ran away with a minor (girl) last year and is very degenerate. I would like to protect them myself but there are private reasons why I can't. He is a nasty customer and you should try to catch him by surprise.

Sincerely yours,
A Friend

*

It was evening in the Glen. Casimir had dropped by to borrow coffee and ask about Jane whose lighted windows he could see from Carla's kitchen.

'How's the house?' he asked. 'How is she?'

'Fixed up,' Carla told him. 'As well as can be expected.'

'Which?'

121

'Both.'

'I'm confused,' said Cazz, 'about my own feelings. I know you think badly of me.'

Carla said nothing. Leo was upstairs helping Maurizio with his homework and she didn't want the two men meeting again. She would have asked Cazz to leave if it hadn't been for Jane who was fretting, hurt, furious and, Carla suspected, eager, under all that, to have him back.

'What can he be doing with that slut?' she'd asked Carla. 'Do you suppose he fantasizes that he's an old Polish feudal lord sleeping with a serf?'

'Well, you did give him a hard time. It must be a change to be with someone he can push around.'

'It's true,' said Jane, 'that he never liked being dependent on me. But he wasn't very supportive either when I got cancer. Well, to be fair, he was good at the start. I remember his saying: "Look, Jane, this changes nothing; we're still us." That moved me,' Jane remembered bitterly. 'I cried. The trouble,' she mused, 'was that the old us wasn't very united.'

Cazz had bolted from the house while Jane was in hospital.

'Can you imagine what it was like to come back and find him living across the road with,' Jane took a deep breath, 'her?'

'He couldn't bear to be alone while you were being operated on.' Carla tried to be comforting. 'He didn't go far either. Maybe he's waiting to be summoned back?'

But Jane was bruised and couldn't be callous even towards Wanda. If she took Cazz from her mightn't that bring bad luck? 'I'm an idiot,' she told Carla, 'pay no attention to me.' Then she'd burst out crying. 'The only reason I want that bastard back,' she sniffled through her tears, 'is that he's the only person I know who is totally but totally weak. I like being the strong one. Do you understand that? He has appalling dreams.'

'Why don't you go and see her?' said Carla to Cazz. 'Ring her anyway. She had a major operation after all.'

'I did send her flowers,' he said. 'Jane's quite tough. It wouldn't surprise me if this hadn't made her tougher. Illness does. It gives people an excuse for egotism.'

'Like being a refugee?'

'You're so predictable, Carla.' Cazz arranged his features in a boyish *moue*. 'I guess it's why you attract me. I can see right through your defences. I see through all defences, but I like them to be there. I feel pain in you, Carla. Don't think I'm insensitive. All that housewifiness is a defence: the oyster pearling over the intrusion that menaces its secret flesh. I love to watch you at it.'

Carla was disgusted. 'What about Wanda?' she asked. 'You're not so sensitive when it comes to her.'

'Has she been crying on your shoulder?'

'She doesn't have to. I live next door. I'm not blind or deaf.'

Wanda and Cazz had the sort of rows Carla remembered from hot nights in the older and poorer parts of Florence when, walking down streets like gullies, you might suddenly see a silhouette at a window or a shadow on an opposite wall: wavering blow-ups of the sort children make with fists and handkerchiefs. The crack of splintering furniture might then ricochet up and down the sour old street. Sometimes a scream, shrill as a razor, would zip through followed by silence. Windows had always been open in that hot, communal darkness. Nothing Cazz or Wanda did was new to her. Neither was Wanda's gritty laughter the day after one of those nights:

'Hey, Carla, how'd you ever land me with that guy? Yeah, yeah, you warned me. Well, I figure a bit of trouble's better than a lonely bed – but you're the wise one, aren't you?'

There was mockery and incredulity in the smoke signals funnelling from Wanda's nose.

'Well, I guess I'm headed for a bad end,' she'd say. 'I can't quit smoking and I can't quit the other thing either.' Brightly done up in Salvation Army pickings, she'd waddled off with a wag of fringed lurex. Gingham and polyester had given way to fancy dress.

'She'll land on her feet,' Cazz assured. 'I'm not the first, you know. There was plenty of extramural activity before I came along.'

'Who hit her?'

'What are you talking about?'

'Her bruises. Who gave them to her?'

Cazz mimed polite incomprehension. 'Carla, you bemuse me. Are you speaking in code?'

'Can you find your own way out?' Carla pointed at the outer door. 'I've got to keep stirring this caramel or it'll stick.'

'Want me to get the phone then?'

It had started to ring.

'No.'

But he'd picked it up. 'Hullo? Yes, right, this is the Verdi residence. What's that? Who am I? You mean who are you?'

Carla had spilled some caramel. Pausing to scrape it up she heard Cazz say 'Oh, it's Marco?' and her heart leapt.

'Hi, man, hi, high too I hope,' Cazz was chattering on. 'Cazz here, *Cazz*, you remember your old buddy Casimir ... Yeah, well she's right here too keeping the home fires burning till the boy comes home. Whaddaya mean whaddo I mean? She's got something cooking that's what ...'

Carla grabbed the phone. 'Marco, darling, is it really you?'

A crackle of Italian sputtered like hot grease in her ear. She'd forgotten how excitable Marco could be.

'There's nothing wrong, is there? You're not ill?'

The sputtering, incomprehensible at first, now began to make unwelcome sense. Marco was in a rage. His first clear question was: 'What's that creep doing in the house? Carla ... Look, how's Maurizio? He wrote me a most disturbing letter.'

'Who?' She heard her voice fly upwards. Maurizio wrote a letter a week to his father. Supervised by her and usually too similar to the ones he'd written before. Nothing wrong there, certainly. Marco must be mentioning Maurizio to gain time. What was his real anxiety? Maybe he'd made some awful mistake in business? Maybe they were broke? 'Marco,' she reassured him, 'I love you. It doesn't matter if ... I mean we'll manage if you're in money trouble or something. I could get a job.' He wouldn't let her do the accounts. She guessed that he concealed failures from her. 'Are things going badly?' she asked so as to make it easy for him to confess.

'Maurizio,' said Marco in the falsely patient tones of a man who has been driven beyond bearing. 'I asked you about *Maurizio*. He ...'

'Wrote you a letter? Maurizio?'

'Yes. Maurizio. Your son. Do you remember him? Mother of

124

God,' prayed Marco, 'are you on drugs or something? Has that creep got you on drugs?'

'What creep? Maurizio?'

'Not Maurizio,' Marco roared. 'Casimir the Creep. Maurizio says ...'

'What?'

'Carla!' Marco's voice trembled, buzzed. She imagined it as a voice caught like a bee in a jam pot, dancing resonantly around its confined space: 'Carla!' He released the syllables slowly down the wire as though directing them at an imbecilic child. 'I want you to concentrate. Pay attention. I'm going to speak very quietly. Now. Carla. Don't. Get. Excited.'

She gripped the phone. Could Marco be drunk? Drugged? But that was what he'd said of *her*.

'Just tell me, Carla, can you understand me?'

'Of course I understand you – only you're not making sense, so, no, I don't.'

'Carla, listen ...'

'No!' Indignation leapt in her. '*You* listen! It's been terrible here,' she began. But that was the wrong note to sound. 'We can cope,' she decided to reassure him. 'Only we need to know about your plans, the future ...'

'Carla, how's Maurizio?'

'He's fine. Why wouldn't he be? You can talk to him if you want. I can't imagine why you're so concerned about him all of a sudden. And Cazz, if you must know, came over to borrow coffee. He's living in the shack with a woman called Wanda who ...'

'Maurizio wrote to me. He says he's frightened of Cazz. He says Cazz has been threatening him and he used the word "pervert". Where does he learn expressions like that? Look, Carla, I'm *here*. I can't do anything for him. Are you sleeping with Cazz? When I said "go have experiences", I didn't think you'd expose Maurizio to them. That boy senses something going on. His letter is frankly disturbed. You're doing irreparable damage...'

He was jealous! Marco. Carla wanted to dance. She didn't believe in the nonsense about Maurizio with whom she sat down to meals three times a day and who seemed perfectly balanced to her – well, not perfectly, perhaps, but that was because of puberty and the lack of a father's guidance. Marco was side-stepping blame and – jealous? The word was like alcohol in her blood.

He scolded on. 'I'm busy. I have money-troubles ...'

So she had guessed right. Good! Great! Money-troubles were better than love-troubles. She and Marco had been quite poor in their first years together and, as she remembered it now, she hadn't minded at all – anyway not much. A memory softened her. It was of Marco putting her feet between his thighs to warm them: a heroic act for they had been living on the unheated top floor of a palazzo right on the river Arno whose quays were raked by a razoring winter wind. In spring, wisteria fell from the balconies like shawls of lace; in summer, mosquitoes rose from the drying river-bed and all winter the bed sheets were as icy as Marco's voice which was at this moment hardening into a frigid rage. Should she remind him of how once he had thawed her feet? The past, he would retort, was not the point. It was for her. It had better be. Only the past made her long for the embrace of the middle-aged man whose sour, contentious voice was jabbing at her ear. 'What's the use,' she heard him wind up, 'of talking to a damn junky?'

'Damn you, Marco, I never even tasted a joint, whereas you ...' But one couldn't have a slanging match across an ocean and a continent. She forced herself to stop.

Across her neat, warm kitchen – redwood and Mexican tiles – Cazz stared in frank curiosity. Why didn't he leave? The conversation with Marco was in Italian but Cazz must have caught the acrimony. Hard not to. Marco's screaming spluttered down the receiver like machine-gun fire. She held the vicious, gulping thing away from her. Words overflowed from it: '... *fesso, caffone ... irresponsabile ...*' Then the voice sobered and she heard: 'I'm thinking of sending Paola over. I can't get away myself and ...'

Paola! Here in California! Sent to keep Carla in line! It was laughable. She almost expected to see Cazz laugh – but of course he hadn't understood.

A closer sputtering released whiffs of burned sugar. A flame leaped on the stove. The caramel!

126

'Cazz,' she gestured at it. 'Can you turn that off?'

'What's that?' the telephone demanded. 'Cazz? Is that *farabutto* still there? *Quel cazzo!* He's well named: Cazzo! What's he done? Moved in? Well tell him I'm coming to get him as soon as I can get away. Tell him I'll run him out of Los Angeles County.'

The absurdity was a body blow. He's forgotten us, she thought. He remembers this place in terms of a TV serial: the Wild West. Covering the receiver carefully, she pointed to the stairs. 'Cazz, could you call Maurizio?' The burnt smell was bitter. Some caramel must have lodged on the gas-jet. 'Marco,' she told the telephone, 'this is all in your head.'

'Maurizio says . . .'

'Maurizio is coming to the phone. He'll talk to you himself. I don't know what's the matter with him that he should write such letters, but . . .'

'Don't you read his letters any more? Have you completely abdicated, Carla? God knows it's hard enough to make a living without having to worry about what should be the wife's province too. You've obviously become totally incompetent. What are you doing with your days? How do you fill them? Why is his school report such a disaster? He used to be an A student. Now he gets Cs. Does everything have to fall apart when I turn my back? Do I have to send my ageing, invalid mother out to take charge because my wife is a . . .'

'Aren't you awfully square all of a sudden?' Carla asked. 'What about all those letters you wrote?'

'*Porca miseria*, you soft-headed idiot! *Dio Bacco!* Words fail me . . .' But they didn't. He was still cursing her when Maurizio came to the phone.

'Here's Maurizio.'

Carla left the kitchen.

Cazz was in the hall. 'How's Marco?'

She shrugged. 'OK. He's OK.'

'Listen, I want to discuss something with you.'

'Oh Cazz, this is no time. I've got to go back to the phone. Look, obviously, things aren't OK at all. I wish you'd go.'

He frowned. 'It's quite urgent.'

'How can it be?' She felt exasperated. 'For *me*?'

'It's about Maurizio. Only I'd rather talk to you privately.'

Carla jerked an elbow in the direction of the kitchen where Maurizio was still on the phone. 'Babbo,' his voice came ecstatically through the door. 'Babbo!' It seemed to her he was saying nothing else.

'Well look, tell me when I can talk to you.'

'I don't know. Has he done something?'

'Not really. Not yet, but ...'

'Look, Cazz, another time.'

'OK, OK. See you, Carla.'

He raised a hand and walked away.

Through the side windows she saw him cut through the green dusk, past clumps of bobbing poinsettias, then up the next-door slope to bring his provisional companionship to poor expectant Wanda.

'Babbo!' Maurizio's shriek of filial adoration bounced through the door. Would that reassure Marco? Maurizio worshipped his father – unfairly, for Marco was tyrannical and had often hit Maurizio too hard when he was small. Carla, intervening, had got hurt herself – and felt hurt again now for it was clear that those two would always prefer each other to her. They were mirrors to each other's maleness. She realized too that she didn't believe in Marco's money-troubles. Paola would have mentioned them if they'd been important, but Paola's hints had been headed in another direction.

'No, no, Babbo, not with Mamma ... with Wanda ... Cazz ... *ma si, si ...*'

Maurizio, a domestic spy, was being interrogated. Maurizio had ratted on his own offer of equality. Carla would have been naive to take it at face value. Marco had not left her here for *her* sake.

'Mamma!' Maurizio was rosy with happiness. 'Babbo wants to talk to you.'

Anger stiff in her chest and belly, she went back to the phone.

'Carla!' He had a honeyed, mesmeric voice when he wanted to. She thought of it as a curling voice: as though each phoneme had been caressed in his throat before being released into the telephone: 'C-c-ca-ar-r-rl-la!'

'Well?'

128

'Look, I'm sorry I got carried away. Maurizio seems OK. I over-reacted. OK? Though you should have seen the letter he sent. I think, mind you, that you *have* been losing your grip just a teeny bit. Be honest, Carla, isn't that so?'

A royal pardon would be coming up if she made the right noises. Maurizio, bubbling with delight, leaned against the door.

'Mamma!' He sketched signals in the air. 'Babbo is giving me a ...' Signal. Gesture. What? 'For my birthday. You know, Mamma.' More gestures. Incomprehensible.

She envied his easy egotism, would have liked to smile at him with the tenderness of an old madonna in a field of gold leaf.

Marco's voice harried her. 'It's true, isn't it? It's all your fault. Worrying about your incompetence, I've no energy left for my own things.' The accusation was beginning to sound indulgent, even friendly. She was his handicap and cherished as such, for who could blame a man so impeded for failures of his own? Listening with a new ear, she noted his shift in tone. 'You haven't written for weeks,' he complained in a voice as warmly relaxed as though he had been scratching himself or feeling for a pulled muscle. 'I don't even know what money is in our joint bank account and you're hopeless with Maurizio, more like a child than a mother, Carlita. At least, I've managed to calm him down for the moment, but you seem to have neglected him woefully.'

This was *too* unfair. She couldn't – wouldn't stand for it.

'Maurizio,' she commanded, 'go to your room.'

'But Mamma ... I want to ask Babbo whether ...'

'Go, Maurizio, now.'

He went. The resolution in her voice must have impressed him. This encouraged her and she said: 'I think we should consider a separation, Marco. A legal one.'

'Carla, don't play games with me. This is a long-distance call.'

'Let's consider the idea,' she said and a thrill of pleasure shot up her spine. It was an astounding sensation, novel, heady. I hate you, she thought. It may be temporary, the reverse of love's coin? How know? But I hate your living guts. Maybe it's myself I hate? One flesh? 'Let's ring off now,' she told the telephone,

129

'and don't ring back, Marco, until you've given this some thought.'

The phone gulped. Its squalid, plastic mouth produced sounds of supplication. 'Carla, listen, are you there, Carla?'

'I'm hanging up,' she told the repellent instrument. 'Let's take a few days to think. Good-bye, Marco.'

When she put down the phone she felt manic. Happiness, she was prepared to believe, was an illusion, socially disruptive and not for her. But she was enjoying her rage. She felt it gush up in her: sudden, black, rich, alien and forceful, like oil released from some subterranean well. Rage, she thought, *rabbia*, and yielded to it the way children did. This made her feel primitive and passionate, the sort of person people think twice about offending.

'Divorce!' she whispered the word with a thrill of self-esteem, for it had always frightened her and she could scarcely credit her nerve. 'I'd divorce him for two pins!'

When Maurizio had gone to bed, Leo joined Carla for a drink and she couldn't help telling him what she'd done.

'I think I'm mad,' she said, thrilled by her own boldness.

He misunderstood. 'You'll easily make it up,' he comforted. 'Married people must be constantly taking back ultimatums.'

Did he think her cowardly?

'Don't you love him?' he asked.

'I think I loved a memory: a titivated one.'

'But he's only been gone a few months.'

'People change even when you're with them. It can happen without your noticing. You think you love the man you're living with but your love really was for someone lost and gone. That makes a nonsense of fidelity, doesn't it?'

'Loneliness,' Leo guessed, 'may have upset you both. You mistake it for resentment. You say you haven't been answering his letters?'

'Are you scolding me?'

'Mayn't I? A compatible marriage strikes me as a marvellous, enviable thing. I imagine you're so attuned that in normal times

130

you don't even need to talk. An outsider might even think you dull together. I *envy* that dullness, that understanding.'

'It wasn't showing tonight.'

'Ring him back,' he advised. 'Now.'

'Oh, no, now I'm angry.' After a minute, she admitted: 'It may be less Marco I'm angry with than marriage. The institution's been modified – like your own institution perhaps? The Church? Once anything's been changed in a system like that, the whole deal is up for grabs. Trust becomes unreal. You can mimic it – and that's what *I've* been doing.' The truth of this shocked her. It was as if she'd lifted a heavy shutter. There was no end to what daylight might reveal.

It was only a little after nine. Leo, however, swallowed his drink, refused a refill and said he must be off. He had things to do, he explained vaguely, but it seemed to Carla that he rushed out of the house. She was disappointed. Needing to talk, she had hoped to consult him about her future and ask what would be the wise move now for a woman in her position. Perhaps he didn't like counselling in his free time? She felt at a loss as she wouldn't have done if she had had a chance to think up new options for herself and try them on, like dresses, in the mirror of his concern. As it was, she was brought face to face with her undressed and unnerved self at the very hour when the Glen reverted to wilderness, coyotes screamed and the only phone calls were from heavy breathers.

Marco rang back the next day.

'Carla? Marco here. Listen.'

She didn't listen.

'Does this mean anything to you?' he asked at last.

'Of course. It always has.' This was probably true, but she hadn't heard.

'Well then?'

'What?'

'Darling . . .'

'I don't want to talk to you, Marco. I'm thinking things through.'

'Oh in that case . . .' Implicit laughter. She supposed he felt she

131

was delaying for her dignity's sake. 'I'll write you a letter,' she heard.

'Yes. Do that. Don't worry about Maurizio,' she added. 'Everything is under control.'

'Of course, Carla. I trust you.' If he'd trusted her, he'd have been yelling and cursing her. Because he was worried, he was treating her with care. Ah well. Now, when it was perhaps too late to matter, she was learning how she could have handled him.

'I need time,' she told him. 'I'm confused. You caused it all . . . You . . .'

'All right,' he said. 'All right.'

Later she began to worry about him, remembering his nervous stomach and the doubts which sometimes assailed him in the night. But she told herself that these were excuses, side issues conjured up to save herself from facing a more central one of which she was afraid.

She went to the beach and waded ankle-deep in foam. Ahead and further out, Carlomagno bored through breakers at an undulant gait. He had recently grown assured, even aggressive, approaching other males with a swagger and even starting fights. Now he was after his favoured prey: the gulls and pelicans which flew along the shoreline, sometimes dipping to fish or perhaps inspect this boisterous, barking creature which kept challenging them from below. Did he want to catch them? Once, when a sick or careless gull let itself be taken, the dog's bewilderment had been comic. The game had for so long been a matter of race and splash, bark and fly, and how could this limp mouthful contend? Carla screamed at him to drop it and had the sensation that it was with relief that he obeyed her.

'Let's hope you really have a soft retriever's mouth!' she told him, plucking at the loose skin on his neck. 'Else what was the use of sparing it? You could have fed like a hunter.' But there must have been generations of domesticated dogs between Carlomagno and any ancestor wild enough to prefer feathery gull-meat to a tin of dog food.

Chapter Six

Maurizio had seen films about pushers and what they did to people who ratted on them. The fact that Cazz had done nothing yet was no comfort because at any moment he might get into trouble with the cops *and then* he'd blame Maurizio. The strain of worrying about this was affecting Maurizio's sleep. His father had got so upset on the telephone that Maurizio had let himself be persuaded into thinking that his fears were childish. His father needed to think that Maurizio thought this and for a while Maurizio had actually managed to think he did think it and had even felt happy while the belief lasted. It had faded now and so had the happiness, and everything looked blacker than before. Cazz probably *was* a villain out to get his hands on Evie. His being a crony of Maurizio's father no longer made this hard to credit since it was clear that Maurizio's father didn't see what didn't please him and no more did Evie. She *liked* Cazz. Maurizio supposed that the explanation for that was sex-appeal, which was a mystery and something nobody could understand apart from the people who felt it. Maurizio sometimes had the feeling that he was playing a game of Blind Man's Buff where everybody but himself had bandages on their eyes.

He had thought up a plan in three parts – joke? Serious? He

133

hadn't decided. Three parts then: one, spread rumour that Evie has been seen hitch-hiking. Two, persuade her to hide until everyone thinks she's disappeared. Her father would then come back here to help look for her and this would scare Cazz away. Her parents, if Maurizio knew anything, would not worry about her for too long. They'd leave soon and Maurizio could proceed to stage three of his plan: Evie could show herself to Maurizio's mother – to his father too if he was back – and the business of their adopting her could be seriously raised. Maurizio expected difficulties but if even half the plan worked – the bit getting rid of Cazz – it would be worth while. He had worked it out in the sleepless nights since his spat with Cazz and knew that there were elements in it of childishness and dream and prayer. Still, the more he saw of adults, the more unpredictable they seemed to him to be and he felt that he would be giving them a chance to do something worth while and laying a trap for their better natures.

So far he had not presented the plan to Evie as anything more serious than her holocaust game. On those terms she played along. Reality, Maurizio had noticed, scared or bored her, but on anything fanciful she would work like a mad creature. Now she had agreed to help collect the things they'd need when and if the time came to fix up a hideout for her. For now these were in the cellar of her house: a messy glory-hole into which nobody ever went. Maurizio had brought tins of food from his mother's larder, and from unused rooms in Evie's place they'd brought bedding and an old oil lamp. Wanda was such a hopeless housekeeper that she'd never notice the loss, and the stuff did double duty when they played the holocaust game.

Leo missed three appointments to teach Maurizio and told Carla on the telephone that he had a touch of flu. When he came again he seemed depressed and said, when asked about this, that he was missing the parish and beginning to wonder if giving up pastoral work hadn't been a mistake. At least *there* he had been connected to people ... His voice trailed off as though he had indeed lost the knack of making contact. The flu had shrivelled him. His eye was dull. He droned on about difficulties he'd had with his pastor, a dry stick and upholder of dead structures – yet, he worried, wasn't blaming authority for one's own spiritual failures all too easy? He argued as though demolishing some imaginary opponent. His knee jigged. He moved like a man whose skin has ceased to fit.

Carla sat sipping brandy and following the warmth of its passage round her palate and down her throat. She was not following his monologue and was by now used to the jets of excitement crackling through it. He was using her, she guessed, as a sounding board. Love as a doctrine, said Leo – and it *was* the doctrine of Christ – was dangerous and terrifying. He faced her with eyes deep in the hollows of their sockets and fierce with obscure, singeing emotions.

Carla stabbed with her toe at the softly heaving stomach of her sleeping dog. Was Leo talking to or at her? Dog and man seemed equally remote and she had an impulse to rouse them both for a drive to the beach – an impractical plan since she couldn't leave Maurizio alone in bed, and the beach was dangerous anyway, being frequented by junkies at this hour and patrolled by police helicopters with searchlights. She would like to run along it though, watching waves cut and chop the dark sand and feeling the wet suck of it on the soles of her feet. Impatiently, she gave a little kick to the sleeping Carlomagno who half groaned, half opened an eye and went back to sleep. He had lost all wildness and fear.

How, asked Leo, could Christian love be kept abstract? Yet to particularize it was to enter a quagmire of questions which conservative churchmen had never had to face.

Carla had no opinion to offer. 'Listen,' she proposed, 'I'm going to cook something finicky but good. Like to help?' She led him into the kitchen and set him to powdering almonds by hand. 'They're better done that way,' she explained, 'more aromatic.' The sense of control she got when cooking bolstered her sense of herself, and Leo was better company and easier to deal with when busy. After the almonds, she got him to peel the thin outside skin off an orange, then slice it into julienne strips for glazing. It would decorate the cake which he might meanwhile watch her make.

'I've always liked learning new things,' he told her, 'games, languages, theology. I like knowing how things work.'

135

When the cake was in the oven, he went back to his abstractions. 'Santa Juana de la Cruz,' he told her, 'wrote of the Narcissism of God who created human beings in his own image, then loved himself in them.'

'Like Sybil loving him in you,' she remembered. 'Have you seen her at all?'

'Why do you keep bringing her up?' he quarrelled. 'Do you enjoy making me feel like a heel?'

'Sorry.'

'No, *I'm* sorry.' He put a hand on her arm then, to her amazement, laid his head on her shoulder. 'I've fallen in love with you,' he told the hollow of her neck. 'It's got out of control. I can't help myself.' His nose was hot on her skin like an ailing dog's.

'Oh God,' she thought. '*Mamma mia!*' She should have foreseen this. The signs – in retrospect – were pathetically obvious, yet she had persisted in misreading them, taking what was after all a familiar language for an alien code. His head was heavy and wooden and it was clear that he couldn't think what to do with it next. Neither could she. Emotion was no guide. She felt none. Nothing. Her feelings – absent? paralytic? – were clearly unprepared to be summoned like this. They needed prior warning, a limbering-up period in some locker room of the unconscious. Inappropriate amusement mingled with her shock as she stood, numb as a piece of furniture, waiting in her vacuum of feeling until guilt, which runs to fill vacuums, made her feel inhospitable and that it would be polite to say something.

Leo had meanwhile collected himself, removed his head from her shoulder and put some distance between them. 'Do you want me to leave?' he asked.

'I thought you were *safe*,' she said, 'a force for stability.'

'I thought *you* were. It was only when I knew you weren't getting on with your husband that my feelings began to act up.'

Her own feelings were still off duty.

'I shouldn't have come,' said Leo. 'Shall I leave?'

'Well not just like that. Probably we should talk, don't you think?'

'I don't know. I'm inexperienced. This goes against twenty years of conditioning.'

'Perhaps we should have another drink?' Carla had begun to

136

shake and shiver uncontrollably. 'I'm shaking,' she informed him. 'I don't understand it. Do you suppose it's shock? Even my teeth are chattering.'

'I'd like to think it was something more promising.'

'Lust? Lechery? I don't recognize it as that.' The biblical terms were suddenly the only ones available, as though ordinary ones – what *were* they? – had been confiscated by some censor in her brain. 'My brain,' she said, feeling full of interest in her symptoms, 'feels perfectly calm. But just *look* at the rest of me.' This sounded self-absorbed, so she asked politely, as one invalid to another, 'how about you?'

'Well, *I*'m not taken by surprise. I began to feel this the night you had the row with Marco on the telephone.'

She didn't like him calling Marco 'Marco'. 'You were full of holy advice,' she recalled, 'about the marvels of a fifteen-year marriage. I thought you a bit priggish.'

'I'm glad I managed that.'

'A last tribute to virtue?'

'Oh, it may not be the last. But I don't see love as wicked – unless you do?'

'I don't know what I see.'

'You said once – in connection with Sybil – that you had gone off sex.'

'Yes.'

'Are you still off it?'

'In the abstract?'

'No.'

'I don't *know*, Leo. If you want the truth I'm shocked – in shock and shocked too.'

'Can I ask why you went off it? I don't want to pry – I mean I do want to, but not if you won't let me. That probably sums up my position generally.'

Carla laughed. 'We sound ridiculous. I'll tell you about the sex. It's because of Marco. He – oh dear, do I want you to know this? He wants me to sleep with other men. He keeps writing letters suggesting it.'

'And that puts you off the idea?'

'Yes.'

137

'I understand that.' There was a pause. 'May I come and sit beside you?'

'Oh Leo, you're gauche.'

'I know I am.'

'And I'm not helping? Look, we'd better give up for this evening. Let me find out what I feel. Give me some days.'

'*Days*?' He looked disappointed, hopeful and, she couldn't help feeling, unmanly. His fine eyes – they *were* fine, she noted, surveying him as assessingly as she had done with dogs in the pound – were, like the pound dog's eyes, too humble. A learned expression? Almost certainly. Obedience, he had told her once, was the prime virtue taught in seminaries. With it would go that submissive air thought in anticlerical jokes – she had been brought up on them – to signal hypocrisy in priests.

'Don't *beg*, Leo,' she bullied, then apologized.

'It repels you, does it, my manner?'

'A bit.'

'Can you tell me why?' This was said without rancour. He simply wanted to know – was an apprentice, diligently learning a new thing.

'I feel – it makes me feel, that there's something sleazy about this scene. It recalls Tartuffe, Malvolio, stories of priests covering furtive urges with oily, holy manners.'

He turned his back on her.

'I've offended you?' she asked.

'Yes.'

'Well, take it as a test. If you can't stand being offended, you're not ready for ordinary relationships.'

Her harshness was also a test of herself. When would she begin to know what she felt?

He guessed this. 'You *are* shaking!' he marvelled. It was now very obvious.

'Once,' she remembered, 'the dentist gave me a pain-killer containing a very small amount of adrenalin and I was like this. Apparently I react abnormally.'

'And I affect you like a dentist?'

Their laughter embarrassed them. They stopped.

'Why don't we try to make love?' he asked shyly.

This put her off. One should, she felt, be swept off one's feet.

'Do you think of me as a sin?' she procrastinated.

'Of course not.' He was angry.

'I think,' she decided, 'that I think of *you* as one: not a religious one, but we all have our codes. I've never slept with any man but Marco. He's a bit ... overbearing. When I'm with him it's he who decides things. I'm thrown by being expected to take responsibility. I know this is absurd.'

'It isn't.'

'Well, it's nice of you to see that. Perhaps you're *too* nice? Let's have a moratorium: time to think about things – like that time with Sybil. By the way,' it struck her, 'why with me and not with her?'

'I'll leave you to work that out for yourself. You're fishing for compliments.'

'Well, if you knew your interest you'd throw me some. Remember I'm married to a macho male.'

'That's why I prefer not to use his weapons.'

A tremor of irritation rose in her – loyalty to Marco? She liked a man with a bit of bluster, a gambler, a man with dash. Besides, at her age, you *needed* compliments. 'Good night,' she said, testing him.

'Do I have to go?'

'Yes.'

He left.

In bed, the shaking persisted and pleased her since it was clearly not for Marco. Muscles twitched. An unreadable part of herself seemed to have taken over and communication between mind and limbs appeared severed. She didn't know what she wanted or what her body's involuntary language meant. How could she? She had never paid attention to it. It was a new-found land, threatened, like California, by seismic disturbance.

8 a.m. A child packaged in emblazoned worsted – *cogito ergo sum* the label claimed – was on the look-out for Carla. She was wanted in the Lycée parking lot. Who by? The child didn't know.

'By a teacher?' Carla prompted. 'Think.'

Shrug. Sun snipped at the gold thread of *cogit* ... blinded out the rest. No thought. No child. It was gone with a flip of black-

139

soled sneakers. Time for gym, hymn or some such start to the school day. Mothers briefly parked, let out their children, then drove away into a radiant, child-free morning. Carla turned off her motor.

'Have you been getting into trouble?' she asked Maurizio.

He opened the door. 'I'll be late.' He jumped out.

Carla drove into the parking lot. It was empty except for Cazz who, half astraddle, half supine on his motorbike, was eating an apple and staring at the sky.

'Cazz?' She rolled down her window. 'Was it you wanted to see me?'

'Hi Carla, like an apple?'

'No.'

He slid his bike alongside her car. Sun blazed on the bike's chrome and paled his hair to a frosty transparence. He looked like a deteriorated angel.

'Stop being nervous, Carla, you're making fists.'

'What do you want? Couldn't you have called at the house?'

'Quit worrying, Carla. I just want to talk to you about Evie and Maurizio. Did you know those two play pretty sick games together? Hey, stop stiffening, I don't mean what you think.'

'What do I think?'

'Sex-play and stuff. Think I'd care?'

'No,' she supposed. 'But then what is it?' She resigned herself to hearing some of the wisdom Cazz picked up in his therapy groups. He disbelieved it, derided it, yet, like a man giving away something which doesn't suit but for which good money has been paid, would sometimes apply it earnestly to his neighbours.

'He beats her up,' said Cazz.

'What rubbish!'

'She likes it. Listen, I *know*. They're acting out all sorts of repressions. My guess is that it's a coping mechanism for Evie. She's seen her father beat up her mother and I figure she feels that if she can take it her mother can too. I'd lay money on her to survive better than Maurizio. Everything's out in the open in that family. There are no cupboards to put skeletons in. Everything hangs out so people are forced to deal with it.' Cazz spoke fluently. His face was impassive.

'You're trying to upset me.'

140

'Yes, but it's for your own good.' He had the Honest-Joe look of an actor making a pitch for Mutual Savings. 'What's *wrong* with Maurizio?' he asked in the voice of a concerned educator. Carla had no sense of there being a continuous person here at all.

'I should have thought,' she said, 'that Evie could take care of herself. She's older, isn't she?'

Cazz shook his head and his halo of sunlit hair. 'Carla, Carla!' He was sober now as though selling plots for Forest Lawn Cemetery. 'You don't see what's staring you in the face, do you?' Sigh. 'Listen, Maurizio's angry. He's getting rid of anger when he fights Evie – and do you know the source of his anger? I'll bet you do even if you won't admit it. Keeping up a front is important to you, isn't it? That's why you sweep things under the carpet. Listen, more harm has come to the world through keeping up fronts and repression than from anarchy and letting rip. You don't believe me, do you? But your way problems fester' – Cazz pronounced 'problems' – 'until one day *Boom!* the whole thing explodes. Now Maurizio knows everything isn't fine and dandy at the old homestead ...'

'Cazz, I have to be somewhere in ten minutes and this seems very fanciful to me.' She turned the key in her ignition.

Cazz reached across her and turned it off. He put a hand on her wrist.

'Carla, don't be nervous. I already know.'

'Know what?'

'You're playing around with a priest. That's nothing to me but I can't help knowing what I know. We're neighbours, after all, and ...'

Had she heard him right? Invented the words? Did they come from inside her own head? What a devil he was! She didn't want him talking and spreading his horrid vision over something which – mightn't ever happen at all. She pulled her hand angrily from his grip.

'I've got to go,' she said, but didn't.

Cazz's voice filled the shell of the car '... face up to where you're at,' it scolded. 'Guilt is corrosive and there's nothing so terrible about ...' It hissed insidiously in her ear. 'Listen,' it said and she did listen, mesmerized in spite of herself, as rabbits are

141

said to be by snakes. 'This guy, this priest,' said Cazz, 'will have his own load of guilt. Don't add to it, Carla!' Unctuous in his moment of power, Cazz lectured her. His mouth was surprisingly expressive. It had a median line which could quiver like a tadpole then firm up in a straight erasing stroke. 'Guilt is manipulative,' he preached. 'All those organizations I've tried out make use of it. That's their strategy. That's what I've learned. But if you're honest they can't get you, Carla. Make no promises, keep up no front and then you're free. Go when you need to, just split and carry no load of bitterness . . .' The mouth danced and wormed. Its corners twirled like the tail of a minuscule fish. 'But you . . .' he said and she saw that the fish was herself, hooked by his interest in her. Self-obsessed suddenly, she wanted attention paid to her and advice even from someone like Cazz. 'Manipulative systems devour the soul,' he told her, 'and what's more the process perpetuates itself. I'll bet your own mother was repressive and now you're repeating the pattern with Maurizio, cranking up the pressure on him so as to make up for your own caperings. You'll turn that boy into a nervous wreck.'

'What business is this of yours, Cazz?'

'I'll tell you what business. His mind is running on drugs. Did you even know that? He's a great little law-and-order man. Wants to tidy up the world. Just like his Mom. He too is trying to compensate for shortcomings he may sense or know about, Carla, and the danger – which is why this *is* my business – is that he may shoot his mouth off about some activities of mine. He's threatened to turn me in to the cops, did you know that? Now, you'll appreciate that, great as my sympathy is for Maurizio, a guy's got to look out first for his own ass and there could be circumstances in which I mightn't be able to act like a gentleman. My advice to you *therefore*, Carla, is to get the pressure off the kid, to control him and look out for all our interests, right? Why make trouble? I'm sure none of us wants any?' Disclaimingly, Cazz's hands fluttered then landed on his handlebars. He slid the bike away from the car, drove round in a little circle, then paused and began to sing: 'For everything there is a season and a time for everything under the sun. A time to love, eh, Carla? A time to step out on your old man?' He laughed. 'Hey, I didn't think you had it in you. Scout's honour. But I like that. I like surprises. Well, see you round!' He flipped his fingers, revved the bike and was gone in a flaming glitter of sun and wheels. A trail of exhaust stretched behind his rear wheel like a tail and a smell of burned petrol lingered after he'd left.

It was Sunday. Terry Steele's guest for the first hour of his programme was a Father Feeny and his topic was the Virgin Mary who, though people tended not to realize this, had been virginal not only before and after but *in the very act* of giving birth to Jesus Christ, true God and true man.

'Why do you think, Father,' asked Terry Steele, 'that people have trouble accepting this vital doctrine?'

'I'm afraid,' said his guest, 'their reasons are consistent with their own desires. You see the Virgin Mary serves as a role-model for Christians in the virginal life.'

'I believe there's a lot of back-sliding these days?'

'Well, Terry, people of modernist tendency often have conflicted needs. They want to sin without feeling guilt, so they discredit the dogma. I am told that in our seminaries it is one of those most frequently denied.'

'Do you think, Father, that the media are to blame for our tepid faith?'

'They may be in part, Terry. Another reason is the emphasis on science. There are scientific truths and truths not amenable to scientific proof.'

'And passion, Father? Would you say that that was a root cause?'

'I'd say it was certainly a contributing factor.'

'Well there you have it,' cried Terry. 'Sex, apathy, pride. One thing leads to another. Where will it end? Phone in and give us your thinking on this. We'll be back after doing a bit of business.' Without missing a beat, his voice brightened and launched into sincere-sounding praise for a variety of consumer products.

The phone rang and Carla turned off the radio. It was Leo. 'Well?' he asked.

'I don't know.'

143

'What's the trouble?'

'Oh, your status, your God. I don't know that I want to take on such a package deal.'

'I'm just me.'

'I don't like the responsibility,' she scolded. 'It makes me feel like a seducer. Like a male, like Marco. Sorry,' she added. 'I'm being horrible. I can't help it. It's my hypocrisy. I'm more of a hypocrite than you are – you aren't one at all.'

'May I come round?'

'We might fight.'

'I'll risk that.'

In that case, she said, he should have dinner.

In her bath, preparing for the evening, she considered the veins in her thighs. They were like the texturing in an autumn crocus and the same colour. How ugly were they? And what about cellulite, bruises, faint marks and maps of living which had accumulated as on a ledger? Oh dear. She tried to assess a body which she had thought of for years as a support for clothes, something needing to be kept in sufficient trim to be got into a size six and, when well masked in a privately acquired tan, a bathing-dress. She had not since her wedding night considered exposing it to a new and intimate scrutiny. Was she now? She shrugged the doubt away, massaged cream into elbows and feet, checked places-which-might-sag for sag and spoke to her own, mildly neglected body as she might have to the yellow dog.

'Poor thing,' she commiserated, 'you poor, neglected thing.'

The house was now charged with potential or remembered turbulence. The telephones particularly – there were four.

Outside her window, a squirrel began frenziedly to scratch and bite at its belly, head, armpits, back and tail. Some appalling infestation must be tormenting the creature, for its round of its own surfaces was as vigorous as that of a man on drums.

At dinner Leo and Maurizio talked about sport. Carla listened with pleasure to words being bandied with the same ritual skill as the ball must have been in the games they were discussing. They fielded each other's comments, laughed, echoed and got nowhere any more than a piece of music might or a dance. This sort of chat was a male art which she was happy to see Maurizio get a chance to practise at their own dinner table. *Her* exclusion was part of the ritual. So were their half-hearted efforts to explain things to her.

'*Crunch!*' cried Maurizio. 'Jabbar really creamed those guys with that last slam-dunk!'

'And remember that turn-around jumper he made one minute into overtime?'

'Boing! Right in the hoop.'

'He gets more rebounds than most guys in the NBA and in Saturday's game he made fourteen baskets.'

'Boing! Boing!'

'Talk English,' Leo recommended. 'Your mother will think we're a pair of half-wits.' Later he began to tease Maurizio about his liking for his mother's cooking. 'It's too healthy,' said Leo. 'Too good. How are you going to compete with guys fed on junk food? They're jumpy and nervous and full of every kind of disease-producing substance. They're developing immunities; they're hyper-active; their bodies are battlegrounds. They'll leave you in the dust.'

'I'd better start drinking Dr Peppers and cokes.'

'And eating at McDonald's.'

'Getting a balanced diet.'

'Yeah.'

'Right.'

'Jabbar probably eats junk food.'

'You bet he does.'

'Popcorn.'

'TV dinners.'

The words were hollow and bouncy; the dialogue was circular. It meant nothing. It was a form of sport. 'Boing!' said Maurizio from time to time as though scoring a goal or drumming out a beat. He was relaxed, happy and Carla's last, tenuous anxieties about what Cazz had told her dissipated. Cazz, animated by malice and private follies of his own, had been peddling fantasy.

Leo, it struck her, had skipped the courtship phase and become a domestic fixture: fatherly, teasing, jaunty. It was his talent. Maybe he was mistaken in thinking he wanted anything else? She said so to him after Maurizio had withdrawn; lightly, imagining that she was hitting the same jokey note as the two

145

males had been playing all through dinner. Apparently, she missed it or else it wasn't licensed for female use. Leo was hurt. Did he have to sleep with some hooker, he asked crudely, and lose his virginity before she would take him seriously?

'You make me feel like a monster,' he accused, 'or a freak. Religion is not some substance smeared all over me which has to be scraped off. You seem to take a weird, folk view of it.' He asked if he seemed unmanned to her and she said no but that they couldn't go to bed here and now, even if they'd wanted to, because of Maurizio.

'Well, can't we just talk pleasantly? Like before?'

'I don't think it can be pleasant now,' she said. 'I think we *are* trying to scrape away the layers of thought that reflect old commitments. At least I find myself doing that with you. You don't seem to mind my having Marco's ways and tastes about me.'

'Why should I? They're part of you. I like them. I'd probably like him.'

He tried to sit beside her and put an arm around her but she kept worrying lest Maurizio came back downstairs. The house was open-plan and a balcony ran around the upper floor overlooking the room they were in. It was like being a teenager in one's parents' house. Only now *she* was the parent hiding from her teenage son.

'What about your apartment? Is it safe?'

'It's bare and Spartan and rather scruffy,' he said, 'because you refused to help me decorate it. But it is safe.'

'When can I come?'

'Any time.'

Carla kept tuning into the Terry Steele Show and wondered why she did. Did its faintly nutty ingredients reassure her? Steele's mock-English voice, rich with the rhythms of the King James Bible, implicitly laid claim to a wisdom which his words never delivered, and the bluff discredited the principles championed on his show. They had been hers. Was she pleased to see them falter?

'Today,' said the voice and throatily suggested a last gargle of port or perhaps communion wine, 'I'm guesting with Dr Sunmaker who's right here in the studio with me, live, and we want all of you out there in the Southland to phone in if you have any questions on parenting: our topic for the hour. We're going to talk to you of Discipline's Divine Design and we'll start with spanking and how parents today are so unsure of their role that they are afraid to spank or, if they do try, just give the child a few swats with the hand. This is counter-productive. You must spank with confidence and the correct instrument. The Bible says "spare the rod and spoil the child". Now a rod is a psychologically neutral instrument and therefore correct and by rod,' said Terry Steele in his elocution-class English, 'we mean stick, cane, birch, whip or even the homely ruler. There is also an appropriate place to spank and that is the butt. Dr Sunmaker has gone into details in her book *Do You Dare to Spank?* published by the Christian Homes Press. Be thinking of your question on this relevant but rarely treated topic, while we take a commercial break. We'll be right back.'

Sponsors for the hour were a direct-import diamond business, a photomat store and a car manufacturer eager to vent annoyance with 'our friends across the Pacific' whose too popular vehicles were so undersized that any American of normal stature would have to assume a foetal posture to fit inside one.

Carla felt her personality dissolve. Once she decided for or against an affair with Leo, a new one might emerge. Meanwhile she was dislocated and adrift.

When not driving Maurizio somewhere or supervising his homework, she let herself slip into a trance. Daily, she chased her blond dog up the beach, letting his dementia camouflage hers until her throat was raked sore by salt air and she could run no more. Then she let herself fall on her back and lie that way until the wet nudge of Carlomagno's snout informed her that he had worn himself out chasing seabirds and wanted to head for home and his drinking bowl. The throb of his thirst paralleled her own.

Her life had been structured by rules as easily tested as a recipe for sauce. Now what? What did happen to a family when the mother gave these up? Surely it must collapse like an umbrella with a broken spine? Like a belly released from a corset or a stern old society robbed too suddenly of hierarchy and belief?

She confided in Jane about Leo and about asking Marco for a divorce.

Jane was dubious. Surely the two things should be kept separate?

'You're not thinking of *marrying* Leo, are you?'

'No, no – I don't think so. It hasn't come up.'

'Well hang on to Marco then. What's sauce for the goose is sauce for the gander. *He's* stepped out on *you* often enough,' said Jane, upsetting Carla, who hadn't known that this was common knowledge. 'Priests are sure to be bundles of problems,' guessed Jane. 'And what could Leo do if he left the Church? What would he live on?'

It was the cold voice of the street-smart but left Carla with the wilful notion that if life with Leo was to hold hardship, then choosing it could be morally condoned.

Jane herself was in better fettle than she'd been for a long time. She'd had a visit from Cazz, had got a small part in a film on parapsychology and her house was being rebuilt with the help of an interest-free loan from the city.

A woman rang the Terry Steele Show in tears. Her problem was not relevant to the chosen topic but her need seemed so urgent that it was decided to stretch a point and talk to her. She had no self-worth, she told Dr Sunmaker and Terry Steele, no confidence. 'Sometimes,' she said, 'I think of ending it all.'

'You're playing victim,' said Dr Sunmaker severely.

'I'm not playing at all,' said the woman. 'It's how I feel.'

'What's your first name?' asked Dr Sunmaker. 'How old are you?'

'Wanda. I'm thirty-nine.'

'Well, Wanda, when I say you're playing victim, I mean you're emphasizing what's wrong. Think of what's good in your life. Focus on the positive. You must have something to be grateful for. Do you own your own home?'

'No,' said Wanda.

'Have you your health? A job? A loving family?'

Wanda burst out sobbing worse than before. She had none of these things.

'Well, how do you live, Wanda? Tell us something about yourself.'

'I was living with a man and he's gone. I think he's gone. We had a falling out and he left and took his stuff and hasn't been back for three days.'

'How long were you living with him?'

'Two months.'

'Well it was hardly a life investment you'd made there, Wanda. What were you doing before you met this man?'

'I was with my husband but *he's* back in Kansas.' Wanda's sobbing was now so bad that she couldn't speak. 'I'm sorry,' she said. 'I'm sorry I rang.'

'Don't be sorry, Wanda. Sorrow is counter-productive...' Dr Sunmaker began but Wanda had rung off.

'We lost that one,' said Terry Steele.

'Buy Firestone tyres,' said a confident, friendly voice. 'All our outlets are freeway-close.'

'It's that new girl on the phones,' said Terry Steele's voice through the commercial. 'She's been pressing wrong buttons and letting losers get on the air, people you can't deal with. It's bad for the show. Better say something positive when we come on after the break.'

'We *are* on,' said Dr Sunmaker.

'Hurry to your nearest neighbourhood dealer,' said the ad, 'this offer ends Sunday.'

Wanda had made or pretended to make another suicide attempt. Or threatened to make one. Maurizio couldn't get it clear. Evie and her Aunt Joanie had been up all night walking her and trying to make her vomit in case she might have taken an overdose of pills.

'I was out,' Evie explained. 'Then when I got home there was my aunt half *carrying* my Mom back and forth across the room. We fed her black coffee and took turns making her walk. That's what the suicide hot line told us to do but it turns out she hadn't taken anything at all. No pills anyway. Just gin. Well, the laugh's on us! The two of us were so wore out, I can't tell you,

149

bushed. My Mom's no feather-weight – and then to find all she'd taken was gin!'

'So how come Joanie ...'

'Oh my Mom had been threatening and ringing the hot lines. See, she'd done it before and so when my aunt found her passed out in the bath and the water overflowing, well,' Evie shrugged, 'she figured she musta done it. The real bad thing – seeing as my Mom's OK – is that my aunty phoned my Pop. She got to worrying last night, so she phoned him and now he's coming to take us back to stay with him. He's in some real crummy place that's nothing but a work camp, but he says we'll have to go because my Mom's unfit to look after me.'

Maurizio talked urgently to his mother about the need to adopt Evie. *Her* mother, he pointed out, was unfit. Her father too. Hadn't he dumped them here and wasn't he now threatening to take them back whether they liked or not?

'It's like taking a *dog* to the *pound*!' he said, shocked. 'You'd rescue a dog – you rescued Carlomagno. Why don't you even *think* about rescuing Evie?'

But his mother said that they might be going back to Italy and that Evie's parents would probably be furious at the idea.

'They don't own her!' Maurizio started to tell how Wanda fed Evie dog food out of a can. But this just started his mother wondering whether she was making a terrible mistake in letting him spend time with such people. He had to backtrack like crazy.

'Mamma, what would happen if she ran off? Like that girl who ran off to live with Cazz?'

'She was put in a reform school, Maurizio. Don't you remember? She had to stay there until she agreed to live with people of whom her parents and the police approved.'

'You *see*!' he drove home the point, 'her parents let her go in the end. What Evie should do first is run away.'

'Maurizio!' His mother was worried now. 'Evie's parents are very different people. Her father may be violent. From what I've heard he drinks. He might injure the girl if he caught her – if she had run away. That happens. Haven't you heard of "battered children"? Children injured or even killed by their parents? It's

150

a well-known problem.' His mother sighed. This was the sort of information she hated giving out.

Willowy as fish, a group of roller-skaters spun past: a traffic hazard. Enclosed in their own rhythms, they wore headsets over their ears like ear-muffs.

Maurizio and Carla were taking the dog to a park officially off-limits to dogs. Owners, poised for a quick getaway, had to keep an eye out for policemen and train their pets to come smartly to heel. Carla hoped this mix of enforced obedience and disobedience wouldn't confuse Maurizio whose severity with the dog surprised her.

'*Sit!*' he yelled and shoved Carlomagno's haunches to the ground. '*Stay!*' He smacked him on the nose.

This, he insisted, was for the dog's own good. Undisciplined, Carlomagno might fall into the clutches first of the dog-catcher and then of vivisectors. This Strewel Peter view of things came from Leo who had a German streak. Maurizio took to it with an eagerness she would not have foreseen.

Why, she had heard him ask Leo one evening, had Leo become a priest? She, busy in the next room, let them get on with their man-to-man session.

Leo's answer pivoted on the Vietnam War. He had entered the seminary at a time when men his age were being forced, in large numbers, to fight against their convictions. 'The *radical* solution,' he told Maurizio, 'seemed to be joining the one institution which tries for the only real victory open to humanity: the coming of God's Kingdom.'

Squeamishly, Carla turned on her egg-beater. There were hypocrisies latent here and pious talk embarrassed her. No. That was unfair. Leo was talking about the past: simply and accurately telling Maurizio why he had done what he had done *then*. Small accuracies were often all one could hope for, half truths – another word for lies? What did Leo believe *now*?

When the eggs had achieved the required fluffiness, Carla turned off the machine and heard Leo distinguishing, harmless ly, between rules like keeping dogs out of parks and ones like loving your neighbour.

151

'*There's* a principle,' he told Maurizio, 'that's forgotten in wartime and doesn't prosper much in peace either.'

Maurizio, though a bit baffled, was clearly stimulated at being talked to as an adult. So what about the Kingdom of God? he asked. When was it coming?

The Kingdom, said Leo, was an ideal to keep in your sights. Without it, brutality took over. Avarice. Indifference. Not just in Indo-China. Right here. Leo, as a small boy in Oregon, had seen these at work in the families of rural boys with whom he went to school. His Sicilian grandfather's stories of *his* child-hood painted a darker picture still, and the grandfather himself bore scars. Though warm-hearted and funny, the old man was driven by a savage temper. The Church, Leo had felt, was the only force for gentleness around.

Had felt? Felt?

'Oh,' Carla was impelled to interrupt, 'but you're talking of *peasants*, people who haven't evolved a humane, secular code – and never will while the Church keeps them dreaming of a life-to-come.'

From the look the other two gave her she knew her voice had been too agitated. Did she want or not want Leo believing what he'd said? She certainly didn't want Maurizio believing it – but must beware of coming on too strong against religion with him. *That* could provoke a reaction. In her mind's eye the Church bulged like the blood-gorged tick used to symbolize it in turn-of-the-century cartoons. These had sprawled and billowed across the yellowing pages of *L'Assiette au Beurre*, an anarchist paper which her Roman grandfather had kept stacked in a glass book-case not a stone's throw from the Vatican. Obsolete images? To be sure. Besides, her present feeling was too fresh and murky to spring from memory alone. Perhaps she was seeing the Church, Leo's old commitment, as a rival? Piety, though, had always embarrassed her. In her family, it had been tolerated only in grandmothers and spinster aunts. She remembered recoiling as a child when one of these slipped in a 'God bless you' with her goodnight kiss. Reproachful contraband, the words had an ooze to them. They suppurated and were not properly contained. Had the aunts' hairy chins, moles and old women's smells per-haps been caused by this insidious contagion?

152

Leo, answering what she'd said about peasants, told her: 'Working in urban parishes here in Los Angeles, I've seen brutality which would turn your blood to pudding.'

They dropped the subject.

Some days later, like an ill-digested meal, it returned sourly to the fore.

Leo, in moral disarray, reported to Carla that Maurizio had asked his help to get his parents to adopt Evie, a victim of brutality, who would be at risk once more when her father got back.

'Talk to my mother,' Maurizio had urged. 'She'll listen to *you.*' Surely Leo, after what he'd *said* about loving one's neighbours could not refuse to help? 'She's a neighbour, isn't she?'

'He had a point,' said Leo who felt nailed by it. 'I could hardly tell him that as my aim is to break up his family by taking away his mother, it doesn't suit me for her to accept responsibilities which would tie her down even more. You see,' he told Carla sadly, 'there you have the argument for celibacy in a nutshell. As long as I suppressed my own needs, I could be trusted. Now I'm a would-be predator, a worm in the fruit . . .'

Worming and slithering, he took her back through the talk he'd had with Maurizio, reviewing his performance with disgust.

'The kid saw through me. He had that disappointed look. By the end he wasn't listening. Words were beside the point. We both knew it. Mine were pure casuistry.' Leo mourned his innocence and sank into gloom.

'The point,' Carla spoke with the scant sympathy of one long inured to craft and compromise, 'the point, Leo, is that the question was a non-starter. Marco would *never* adopt that girl. There's no need to torment yourself.'

But Leo did. Shadowed creatures both, they chewed through their apple of self-knowledge.

'If it's Evie you're worried about, the practical fact is that none of us can help her.'

'There'll be other Evies and I'll be no good to them either. I've grown selfish.'

'Ah, now you're worrying about *yourself*: really selfish.'

'Oh, pride is the celibate's sin,' he admitted. 'It has to be. "Look how self-sufficient I am", you've got to think – in human terms.'

153

'And are you?'

'You know I'm not.'

'Well, you'd better get over hating yourself for *that* or you'll have nothing – neither of us will.' She had not decided whether she could bring herself to have the affair with him. He was refraining from pushing her. She was grateful for this, yet felt pressured since it meant that she owed him equal courtesy and concern. These were cold words and whenever she tried to bring herself to decide one way or the other a numbness seemed to paralyse her.

'I hate thinking,' said Leo, 'that I've lost Maurizio's trust.'

'You probably haven't. You may just have been demoted to the ranks of ordinary adulthood! Take him to see another basket-ball game. Cupboard love *is* love, after all. Affections are grounded in the senses, aren't they?'

'That's what *I* keep telling *you*.'

She laughed, blushed, shivered, laughed again and felt the numbness creep icily through her brain. Was it desire? Fear? What?

*

Dear Babbo,

I miss you a lot, especially now because I have a serious problem which Mamma can't understand. She thinks I am just a child, but in many ways, especially lately, I have been getting mature. What it is is that I have a friend who is a girl – not a girl friend, a friend who is a girl. I told you about her. Her name is Evie and she lives next door with her aunt who is a moron and her mother who is in love with Cazz. He has split now and Evie's mother tried to commit suicide and passed out in the bath. Evie was pretty burned up. Then the dumb aunt called Evie's Pop who is a man-slaughterer (he killed a man by splitting his skull in a fight only he got off) and beats Evie black and blue. He said he will take Evie off to his work camp because Wanda is unfit, but he is more unfit. I want us to rescue Evie and adopt her. Mamma says it is not up to her. Who is it up to? Babbo, this is serious. A girl may be going to get killed by this man-slaughterer and baby-batterer (= fathers who kill their children). I know you are not uptight like Mamma. I am not criticizing her. I love her, only she thinks I am only a boy and I see her not taking me seriously. It wouldn't cost much to adopt Evie. She goes to public school. I think it is too late for her to start in the Lycée because she knows no French. I will share things with her if we adopt her. Please think about this, Babbo. Please. I have never been so serious about something and it is getting so serious that I cannot sleep. Please answer or come as fast as you can.

> *Lots of love,*
> *Maurizio*

*

Leo wanted to contribute to the meals Carla cooked – bring ingredients or perhaps buy wine? He didn't think they should eat together in a restaurant – scandal – but would like to buy some food if Carla would tell him what to get.

'I can't go on letting you feed me all the time,' he said.

It struck her that there was a delicate moral problem here – for why should Marco contribute food-money towards his own cuckolding or to Leo's attempts to bring this about? Why, on the other hand, should the Church?

'Is your money your own or the parish's?' she asked, deciding, as she spoke, that the Church could stand a little bleeding in return for all the bleeding *it* had done over a long innings. *Écrasez l'infame*, the Voltairian slogan, was perhaps a touch extreme, though it had been endorsed by Carla's father and grandfather. Letting Leo pay something towards his dinner wasn't exactly *crushing* the infamous outfit, though, was it? 'I ask,' she felt it fair to explain, 'because, whereas I don't want to beggar you who may be on short commons, I wouldn't mind getting something from *it*.'

'Are you anticlerical then?'

'One of my best friends is a priest.'

'I don't like your attitude.'

'Well, but now you know it for what it is.'

Leo started bringing food from time to time.

'So when's your Pop coming?' Maurizio asked.

'He won't break a leg getting here. He'll come when he's good and ready.'

'Evie, why don't you hide while he's here? In our basement?'

155

Evie's Pop seemed worse to Maurizio now than Cazz: violent, murderous. He'd have dirt in the lines of his hands and black-heads like nails on his nose. Maurizio had seen guys like that on the city buses. Nobody travelled on these except kids, pensioners and the freaky poor. You had to have something really wrong with you not to drive a car in LA, where owning an old clun-ker made all the difference, so what you saw on the buses were often junkies and winos: bodies that looked as if a bunch of Disney figures had got broken and stuck back together in the wrong way. He imagined Evie's father as a cross between Grumpy the Dwarf and Long John Silver.

'Evie,' he implored, '*think* about it!'

'Don't be a ding-a-ling, Maurizio! They'd find me right off.'

Maurizio had heard from some Lycée friends – Catholics – of a rock mass to be held in the open air with guitars. Leo was to be the celebrant.

'Hey, why didn't you tell me? I'd like to come.'

'Come,' said Leo. 'If your mother agrees.'

They were having dinner.

'Why do you want to go?' Carla asked. The notion affected her unpleasantly. '*You*,' she turned to Leo, 'are going to say a *rock mass*?'

'Why not?' Tranquilly, he coiled a skein of spaghetti round his fork and neatly ate it.

How could he be planning to make love to her and say a rock mass too? But, come to think of it, he must be saying mass every day – and what grounds had *she* for complaint?

'I'm interested in religions,' Maurizio was answering her. 'And I'll enjoy the music.'

'What do you mean you're *interested*?'

'Well, I ought to know about them, I think. They have some answers. I have some questions.' He laughed. 'They may match up. Some of them.'

Oh God, she thought, he makes it sound like a game: balls and hoops.

'What kind of questions?' Nauseated, she felt unable to directly confront Leo, a wolf in shepherd's clothing, who seemed unscrupulously ready to try and hook her son.

156

'Why not a rock mass?' Leo gave the word 'rock' a light emphasis as though that were the source of her surprise. 'Your mother,' he told Maurizio, 'imagines us still back in the days of Latin and ladies in lace mantillas. Listen, Carla, why don't you come too? It will interest you to see the changes if nothing else...'

What else? To see him false-changing his congregation? Dispensing sub-standard spiritual goods? The proposal outraged her. She didn't want the religious dimension entering her relations with Leo, either as kink or scruple, didn't want any discussion of his old and – it now transpired – still active affiliations. If he came to her, let him come as an ordinary man, not trailing ecclesiastical panoply. Why did he want to draw Maurizio into a fold he himself was leaving? *Was* he leaving? On what basis could he stay?

She couldn't bear to raise these questions, but, because of Maurizio, she might have to.

Leo was still perorating about change and the excitement of cracking the dead shell of old doctrine to find relevance and human truth fresh inside. He seemed to be talking to Maurizio about rock masses and to her about love. Why did she think that? He talked of accretions of dead ritual and the resurrection of the body. Smiling at her over his wineglass. Open-necked collar. Winning voice. She had to suppress an urge to tell him to shut up or even to throw something at him: violent, conjugal impulses which revealed that she was connected to him now.

Two pairs of bright, solicitous eyes considered her across the dishes: erratic female. They were making allowances. Leo and Maurizio. Oh dear! Oh God – no, *not* God!

Later, she saw that what had upset her was not Leo's continued allegiance to religion but his shiftiness. He would have explanations. She had heard several; but no amount of talk about reinterpretation and renewal could dissipate a feeling that he was living by marked-down values: an unlikeable trait in a lover.

Chapter Seven

Cazz had come back and had lunch with Wanda. Now they were having a fight.

'Go back to Lady Jane then, why don't you?' Wanda was screaming. 'She's got dough. She can keep you. I can't.'

'No,' said Cazz, 'you're not your lover's keeper at all, are you?'

The two were cleaning up after a barbecue meal which Cazz had cooked to celebrate his return. First they ate the remnants. Then they stacked the plates. Nothing got thrown away.

'Go then!' Wanda threw a plate at Cazz. 'For all I care!' The plate hit him on the shoulder.

'I probably will,' Cazz told her, 'as a matter of fact.'

Minutes later, his Honda zoomed down the Glen.

Maurizio peeked at Evie to see how she was taking this but her face showed nothing and he didn't dare ask.

Fifteen minutes or so later, Wanda cooee'd across the fence. She was wearing a Hawaiian beach dress.

'Hey, you two,' she yodelled. 'Wanna get off your asses and come to the beach? Get your things, why dontcha? We'll go to the Santa Monica Pier and see the action. I'll stand you a coupla cokes and tacos.'

158

'She's stoned,' Evie whispered. 'Better not let her go alone. She'll be picking up men,' she added furiously.

The sea was toothed. Rollers like reaping machines came grinding up the beach. Further out, surfers in wetsuits rode their boards along cresting breakers, slicing blade against breaking blade, then coming to ground in what looked like a smash of splinters.

Maurizio rested his chin on the sand and wished his stomach would settle. Cazz had poured him a beer earlier and now it was struggling inside him with the greasy taco Evie's Mom had bought at a beach café. He hadn't wanted it but she had been too busy flirting with the counter-hand to hear his refusal. She was in a tavern now, a place as dark as a gopher hole.

He should go back. His mother would come home and worry about him.

Evie sat, lumpish as driftwood. 'You go. I'm staying.'

Duties divided Maurizio. The sand shone like salt. Evie was certainly not great company, but he hung on until a breeze started up, turning one side of him cold.

'Maybe,' he said, 'we could stick our heads in the tavern door. Your Mom might come out.'

They rose, trudged across the board walk to the Shamrock Tavern and opened the door. All they could see in the blackness was the lit panel of the jukebox. A barman stood, dark against a gleam of bottles.

'Those your kids?'

'Oh boy!' Wanda's voice. 'I guess they think I'm living it up in this den of vice.' She giggled in a silly way.

'They can't stay here,' the barman told her.

'Hey,' Wanda wheedled, 'wanna wait for me a minute outside? Just a weentsy minute, OK?'

'My mother's waiting for *me*,' Maurizio told her.

'Honey, I won't be a minute.'

The two backed out and sat on a bench outside. They were opposite Muscle Beach, a roped-off bit of ground where stuntmen and stuntwomen worked out. A weedy-looking woman with thighs like stirred yoghurt held two, then three men above her head. Maurizio thought she might be fifty, though it was hard to tell. Maybe she'd got so beat-up-looking from straining so hard?

'If you had to choose between being beautiful and very strong,' he asked Evie, 'which would you pick?'

'Strong.' Zestlessly.

'Want to go for a walk?'

'Nah.'

They sat on, hunched, cold, staring at bits of orange rind, paper cups and bottle tops. Feet passed. Black feet had dirty-pink soles, white ones a layer of grey callous. A glitter of damp had dried on the concrete, leaving flounces of tide marks and trickly lines leading to a central darker blob.

'What do you see in that shape?'

'I see a spider,' Evie said, 'devouring a pale-coloured thing. A dark spider eating a moth.'

He wanted to enfold Evie, poor moth, in the great strong arms he didn't have. A forecast Maurizio, ghost of his future self at, say, age eighteen, waited often in the corner of his brain or eye, jumping the gun and getting in the present Maurizio's way. Desperation empowered him to grab her hand which she let him have. They sat there then, waiting for her Mom who did come in the end.

'Oh brother!' She chuckled, rocking on her heels, then made for the parking lot. She must have got something going with someone in the tavern or was perhaps too drunk to know the difference. They followed her to the car and, since Evie was now sulking with her mother, left her alone in the front seat. Wanda had trouble backing out and began weaving the minute she got on Ocean Drive.

'Mom! Look out!'

'Boy, these gears!' Wanda struggled. The car skidded and Maurizio found himself on its floor where he did what he'd probably been needing to do all afternoon: he vomited. The car had stopped dead. Evie was quickly out and pulling at her mother who was slumped over the steering-wheel.

'Mom!' she was crying, 'Mom!'

It came to him that she should have sounded angry and didn't, so maybe Wanda was hurt. He climbed out and around the front but by the time he got there Wanda had come to.

160

'Sss OK ...' she groaned. 'Be OK in a minute. Just wait a weentsy minute, kids ...' She closed her eyes.

He was shocked by the relief on Evie's face, seeing, as he hadn't until now, that Evie loved this ridiculous mother. His throat pained him at the hopelessness of everything and he flopped leadenly on the front seat, keeping away from Evie because he must smell of vomit.

A highway patrol car turned up. Sent for? Arrived by chance? Maurizio couldn't tell but saw, now that blame was about to fall, that Wanda had driven across a pavement and into a post. A one-car accident. She had no excuse.

When Carla got home, the scene in her yard was like a Douanier Rousseau viewed through a red filter. A leonine Carlomagno, moustache and fur washed sunset pink, jumped in a jungle of poinsettias. These grew close to the fence and, in his efforts to get over it, he had broken several. His tail bludgeoned stalks, making the red petals flap with the pep of a May Day parade.

'Carlomagno! Who fenced you in? Is nobody home?'

Nobody was.

'Poor dog!' she comforted, 'have you been alone long?'

To judge by his excitement, he must have been.

She went next door and rang the bell. Wanda's sister answered.

'There's nobody here. I just got home from work. I don't know where they are.'

Carla went home, fed her dog, then telephoned Jane.

'Darling, they went off in the car with the slut! I supposed you knew,' said Jane, 'or I'd have stopped them. I heard her yell that she was going to the Santa Monica Pier and the Venice board walk.' Cazz, she could not forbear telling Carla, had rung her again.

Carla drove straight for the coast and a conflagration of red sunset which suggested wrath and penalties. In her rearview mirror, snow-covered mountains figured a lost past. Love contaminated: love of every sort. Once, years ago, in Florence, a married cousin had begged her to store her lover's letters and Carla had hidden them on a high shelf behind jars of preserved fruit, reaching them down when her cousin came for a re-

reading. Loath to pollute her own house, the cousin always wrote her replies on Carla's sewing table. Her lover lived in a town an hour's drive from the city and for several years she met him on regular, clandestine afternoons between four and seven. That was the old way of conducting an adultery. The new one was to arrange one's loves serially. Carla, opting so far for neither, felt awash in treachery: *frode*, categorized by her co-citizen, Dante, as the most noxious sin. Her mind was a dance of doubt and surely, at such a moment, with psychic defences weak, Fate might be tempted to strike?

Carlomagno, riding shakily in the back seat, skidded on mock leather and leaned his snout into her neck.

'Down!' she barked at this and all infractions of discipline.

They reached the old wooden pier at Santa Monica which was lined with fading and disheartened booths containing slot machines and cafés smelling of cheap frying-oil. At the very end, a fish shop glittered icily.

Carla cruised up one side and down the other looking for the children or a sign of Wanda's car, then drove on to Venice, parked and walked along the board walk.

'Gotta dime?'

A Leonardo grotesque grinned from under a panhandler's hat. The hybrid light – neon infused through powderings of moon and dusk – lent a starfish delicacy to the gingerbread, gave façades a zany lurch and endorsed the Disney Gothic. A shop was open: candle-makers. A young man was demonstrating his craft. A row of wicks dipped into molten wax, rose, dipped again, rose. Further on, old men sat on a municipal bench playing chess under the street lights and further still a row of old people spoke softly in Yiddish. Kosher shops sold groceries. She looked in. No Maurizio. Across the board walk was a dance hall. A helicopter passed, its searchlight raking the beach. The police. 6.45. Was it late enough to ring them? The children had surely been gone long enough to justify alarm. She turned the dog round and made for home.

Neither police nor coastguards knew anything. She rang Leo, who was at once all helpful zeal.

'May I come?'

'Oh please.'

He was in her kitchen within the half hour, dancing around, rummaging in the refrigerator, making her a sandwich.

'And wine. Wine's good for you. Calm you down.' Not mocking nor scolding nor seeking attention for himself, he made her feel cossetted and safe. How, she wondered in disloyal amazement, had she lived for fifteen years with a bully?

On the table was a small gift he had brought: a box of Perugina chocolate kisses wrapped in silver foil. He made more phone calls. Nothing.

'Nothing's *good*,' he insisted. 'If there'd been an accident the cops would know.'

But Carla thought of the scrub-covered cliffs along the freeways, interstices in the neon-lit metropolis, down which a car could slip and be lost as effectively as in a desert or jungle. This ill-finished city was full of menace.

'You're fathering me,' she realized; then, with a swing of mood: 'I haven't been mothering too well lately.' She had meant him to feel reproached but was glad when he didn't, even though his making free with phone and fridge in what, after all, was Marco's house, upset her. She felt cowed by her landlord's furniture. In the dining-room, chairs, erect as choir stalls, gleamed darkly at her and found her wanting. Order, she tried to explain to Leo, was insured by the closeness of fit between the inner and outer woman. People must be seen to be what they were. Else how could families be safe?

'You're a bundle of superstition,' he said and tried to put his arms around her. 'People without religion are often like that.'

She slid away from him and they might have had a row but for the fact that, as he told her, he could see she was not herself and moreover – 'I'm getting to know you!' – trying to provoke him into behaving like Marco who had bullied her into a state of helplessness. 'But you're not helpless. You're a bright, shrewd woman.' He told her to pull herself together. 'I thought you'd have had more guts!'

He meant that, she saw, seeing herself suddenly with his eyes as carrying on like some histrionic creature from the Italian south.

'Sorry,' she said briskly. 'You're right. All over now.'

The phone rang. Leo took the call. 'Yes,' he said. 'We'll be

163

right over.' He put the receiver down. 'It's OK,' he told her, 'farce not tragedy. Wanda took them for a drive, got a bit drunk and ran the car into a lamp-post. Nobody hurt. Relax. Nobody.'

'Where are they?'

'At the Santa Monica Police Station. They've been there since four.'

The Police Station was not exciting. Maurizio and Evie were separated from Wanda and left to sit on a bench where nobody took any notice of them except once when they were given coffee in paper cups. For a while Maurizio entertained himself by staring at a picture frame which held samples of drugs: leaves whole and crushed, powders, coloured pills. As Evie wouldn't talk, he studied these and learned off the printed information so as to impress people in school with his knowledge. Getting bored with this, he began to feel tired and, lying down on the bench, fell asleep. It was only when he woke up that he thought of asking whether anyone had phoned his mother. As soon as he did, it became hard to see why he hadn't earlier. She'd be flipping out with worry. She must have got home between three and four and now it was eight o'clock. He felt really bad. He must have been drunk, or anyway a little drunk, earlier on the beach, and once he was in the hands of the police he'd felt things were up to them. Anyway, when he told them that he wasn't Wanda's son but the son of someone quite different who'd be half out of her mind with worry, the guy on duty agreed to phone her at once.

A minute later the same guy stuck his head round the door and said: 'We got your Mom on the phone. She's coming to get you both. *Your* Mom,' he told Evie, 'will have to spend the night. She can't raise bail.'

It seemed they'd got through to Evie's aunt, Joanie, too, but Joanie had no dough. Then Maurizio's mother turned up with Leo and seemed terribly relieved to have him back and neither drowned, drugged nor mugged as she'd been imagining.

'Your aunt will be home right after us,' Maurizio's mother told Evie. 'She's with your mother seeing what she can do for her. They won't let your mother out tonight though. It seems she's had a previous conviction. But she'll be all right. She'll appear in court in the morning and then she'll be home. Why don't you have dinner with us? Your aunt too when she gets home.'

Evie said 'OK' and 'thanks'. She was terribly down. Maurizio could see.

'What if I'm in your place and my Pop or someone telephones?' she asked suddenly. 'Or the police?'

They talked that over for a while, then Leo had a neat idea. Why not take the phone from Evie's house – it had a long extension cord – and pass it out the window, across the fence and into the Verdis' yard?

'Brilliant!' said Maurizio. 'We'll leave our side door open so that Evie can run out if it rings.'

When they reached the Glen, Maurizio's mother said that if she didn't get started on the dinner none of them would eat before midnight. She went into her kitchen and the other three went next door to get the phone. The business of moving it took Evie's mind off Wanda and she and Leo were laughing over some joke, while she helped him uncoil the cord, when Maurizio, who'd been watching them, got a cold feeling in the back of his neck. He turned and got a humdinger of a shock. You might have thought he'd have been shock-proof after all the things which had been happening – but this one topped them. Three feet behind him stood Evie's Pop. Maurizio knew that that was who it was because – Jeez, maybe because it was the worst thing that *could* happen. He was smaller than Maurizio had expected but just as mean. He was one of those knotty, nut-faced guys with black wrinkles cut deep into their cheeks like knife scars and he was paying Maurizio no attention at all but looking past him at Leo with a look Maurizio knew from the movies.

'Who are you?' Evie's Pop asked Leo in an insulting voice: sort of raspy like a blunt saw.

Evie gave a little scream. 'Pop!' She kind of vomited out the word. 'Pop, Mom's at the police station.'

'You be quiet, Evie,' her Pop told her. 'Who are you?' he asked Leo again. 'What are you doing in this house? As if I needed to ask?'

Leo stood up. He'd been crouched down, unravelling the telephone cord. He couldn't have thought the guy was friendly,

165

but he had no way of knowing just how unfriendly he was. Maurizio could have filled him in on some of Pop's past record but there wasn't time.

Suddenly the little guy started swinging. He hit Leo in the face.

'So you're the one she took up with!' His voice was surprisingly high as though the blunt saw had hit metal. 'While a man's off earning his honest living ... sneaking into a decent house ... decent ...' He kept dancing round, taking shadow punches. But some hit home. Leo's nose was bleeding. Maurizio hoped it was only his nose.

'They warned me,' the maniac shouted. 'I got information. A letter,' he screamed and Maurizio's stomach folded inside him. His letter! Oh, no! Now what had he done?

'Mister! Mister!' he heard his own shriek. 'You're wrong. This isn't him.'

He might have been invisible. The maniac drew a knife. This was a lot more frightening. Leo had somehow managed to get in a sideways blow and draw blood. He was holding a chair.

'Hit a man in his own house!' yelled Pop, but as though he was glad and had been wanting the provocation. Blood dripped past his eye and he had a kind of grin on his mouth. Bent at the hips and knees, he held the knife and didn't move. But his stillness was like a snake's. You knew something bad was coming.

Maurizio ran to the window. 'Mamma,' he screamed. She was on the terrace. She must have heard the noise.

'What is it?' she called. 'Maurizio? Are you all right?'

He yelled in Italian. 'Call the cops, Mamma. Evie's Pop is here. He has a knife. He's attacking Leo. He's insane. *Chiama i carabinieri.*' He turned back to the room where Leo had dropped the chair and was keeping the dining-room table between himself and Pop.

'I don't know what's on your mind,' he was saying while dodging round this. 'This is the first time I've been in this house,' he told Pop. 'I'm a friend of the lady next door. As a matter of fact,' he added, 'I'm a Catholic priest.'

'That's right,' Evie and Maurizio shouted together.

Evie caught her father's elbow from behind but he jerked it into her stomach and sent her reeling.

166

It was then that Joanie walked into the room. Maurizio had always thought her dumb and maybe she was ordinarily, but what she did now wasn't dumb at all. She picked up a vase of rancid water and threw it at Evie's Pop. It stopped him for a moment and while he was stopped – that house was such a mess that the water must have smelled of old skunks – she yelled: 'That's not the man, Walt, he's this lady's friend,' pulling Maurizio's mother into the room after her. 'Tell him, tell him,' she kept saying. 'He thinks this is Cazz. Tell him he's *your* friend!'

Maurizio's mother was slower catching on. She didn't say a thing, though they were all waiting and staring at her. She just kept looking at Maurizio and opening and closing her mouth. 'Are you all right?' she called, 'Maurizio?'

'Sure,' Maurizio told her. 'Sure – it's not *me* he's after.'

'*Tell* him,' Joanie kept screaming at his mother, but his mother didn't seem to hear.

'I've rung the police,' she said instead. 'They're on their way.'

'This is my house,' shouted Evie's Pop, and rolled his eye in its bloody socket. 'I pay the rent.'

'You've got a record, Walt,' Joanie yelled. 'It'll look bad. You'd better scoot.'

'*He* broke in.' But the maniac was weakening. The hand holding the knife had gone limp.

'*I* let him in.' Evie dodged for cover as she said this. 'With a key.'

'It'll look bad, Walt,' Joanie warned. 'It's the wrong man. Don't provoke him,' she begged Leo. 'He killed a man once.'

'Self-defence,' shouted the maniac, 'and I'm in my own ...'

'Who drew a knife?' Joanie turned to Maurizio's mother. '*Tell* him,' she said angrily. 'He doesn't believe me. You tell him.'

They were yelling at him from different corners of the room and Pop's attention must have faltered because before he knew it Leo had kicked the knife out of his hand and under a sideboard. Maurizio thought that was really something.

'Brilliant!' he yelled. But apparently Leo wasn't all that good on the follow-through for the other guy recovered fast and began aiming blows at him again. Leo dodged back round the table and Pop kept coming after him and the thing might have

167

gone on like that all night with pauses and arguments and Pop making sudden sneaky rushes if the good old police siren hadn't finally come wailing up the street. The noise rammed home the message Joanie had been trying to get across.

The fight stopped completely then and when the cops came in Joanie started up some story of a misunderstanding. There had been no knife, she said, and Maurizio's mother agreed that there hadn't. The children, she said, had got things wrong. Well, officer, they *were* only kids. Yes, she, believing them, had mentioned a knife to the police on the phone. But there hadn't been one, no. And nobody wanted to press charges. It was all a mistake. She was sorry she had bothered them.

The cops seemed sore at this and Maurizio too felt sore at being made to look a turkey, but could see that it was in nobody's interest for Evie to end up with both parents in the slammer. Leo probably couldn't afford trouble either. One cop said something about phony calls and their time being valuable but Maurizio's mother asked if it wasn't better to be sure than sorry and what about their slogan being 'to protect and to serve'? She said that Mr Briggs – Pop – had mistaken Leo for a burglar and been understandably overwrought because of an accident his wife had had earlier in the day.

Maurizio didn't know whether to be shocked or impressed by the smooth way she lied. The others all followed her lead. Evie's Pop kept nodding his head and saying 'Yeah officer, like the lady says. That's right.' The police frightened him – you could see.

Just when everything looked ready to settle down, there was a hitch. Leo had come out without his ID. He'd been in a hurry, he explained, and the wallet with his cards was in the pocket of a jacket presently hanging in his closet at home. If the officers wouldn't mind dropping by his lodgings? Well, Father, said the cop in a voice that might or might not have been doubtful, as a special concession, they'd do just that. They'd also like to phone his pastor – or ex-pastor, whatever, OK, Father? There was a slightly snotty tone to their politeness and Maurizio got the feeling that they weren't too sure that Leo mightn't be trying to fake them out. Leo said they could ring anyone they liked.

Maurizio's mother walked out to the verandah as the cops were leaving and began arguing. He could tell that she was getting on their nerves. Going by a citizen's residence to get his ID, Maurizio heard one of them telling her, was a *concession*, Ma'am, a courtesy, and no part of their duty. Did she realize that they could run Father Hausermann into the station right now for having driven without it? He had driven here, hadn't he? Well ... They left and Maurizio turned his attention to Evie who didn't want to come to dinner any more.

'I can hardly bring my Pop along,' she protested sullenly.

Maurizio, unsure how to handle this, was wishing his mother would come back in when a weird thing happened. The redneck father began to cry.

Below in the roadway, the revolving red light of the patrol car might have been announcing a circus or a murder movie and Carla, who had been hoping the worst was now over, began to fear it might not be.

'I'm sorry,' she told Leo and gripped his hand.

'Listen,' he said, 'this is it. I'm going to tell my superiors.'

'What? Tell them what?'

'I was thinking of it anyway. This is a precipitant, a sign.' There was liable to be trouble, anyway, he explained, when the police told, as they well might, of his fight with a man who had taken him for his wife's lover. 'I'll tell them I want out.'

'No, no!' Beseechingly, she squeezed his bruised hand. He snatched it away.

'Yes. I'll phone you,' he said and ran down the slope to where the police were ready to leave.

Inside the house, Evie's father sat smearing his mouth across a sleeve. Red wetness gauzed his face as though it were one enormous, bloodshot eyeball. He swivelled it towards Carla. Behind her, the dog butted against the screen door. Bumping inwards, its nails tore at wire netting.

'*Stay!*' she commanded, glad of the buffering moment. 'Here,' she offered Briggs a handful of Kleenex from her purse. He slapped one on his face and it grew transparent. 'Thanks,' he said, surprising her by his formality. Maurizio and Evie looked

169

worried, lurking, it seemed to her, in a corner. Joanie too. Furniture seemed, suddenly, to be primarily there for defence.

Briggs was in the middle of a monologue which she had been hearing but ignoring from outside the door. 'Folks get one impression,' he droned, 'but there's another side to the story ...' He wiped red threads from his chin. 'Always is, right?' He paused, then went on laboriously, ' "Dumb drunk," they say, "always gettin' into fights. Wife couldn't stand it so she took her kid and left." That's how she tells it, I know.' Wet oozed as though his face were a piece of defrosting meat. Leo must have inflicted almost as much punishment as he'd got. How much had he got? Carla tried to reconstruct the fight in her head.

'Are you OK, Maurizio?' she hoped.

'Sure.'

'Course he's OK. I didn't touch *him*!' Evie's Pop's eyes squinted indignantly. Accusingly, they nuzzled at her, gleaming with a demand for respect – yes that was the word she'd been hearing from the verandah. 'I don't get no respect. That priest said I was an animal. An *animal* because I won't have my wife sleeping with every little punk ...' Tears blotted out the mad light in the small button eyes. He must have been drinking, she realized. '*He's* OK, aren't you sonny?'

'Sure.' Maurizio nodded in a squirm of embarrassment.

'Why don't I go home and cook us all some spaghetti?' suggested Carla. 'I can bring some over to you,' she told Joanie. 'I'm sure you're too tired to start a meal.'

'A good woman,' intoned Mr Briggs. 'Not like my wife. Listen, Ma'am,' he said, bidding urgently for Carla's attention, 'that female's been a layabout since the day I took up with her. Can't keep the young punks out of her pants. So what am I supposed to do? Smile? Say "Help yourself, punk, it's going free"? Huh? I can see *you're* a good woman, Ma'am, and a good woman is what makes a good man, am I right?' he heckled. 'Am I? Willya give me an answer, heh?'

Carla soothed. 'Yes,' she said.

'Listen to that, you,' he barked at Evie. 'Takes after her Mom.' He nodded. 'Planning to go the very same way if she hasn't started already. Won't live in the camp with me. *Her* education was the excuse for their bein' here and an excuse is

170

what it was. I got a letter tipping me off. Telling me my wife was
having it off with some guy.' He stared quickly at each of their
faces. 'That sure undercuts a man's self-respect.' He stood up,
moving to head off Carla who had been inching towards the
door. 'OK so I got the wrong guy,' he pleaded with her, 'but
things looked bad. I mean here was I, the old work horse, bustin'
my guts trying to get on top of a drinking problem brought on
by – well the old story, right? Then I got a letter. I'd just like to
show you because it backs me up.' Pop patted the pockets of his
work-shirt. 'Here,' he drew it out triumphantly. 'Knew I had it
some place. You read it, Ma'am. Go on. Read it.'

Carla saw a crumpled piece of her own handmade Pineider
writing-paper – a present from Paola – unobtainable outside
Italy. She recoiled. 'I don't want to read it.'

The refusal annoyed him. 'I'm asking you to.'

'I've got to go.'

'You think I'm some sort of bum,' he said angrily. 'That's
what *they* told you, I'll bet.' He jerked his jaw towards the corner
where Joanie and Evie stood. 'That's it, huh? You've been listening to talk about me and made up your mind!' He focused his
little eyes shrewdly on Carla who felt a shiver of discomfort. The
man's intensity was odd: compounded of indignation but of
quite different elements too. At the back of it, wasn't there
something like a streak of amusement? Glee? As though the
unfortunate relished his role and the limelit moment rare in a
drab life. He had been elected, if only in mockery, like those
carnival kings who enjoy attention during small-town *feste* in
Italy, and are allowed to say their say and drink their fill while
the sport lasts. Powerless and without importance themselves –
who but a down-and-out would take the job? – their burlesque
gives them a taste of the authority it derides.

Waving the hard-wearing Pineider paper – it had a high cloth
content – under Carla's nose, Pop milked his disgraceful
predicament. 'A man's got a right to a hearing,' he insisted. He
had been defending the sanctity of the home, hadn't he? He had.
He had thought in good faith that he had. Here was the
evidence.

She backed away, recognizing, in Maurizio's handwriting, a
writ as much to herself as to Wanda. Leo, lusting in his heart,

had got what was coming to him. Pop, King Cuckold for the day, had hammered one cuckoo in the name of all.

Maurizio avoided her eye. He too had been defending the sanctity of the home, writing letters – how many? Blindly, unknowingly – she was sure he couldn't have guessed anything about her and Leo – he had joined a conspiracy of males: his father, Evie's father, even Leo, even Cazz, who were nudging her into a situation where she was going to have to choose and commit herself before she was ready.

'I've got to go.' Grasping Maurizio's hand, she made for the door. But was going to have to push aside Pop, the hearth's defender, who was barring it and tendering his piece of grey writing-paper. Maurizio's hand felt clammy in hers. He'd know she'd recognized his handwriting and her paper.

The letter, danced, fluttered. Carla pushed it aside.

'I'll be back,' she prevaricated, 'with food.'

Briggs's face leaned into hers. Now what did he want? The face was sweating; its wetness reflected electric light, glowed like a Christ's in passion. He whispered seductively: 'What's his name, Ma'am?' Wheedling. 'Tell me. Who's the guy has been screwing Wanda? I don't want to make no more mistakes. Like I say, it's in the letter but I don't want to put too much trust in that. Not without I get confirmation. If I would've known tonight ...' He paused, fixing her with his stare. 'You must know,' he accused.

'I mind my own business,' she told him.

He was almost toppling over her and she could smell his breath. 'You can't approve of her doing a thing like that! Why're you holding out on me? A Christian woman like you? Bet you're a Christian? Sure you are! So, tell me his name. Who it is. To prevent more mistakes.' He leered. 'C'mon, Ma'am, spit it out.'

Carla felt Maurizio's hand jump in her own. She tightened her grip on it. Quiet, she squeezed.

'Mr Briggs,' she looked Pop straight in his red-rimmed, blazing eye, 'your wife is a decent woman and you should be ashamed to talk of her the way you do. What kind of support or loyalty are you giving her? And if you're giving none, why ask anything back from her? You talk of "respect" and I'd have thought you'd have enough of that to trust your wife over a

172

letter written by someone who hasn't the nerve to sign it? Do you know what sort of people live around here, Mr Briggs? I'll tell you. They're people who like breaking up decent families. It amuses them. They've seen too many movies.'

The red, revolving police-car light gleamed insultingly inside her own head: a circus, night-club or red-light-district light. How dare they come throwing implications over her quiet garden?

'They're children, Mr Briggs!' She squeezed hard on Maurizio's hand. 'Children can't make so they destroy. That's the sort of people who live here. How can you trust them, *you*, a hard-working man, who must know that we can only trust the people near us and hold onto what we know because it's more than *we* can do to rearrange the world? Even if there *were* any truth in that letter, you should remember that you left your wife alone in this place and that anything that may have happened is as much your fault as hers.'

Briggs looked at her with bewilderment. She had been shouting. He rubbed his nose. 'Well, maybe this isn't a good place,' he conceded. 'You may be right about that.'

'I am,' she assured him. 'Take your wife away, Mr Briggs, and take Evie away ...' Maurizio's hand was like a trapped small animal in hers. 'Take them away!' She tightened her grip on the hand. 'As soon as you can.'

Mr Briggs looked doubtful. 'Irregardless of that,' he began, 'I still want to know ...'

'What for?' she interrogated. 'What for, Mr Briggs? To make trouble. Leave fighting to the movies and look after your wife and daughter.'

Maurizio interrupted. 'Mamma, listen, our phone's ringing. Over in our house!' He pulled his hand from his mother's. Delivered, he shouted, 'I'll run and answer it.'

'All right,' she shouted after him. 'I'll be over in a minute. The door's on the latch.' She turned to Briggs, hauling at Carlomagno's collar as he made to follow Maurizio. 'Who do you think writes letters like that?' she asked. 'People who have *your* interests in mind? No way! Troublemakers. Spoilt children of one sort or another. This place is full of them. If something isn't

173

perfect they throw it out. They have no compassion. They don't mend or cure. Wanda needs you, Mr Briggs.'

'Well, I came, didn't I?' She had him on the defensive now. 'Drove all night and most of today, then ...'

'You got to drinking!'

'A few beers. I don't have no air-conditioning and those highways are hot. 'Ssslike driving across – I don't know – a griddle, a hot saucepan. The steering wheel gets red hot and light jumps off the road. You might be *in* the motor, you're so hot and the one thing in your mind is ...'

'Some punk's lie about your wife. That's what *they* wanted, don't you see? To drive you frantic. And you let them, Mr Briggs. You danced to their tune.'

He was fingering the letter, turning it over, questioning it with his touch.

'You a friend of Wanda's?'

'Sure I am. And of yours too.'

'Well, I ...'

'Mamma ...' Maurizio was shouting from their side porch. 'It's a cable.'

'I have to go.' She seized her chance finally, pushing her way past the now hesitant Briggs. 'Remember what I said.'

Maurizio was putting back the receiver as she came into the room. 'I copied it down,' he told her. 'It was from Babbo. A cable. From Western Union. "Arriving Monday at sixteen hours stop love to both Marco." Monday. That's tomorrow,' whooped Maurizio then, in mid-laugh, burst into tears. 'Oh Mamma,' he hugged her feverishly. 'I'm so glad Babbo is coming back. Aren't you?'

Morning. 8 a.m. Carla stared out the window, down the Glen and into space. Leo had rung after midnight to say he had written a letter to his bishop and spoken to his pastor.

'What did he say?'

'To wait. To cool it. I can probably have a leave of absence. The kid-gloved approach.' He laughed excitedly. 'They're becoming very patient these days,' he commented. 'Very expert.' He had been asked if he was thinking of leaving the ministry

174

because he wasn't cut out for it or because of a woman. A standard question.

'So how did you answer?'

He brushed her wonderings aside. They were cobwebs. So was the past: all dust. He didn't want to rehash or root about in it. Not with her anyway.

'I don't want to be an ex-priest. I want to be something new. A phase,' he asserted, 'is finished. It was on the point of being when we met.'

'You never said.'

'Why did you suppose I left the parish?'

'But Sybil?'

'Oh, Carla, wasn't it kinder to keep her in the dark?'

'Marco's coming back.'

'When?'

'Tomorrow – no, now it's today. We got a cable.'

Silence on the line. No click. He hadn't hung up. Perhaps he had laid down the receiver and walked away? She visualized him pacing that little apartment which she hadn't visited. Did she even know it was little? Yes, small and untidy with bachelor mess, it became her own head and she paced it with him. No room here for Maurizio and herself. It would be confining. There would be a shortage of coat-hangers and an unfastidious smell of male laundry kept too long before being taken to the cleaners. Windows would be bare of the drapes she had refused to help him choose. How – Jane's question – would he live now? Who would he be? His face glowed at her in memory. It was dark and brilliant, shiny with a gleam shed by eager eyes, grins and enthusiasms whose highs must surely be paid for by moments of depression? She hadn't seen these, having only met him in visiting mood.

Abruptly, the silent line came alive and spoke into her ear: 'We should have made love.'

'Oh, we should have done a lot of things: spent nights together, had fights – at least one over money. One of us ought to have been sick.'

'Haven't we still time?'

She didn't know. Marco's plans might be imperious. A trial

period with Leo was perhaps no longer possible and leaping before taking a close look at her future daunted her.

Conversely, she was revolted by her caution. How *mean* to hesitate as though Leo were an unreturnable item offered in a sale – yet who but he had told her that statistics on the survival of ex-priests' marriages were unpromising? No, perhaps it was Father Feeny on the Terry Steele Show: a biased source.

'We haven't time now to be casual,' she heard herself regret.

'I should have courted you hard,' he was saying, 'but you wouldn't let me.' He started to do so, framing phrases which reminded her of old Valentines or maybe litanies. 'Joy,' he said shamelessly, 'the most wonderful thing' and 'love'. Fearfully, she heard herself transmuted into a sort of plaster saint of matrimony: Blessed Matron, Hope of the Shipwrecked, Tower of Ivory and Star of the Sea. She, with her thirty-six-year-old thighs, her three capped teeth and the innumerable other minor ills to which her flesh had fallen heir, could hardly take these outpourings as being directed with any accuracy at herself. And inaccuracy boded badly. The man was struggling out of a desert of loneliness and she was a mirage.

Should she gather him up then like a lucky find? Light candles to whatever wayfarers' god or patron had sent him her way? Why not? Would she be any worse for him than, say, Sybil or Wanda or Jane or whatever other random woman he might have fallen in with? A girl would not see his boyishness and would be the less capable of handling him.

'Yes,' she said, to say something, ruminating out of a limbo of doubt, 'yes, we should have made love.'

He took this for passion. Was it? Maybe it was? But he too was a mirage. What underlay the dazzling face and teasing manner? She'd seen him dig mud, grate cheese, tease Maurizio and sustain a physical attack. Indian brides knew far less of the men they married – but then the choice was rarely left to them. Besides, he was mutative. A man of authority, he had become an outlaw, eager to take where previously he'd given.

Was he Maurizio's rival? More son than lover?

'Depersonalized', she heard him say, describing his desert. He was an Adam without an Eve. Love, he said, was life-giving and

176

he had joined the seminary in search of it: love of humanity, love of Christ, but had been left with the cold stone of a dead routine. He talked of drouth and she wondered whether seminaries attracted the simplest boys from every year: grail-hunters, eternal children? He was being true to himself, he argued, in leaving, as true as when he first committed himself. It had been an honest mistake. Yes, she thought, and so would the next one be, for, though she didn't follow his argument, she knew an excuse when she heard one. She would have liked, like a prudent housewife, to preserve his happiness in some sort of jar or pickle. Matrimony?

She answered, however, with something dampening, which was the way to treat excitement.

He could – and did – answer in syllogisms, packaging his folly. They talked until 3 a.m. while she sat in her house in the Glen, hearing tiny rustlings outside with a new ear. 'Hoo' went an owl or mocking-bird, while more silent creatures slunk after domestic prey. His voice was as programmed as theirs and so were his appetites, though to him they seemed astonishingly fresh. He wanted marriage, a house, a car, a job, a family. He was ecstatic with materialism and saw it as sacramental. 'A car,' he said, 'an old jalopy,' and it became Ezekiel's chariot, gilded with humility. He was playing house again, moving on from the first lessons learned in her kitchen. Sleepily, she let her emotions yield to his as the night wore on. He was coherent. Why resist him? Refusal to change, he was saying, spelled rigidity, rigor mortis, death. He had followed the New Church's path away from abstractions and back to the people. But the people, unless personified in one, single, carnal attachment, was abstract still. Logic and loyalty to the thinking he had formerly embraced led him now to embrace *her*. Why not? Why *not*? It was she, not he, he assured, who was petrified in allegiance to an old vow. Her marriage dead, loyalty became necrophiliac. Maurizio was a bright young man. At thirteen a boy was almost fledged. In two years, three, he would be self-sufficient. Was she going to sacrifice her own and Leo's happiness to those two years? Electrically, his voice crackled and ignited her. It was all persausive, semi-true ... Was he then, she asked, ready to marry a divorced woman and leave his Church completely? He said he thought an annulment should be possible, perhaps easy. Why had she only one son? Had Marco denied her more? Slyly, Leo was ready to use one of the Church's more retrograde laws whereby a marriage not dedicated to reproduction was no marriage. Well, the Church was his jungle. She was glad he knew its ways. This proof of practicality was promising. It meant he knew how much to shed and to hold onto when changing spheres.

At 3 a.m., the air seems thin like air on high mountains. Waking thought has some of the risky juxtapositions of dream. She became girlish and hopeful and listened with a receptive ear. His words vibrated like caresses. They were forceful and physical. They lulled and thrilled. After hours of talk, lust had turned to words, as must have happened with the old troubadours. The words carried the contour of the throat which released them. They were flesh and drained their speakers of energy, so that lust withdrew like a beast to its lair to replenish strength.

Following the hoop and climax of verbal love-making, they settled to a post-coital chat about frugal plans whose modesty thrilled Leo, perhaps because smallness suggests beginnings and beginnings youth. He would be doing what he never had. Fresh starts. Modest goals. Togetherness. Hand in hand, he and Carla would negotiate tomorrow. Didn't she want to? Oh, she did, she did. The picture was like that of Jack and Jill in a school primer going up the neat, pastoral hill of honest toil. It was morally irreproachable.

Now, five hours later, at 8 a.m., a cold-eyed slice in the morning's arc, Carla focused on something in the foreground of vision and recognized the outline of the Briggs's pick-up truck. She considered its particulars: peeling paint job, dented fender, rust, a pile of boxes which had once held Cranberry Juice Cocktail and now did service as suitcases. Two dolls dressed in some regional costume dangled before the windshield. The rust, close up, would have the colour and texture of squashed ants. The truck was halfway to the scrap heap. So was Briggs: an ant-dull, baffled man, angry about the wrong things. His poverty had not been liberating. Was it folly to suppose that Leo's would? She was too tired to think. Another sleepless night. White nights: this unconsummated love affair was made up of them. After driving Maurizio to school, she would get some rest before facing Marco whose plane was due to touch down at four.

Chapter Eight

Carla had been living in a blur since Marco's arrival eighteen hours before. He had landed with bustle, but neither his chat nor his projects impinged. They crackled like radio ads which, for all their zest, could, at any moment, be turned off. Her energies went into doing this.

His return was intolerable. For months their joint bedroom had been hers alone. He struck her as a stranger: old, shrivelled, inconsiderate. His bathroom habits jarred. So did his handing her intimate laundry to wash.

She was unable to get hold of Leo. She had tried endlessly from the phone booth outside the Glen grocery but had not got through. Perhaps he was at the chancery? Reconsidering his decision? In hospital suffering from some late-maturing injury? Anxiety whipped up her feelings for him and her doubts as to just where they stood. That heady midnight call could hardly be relied on. She wanted to hear him say something firm and calm by daylight. 'Leo,' she found herself whispering as though his name were a prayer. In the US, Leo had told her, quoting some survey, only four per cent of the population claimed that they had never prayed. As if the Enlightenment and Marx had never been! Yet, if this sort of inner cry could be called prayer, then maybe it was true!

Snatching a quick nap before Marco's arrival, she had dreamed and in the dream found herself spending long stretches of time – hours? years? – looking for a safety-pin. A message from her deep to her trivial self?

Marco was constantly at her elbow.

'Carla, listen, I want to ask you ... Carla, eh! Are you deaf?'

He followed her about with lists of things he wanted her to see to, sell, pack, buy, store, mail. They were, he had decided, leaving straight away for Italy. She had not tackled him even in her head.

'You'd better think about getting rid of that dog,' he said, 'and buy some gifts to take back. Electronic games. Jogging suits. Something typically American. I've booked us provisionally on a flight leaving next week. Sooner would be better. If we're not back for my parents' anniversary, we'll never hear the end of it.'

Crackle, crackle. Time in her memory stretched and dwindled, shooting images into her field of vision: a red-webbed eyeball, Leo's bloody temple. Could he have been hurt more badly than he had admitted? She tried to reconstruct the fight but seemed to have missed half of it by closing her eyes. She asked Maurizio, begged him to say as little as possible to his father – she didn't dare emphasize this – then asked Joanie too, rushing downstairs to waylay her as she pegged a final wash of clothes on the line. The Briggs were packing up and leaving. Carla recognized a T-shirt torn in the fight.

'Listen,' she asked, 'I, ah, how long did it go on? How badly were they hurt?'

The other woman gave her an angry look. 'You should know. You started it.'

'I? How?' But Carla recognized, through a possible confusion, a truth more accurate than Joanie could have guessed. 'What did I start?'

'You brought him round. Trash like him!' Joanie snorted. She was talking about Cazz. 'Wanda's got no sense when it comes to men, but we were getting by until she took up with him. He's the criminal class,' dim Joanie whispered, 'and he's come round again. Lying. Pretending he's from Welfare and Walt believes him. What am I to say? I don't want to start anything. Being I'm an invalid and not supposed to get involved. Well, at least we're leaving.'

So, said Marco, were the Verdis. His sister had rented a house in Milan for them. Furnished. It would tide them over until they found something permanent and his mother was getting it ready for their return.

'I don't know if I can leave so soon,' Carla told him.

'What do you mean? They're pressuring me, Carla. My mother and father and – besides I have to get back to work. Listen, this house can be turned over to an agent. Just pack a suitcase. We'll pay someone to pack and ship anything we can't take. What's the problem?'

'Why do you need me so suddenly?'

'I told you! My mother . . .'

'And why does *she* want me? There's some girl, I suppose. One you might marry. She's afraid of that, isn't she?' Paola's letters had been one long alert: *Your home is threatened. Come.*

'No. Yes. Nothing important. There *was* a girl, yes, but – look, isn't it obvious that I'm here so it can't have been anything?' He tried to put his arms around her.

She ducked out of them. 'It *was* something, which is why you wrote me all those letters.'

She felt no jealousy, she noted. Well.

Marco danced around her, intent on her just as he must have been intent on the girl he had now decided to ditch.

'I've got involvements here,' she said. 'I can't just leave when you click your fingers.'

'Involvements? What involvements?'

He smelled of *Eau Sauvage*. His nails were manicured, the hairs in his nose trimmed, his shirt silk but sober. He had gone back to his Italian persona, putting the Californian one away as one puts away water-skis in winter or the props for some sport one has given up. As he had put away the girl, perhaps. He laughed slowly: 'Ca-arla! You didn't take my advice and take a lover, did you? Mmm?' His hands hovered about her. He could not resist trying to please. '*Dimmi.* Say.'

'It would be my business if I had.'

'*Certo, certo*. Listen, I wouldn't blame you. I gave you the green light after all. And I suppose my motives were mixed.' Smile. Playful curiosity mingled with disbelief.

'How old was the girl?'

He shrugged. 'She's not important. Young actually. But you don't want to hear about her.' He made the gesture of throwing something away: a light, easy flick.

'No.'

'Of course not. About the bookings – what about moving them to an earlier date? Say four days from now?'

She argued about this, gaining time, talking about laundry and dry-cleaning, wondering when she could talk next to Leo. Meanwhile, she flung the trivia of life at Marco. He had left it all to her and now she used it against him.

'Besides,' she wound up, 'Maurizio won't want to leave.'

'Maurizio doesn't count. Who does he think he is?'

'He's nearly fourteen. Children sometimes leave home at that age.'

'Who? Drop-outs? Runaways?'

And who had brought *them* around? But Marco was oblivious of his old enthusiasms. Individualism, he had explained to Maurizio this morning, was all very well in its place but the good of the family as a whole was more important.

'It's like being on a boat, Maurizio. We've got to pull together and you're not the helmsman. I am. When I'm not here, your mother is. If we had no helmsman the boat would go round in circles. You do understand?'

Jovial paterfamilias slapped filiusfamilias on the shoulder.

'Sure you do. You're a bright kid. My, but you've grown while I've been away.'

Maurizio was unsmiling. He held his father's arm. 'Babbo, we're so glad you're back.'

'Well, of course you are. So am I!'

'Babbo, I want to ask you something important.'

'Fine. What is it?'

'You're to take it seriously.'

'Of course.' Marco smiled. 'Well,' he encouraged. 'Come on. Is it so outrageous? Am I such an ogre? You can ask, can't you?

No censorship here, you know. This is Liberty Hall, gentlemen, you may do as you please.' He laughed.

'That's a quotation,' Carla told her son. 'Not to be taken literally.'

Marco frowned.

'I'm protecting my young,' she told him. 'And you too. You might disappoint each other.'

'Does it disappoint *you* that I'm back?' Marco asked her. 'You've been father and mother, haven't you? The all-powerful Mom bringing your son up a Mom-ist. *Are* you a Mom-ist, Maurizio? Do you believe in Mom the Mother Almighty, creatress of heaven and earth, etc. etc.? Hmm? It's the national religion of America, but then you're not American, are you Maurizio?' Marco grinned.

Maurizio looked away. His body, his mother saw, was bunched intently and a tic twitched in his cheek.

'He wants to ask you something,' she reminded.

'Well he doesn't need an advocate I hope? He can use his own God-given tongue, can't he? What is it you want, Maurizio?'

Pause.

'Come on,' his father encouraged. 'Spit it out. Look me in the eye like a man and ask.'

'I don't think I'd better,' Maurizio told him. 'You're not in the mood.'

'What do you mean "mood"? Come on, Maurizio. You're not a child any more, you know. And you're not dealing with a woman who has to be taken in the right moment. We're men, Maurizio, creatures of reason. Like it says on your blazer pocket. Do you remember what it says? Your school motto? Do you?'

Maurizio's tic jumped.

'What is the motto?' his father insisted. 'Tell me.'

'I don't want to.'

'Do you know it?'

'Of course I know it.'

'Well say it.'

Silence.

'You're embarrassing him,' Carla said.

'You keep out of this, Carla. All I want is for him to say three words. Why shouldn't he say them? What is this? A conspiracy? Against me? I must say I'm bewildered. I don't understand. What's embarrassing about saying three words of Latin? One of the most famous sayings of the Western tradition and his school motto. Is he ashamed of his school? Ashamed of being a European? Or does he just want to spite me? Why, Carla? What have you been teaching him?'

'Maurizio,' Carla said, 'can't you see the trouble you're making? Say it, why don't you?'

Marco roared. 'Why do *you* have to ask him? Is he your puppet? What's been going on here while I was away?'

Carla looked at the floor. Maurizio, she saw with the tail of her eye, was doing the same thing.

Pause. Marco tapped his foot.

'Do you really want me to say it?' Maurizio asked in a neutral voice.

'Say it,' his father commanded.

'*Cogito ergo sum.*'

Marco smiled. He was a good winner. 'Well now, was that so hard?'

Maurizio left the room. Carla made a phone call to the rental agency who owned their breakfast- and play-room furniture. The agency agreed to pick it up next day.

'Well,' said Marco, 'we're making progress. What else is on the list?'

'I have to go out again,' Carla said. She wanted to try phoning Leo once more.

'You've been out three times,' Marco said mildly. 'It's only noon. Why couldn't you do all your errands at once?' She supposed he was keeping his temper. Paola would have lectured him on this.

'It's odd,' Carla remarked, 'I felt more intimate with you when you weren't here.'

'Memory cheats.'

'Does it? In my memory you were quite overbearing. I didn't try to improve you. I think the difference was that the remembered you knew all about me, was omniscient, godlike. One minds less being thundered at by a god.'

'And now I'm here I don't know about you?'

185

'Don't want to. Haven't time. I suppose I gave myself the star role in my head.'

'Poor Carla!'

'I'd rather not be pitied.'

'Pity is a form of attention.'

Her trip out was in vain. Leo did not answer his phone.

Coming back, she found Marco and Maurizio in the garden trying to interest Carlomagno in a ball.

'Your dog is stupid,' Marco told her, but his humour was manic. 'Never mind. He was never the family dog. We're a tight little unit: just three people. It's nice to be back together. Don't you feel that, Maurizio? Snug. Just the three of us for the next few years. Then you'll be off. You're getting to be a big fellow. You'll be taking flight in no time. How do you feel about that? You'll be leaving the old folks, right?' Marco threaded his fingers between his son's and began to swing their arms in jaunty rhythm. 'Come on,' he invited, 'march. The way we used to.' He began to hum, clowning, trying to drag Maurizio with him. 'Do you remember when you used to play at going off to war? You had a sword and a cocked hat. Well, it'll soon be a reality.' Marco began raising his knees in an exaggerated military step. 'Left, two, three,' he yelled jovially.

'Babbo,' Maurizio pulled away from him. 'They'll *hear* you. The neighbours. I'm going in.'

'What neighbours?' Marco raised his voice. 'Who cares about neighbours? What's all this human respect? Why should I care what some dull conformist thinks of me? Because only a dull – where's he gone? What's the matter with the boy?'

'He's gone in,' Carla explained unnecessarily. 'The neighbours are friends, Marco. No need to shout.'

'And he cares more about them than about his father? About what they might think? Some dumb Joe Doe who mustn't hear us raise our voices? Does he think I'm loud? An Italian organ-grinder, is that it?' Marco bounded up the side-porch steps.

When Carla got in he had cornered Maurizio in the drawing-room and was explaining how much he loved and had missed him. 'You mustn't think that because I wasn't here I didn't care. I've had business-troubles. It's too complicated to explain now

186

but you see I didn't know if I was coming back or whether I could make a niche for myself – for us all – in Italy. I'll explain it all to you some day. But for now I want you to know that for me the most important thing in life is my family. I'm not ashamed to say it. For that I'll work day and night. I'd lie and cheat for it if I had to. I might even kill. Yes, if I had to I would. Well, here's your mother,' Marco said, interrupting himself and changing his tone. 'We mustn't be so serious. Are you glad to be going back to Italy, Maurizio? Nonno Aeolo and Nonna Paola are thrilled to bits. They're preparing the house. Nonna Paola is. You must make a great fuss of her when you meet. Old people attach a lot of importance to family festivities, you know. It's because they expect to die soon and can't look ahead the way the rest of us do. Will you promise me to be very nice to them, Maurizio?'

'Sure.'

'That's my boy.'

'Babbo, I said, remember, I said I had to ask you something important?'

'That's true. You did. Well, now is the time. Ask.'

Maurizio looked worried. 'It's not easy. I'm afraid you won't listen.'

'Well maybe it's something foolish if you're afraid of that? What is it? Something you want? A racing bike?'

'No.' He sounded sulky.

'All right. I'm listening then. I shan't guess or laugh. Promised.'

Maurizio looked anguished. 'I wrote you about it.'

'You certainly wrote some odd letters.'

'You mustn't think things don't matter just because I'm a boy. Young. I've thought about this a lot and – Babbo, can you adopt Evie?'

'Who?' Marco's receptive expression wavered. 'Evie? Oh the little girl next door? Can I *adopt* her? Maurizio, don't you think you're being a bit juvenile? Why isn't your mind on serious things, your family, the future, going back to Italy, even your school work, for God's sake!'

'This *is* serious. I knew you wouldn't listen. Why must only the things *you* say matter and be serious?'

'Maurizio, you're being rude to your father.'

'Keep out of it, Carla.'

Maurizio's face was un-negotiable.

His father tried humour. 'Hey, this reminds me of the time you kept begging me to buy you a pony. We were living in an apartment right in the middle of Milan. Not a blade of grass in sight and you kept saying, "Babbo, can we get a pony?" You were seven years old. Well you're growing up. It's a big step from ponies to girls, what?'

'I'm not a child. Don't play with me.'

'No? O K.' Rebuffed, Marco could get aggressive fast. 'So you're an adult!' He spoke icily. 'Very well, then stop asking me to provide harems and menageries for you. That's the child talking in you. If you're grown up, you'll know that adults do things for themselves.'

'But I can't. How can I?' Maurizio's face was swollen. Desperation seemed to clog his processes. He looked costive, rigid with despair.

His mother put a hand on his arm. Marco turned on her: 'Carla!'

She withdrew it.

'If you can't do anything,' Marco told his son, 'better forget the notion. It was pretty silly if you think of it. *Dio Bacco*, Maurizio, we're leaving here next week! We can't take anyone with us. We're even going to have to get rid of the dog your mother got.'

'Get rid of Carlomagno?'

'Of course. He can go back to the pound. We have to travel light. We're nomads, you know.' Marco's voice was merry. 'A nomadic family!'

Maurizio was intent on his worry. 'Evie's father is a maniac. He may *kill* her. Really. You can't just let that happen. You can't just care for people in your own family. What about loving your neighbour? He's a murderer.'

Marco laughed. 'Come on, Maurizio.'

'It's true. He's been in prison. He has a knife. A switchblade knife. He threatened a friend of Mamma's with it. There was a fight. And he did kill a man one time. Evie says so.'

Marco was still half laughing. 'You're having me on, aren't

you?' He looked at his wife, then back at Maurizio. 'What *is* this, Carla?'

Carla shrugged.

'Is he being imaginative?'

'Maurizio,' she said dully, 'there's no need to bother your father with every little thing that happened.'

'It wasn't a little thing. It is important. I want to save Evie. The guy is half mad and he has a gun. I saw it this morning.'

'Stop exaggerating, Maurizio. Save her from what? She's been OK up to now, hasn't she? She's survived. The world,' said Carla, 'is full of hard cases. We can't save everyone. I'm sorry, Maurizio, but I don't see what we can do.'

'Oh you!' Maurizio turned furiously on his mother. 'You don't care, do you? You don't care about anything.' He began to imitate Carla's voice, squinting and talking in a high, affected squeal: '"Save her from what?" You know what. You know exactly. You're the one who told me about battered babies and how fathers can kill their own children. Evie's father might. He might really. And you saw what he's like only you don't care. You're worse than Babbo because *you know*! You're a Judas! Mrs Judas, that's you!'

'Maurizio, don't you dare speak to your mother like that! Apologize this minute! I can see it's time I got back. You need discipline and you're going to get it. I won't have you ending up a juvenile delinquent like that kid next door. If this is the result of being in her company, I want no more of it. You're not to see her again. Understood?'

Maurizio's head was bent. He turned away, possibly to hide tears. Marco walked round him. 'Well?' he heckled. 'Is that understood?'

Maurizio turned again.

'Don't you turn your back on me!' his father howled. 'Look me in the eye.' Marco put his hand under his son's chin and jerked it upwards. 'Look at me!' he yelled. 'What have you to say?'

Maurizio's face was bunched like a fist. He jerked free. 'Up yours!' he yelled at his father. 'Did you hear me, Babbo? That's what I have to say to you: up yours, up yours, up yours!'

Marco knocked him down. Maurizio, lying on the floor, bit

189

his father's leg. His father tried to kick him but Maurizio had caught the kicking foot in both hands so that Marco nearly fell.

'*Porco cane!*' he roared. 'You little bastard! I'll show you what a battered child looks like. Let go, Carla, *Dio Bacco*, let go my elbows.'

'Leave him alone, Marco! You can't come thundering in suddenly like a nineteenth-century parent!'

'I'll do what I goddam please.' The elbows hammered her chest.

Carla staggered but held on. 'Stop it!' she yelled. 'You can't turn discipline on and off like a faucet. Try disciplining yourself for a bit!'

'Let go Carla.'

'I will if . . .'

'No ifs . . . Ah!'

With a wrench of his back, Marco pulled himself and Carla to the floor. Maurizio, now free to scramble to his feet, did so, rushed to the front door and threw it open.

His parents picked themselves up and self-consciously brushed themselves down.

Their son plunged past the screen door, paused and shrieked through its wire netting. 'Two Judases!' he shrilled. His voice wobbled and broke: 'Two! Mr and Mrs Judas!'

His father made a lunge for him but he was gone. They heard his feet clatter noisily down the steps, thud along the grass strip near the garage, then fade down the Glen.

'Well,' said Carla, 'I suppose that proves that his home is not much safer than Evie's. In a way your position has been reinforced.'

That had happened this morning.

Carla feared that there would be another scene when Maurizio got home. The longer he stayed out the worse it was likely to be and he had been out now for three hours. In the meantime, she had not found an auspicious moment for her own announcement. Marco seemed to have entirely forgotten that she had asked him for a divorce. This, of course, was a tactic.

'Carla!' He walked into the room. 'What was all that about a switchblade knife and a friend of yours?'

'What?'

'You remember? What Maurizio said when he was trying to make a case for adopting that girl next door. Edie. Evie, whatever her name is.'

'Oh that was some boy's father. Some man from the Lycée car pool who came to borrow an assignment his son hadn't copied. Maurizio's briefcase was next door and when this man went to get it Evie's father thought he was a burglar and began to flash a knife around. I don't think it was as serious as Maurizio said.'

The lie was the corner-stone of community life.

'You still haven't said when I can make those bookings for?'

'Why don't you let me follow later? I have things to do here.'

'What?'

'My dog,' she remembered. 'Yes. I'll have to look around. Find him a home. I'm fond of him and ...'

'Christ, you're not staying here for a goddamned dog? My mother and father are breathing down my neck. They think you've got a lover or want a divorce and meanwhile you hang on here for a – dog! You don't think we want to take that great flea-bitten monster to Milan, do you?'

'No. But maybe I could find someone here to take it if,' she bargained, 'I had more time.'

Marco ground his teeth. 'Time! Do I have to repeat, Carla, that my parents attach importance to your coming back for their ANNIVERSARY which is a symbolic and sentimental occasion? Part of the fucking family cult, get it? And it takes place in ten days time! Thus, *we have no more time!* OK? None at all.'

No time. He might have been punching signals in her skin: no time. None. Where *was* Leo? *He* couldn't ring *her*. Her emotion was displaced, confused. She began to sob.

Marco looked astonished. 'Now what's the matter?'

'Time,' she groaned at random, letting one wound camouflage another, and flung herself on the bed. 'I'm the one without it.' Her hands ran over the flat surface of the mattress on which she and Leo had not lain. Why? What silly scruple had held her back? 'I'll be thirty-seven next year, forty in no time, older and older! I'll get varicose veins, flab, wrinkles, hair on my chin, menopause, hot flushes, brittle bones ... Older women

191

used to die ... in childb-b-birth ...' She sobbed luxuriously. Naming terrors conjured them away. 'That was a mercy. What's the good of surviving your best self?' Now that she had let herself go she couldn't stop. Her body danced drily on the bed. Energy was seeking a release. She could have wept for all the evils of the world, might have been having a fit – maybe was? Leo, Leo, Leo thudded a voice in her head. Where *was* he? *How* was he? Her words camouflaged his name. Or had she let it out?

'What did I do to deserve this?' Marco roared. 'A mad wife!'

'What did I? Could you stand to be me?'

'I told you to get out and live a bit.'

'Too late. You told me too late.'

'What about all the other women in the world? My mother ...'

'She thinks she's immortal. That she'll live again in heaven.'

'We're all going to die. What's so unique about you? If it's too late to live why not go and drive off a slide-area cliff? If you really believe that crap, be coherent. Take the car keys.'

'Oh God,' she groaned. 'American women go to analysts who comfort them for hours. They get therapy ...'

'This *is* therapy. Listen, you silly bitch, you've got a good face and you're ruining it. Stop crying, Carla.' He climbed into the bed beside her. 'Carla!'

'No!' She pushed him away.

'Come on, Carla, *calma, dai!* I know you've got unused to me, but ...'

'No.'

'Yes.' He put his arms around her and now, opening her eyes, she saw that he had pulled down the blinds. The room was dark. He lay behind her caressing her neck and back. Expert hands. She hated and succumbed to his expertise. In the dark, she let him comfort her and let an old, half forgotten excitement flow through and bear her high into oblivion. Treachery, she thought, fighting back from it, but the thought broke like images on stirred water, reformed, then faded into a glitter of bright hallucination. Relief floated away the thinking part of her as she recognized the explosion of colour which had always danced on her inner eyelids at such moments and which she had thought lost to her like the edge of old appetites and the vivid

192

greeds of youth. Marco's body both was and was not familiar and brought back moments in early marriage when he and she had lost their separate selves in a surge of blind tenderness. The memory was ready to tinge the present moment like running dye and she wanted to whisper – as she must have then – words of love. Alerted, an inner image of herself tried to claw itself together, to collect the shreds of self diffuse on that tide still tossing and dazzling, so that her mind could scarcely focus on the image of itself which hung, precariously unjelled, in its own dissolving eye, collapsing further with each flicker of attention, scattering like a shoal of fish then coalescing as the viewing mind – at once net and fish – managed to impose a contour on its elements. I, she reminded herself, must – she grasped at her defining rules – *must* keep things distinct. *This is not love.* To keep back the words, she put her mouth to his. A Judas kiss, she thought, then, as he returned it, remembered Maurizio's last words to them both: Mr and Mrs Judas. But her passion was not yet assuaged and she gave herself back to this conjugal amenity to which she had every right since she had not sought satisfaction elsewhere.

Afterwards, Marco lay back and said: 'You did take a lover, didn't you?'

'What do you mean?'

'I know you did. I'm glad. He woke you up. You make love, *cara*, like a tart. No complaint intended. No reproach. I'm delighted. You enjoyed making love just now, didn't you?'

'I suppose. As usual. It's been such a long time, so how can I . . .'

'Oh, you're a miserable liar. Don't bother.'

'Marco, stop playing. Teasing. I can't stand it.'

'It would be a pity to drive over a cliff and never enjoy this again, wouldn't it? Huh? Not talking? Oh why? Remorse is hesitation after the fact. Silly if you think about it.' Pause. 'I'm not jealous. I promise. What I don't see is why you're so sulky after this display of talents I never knew you had. You didn't fall in love, did you? Break your heart?'

Carla jumped up. 'I'm going for a shower.'

When she returned, Marco was sitting smoking in their bedroom armchair.

'I owe you apologies,' he said. 'I shouldn't have teased. Sorry. I can see you're unhappy. Do you want to tell me about this man?'

'There is no man.'

He shrugged. 'As you like. Well maybe, then, it's just middle-age megrims. Don't think I don't know them. They're hell. But one gets immune, adapts.'

'You're a man,' she accused. 'It's not the same. Don't pretend. Besides,' she lied, 'what annoyed me just now was your going on as though I were a car you'd got serviced and that was getting better mileage. A thing. Something tuned up . . . Not that I have been or . . .'

'Look, if you're going to start crying, let's not talk. I'll go get some liquor. You seem to have drunk all the vodka. Maybe *that's* your vice, after all? Hm? No, don't get angry. It looks as though we're going to have to learn how to talk again. Listen, let me just say that I don't think of you as a tuned-up car. OK? And the fact is that people get satisfaction out of being useful and you are needed by three people in our family. Needed and, however imperfectly, loved. Think of that while I'm out.' He stood up. 'I'll have a look round for Maurizio too. He's been out long enough for his pride's sake. Besides, my looking for him will be a sop to his dignity.'

'I didn't think you knew about such things.'

'I've been a thirteen-year-old boy in my time.'

'Pity you were never a woman.'

'Maybe so.'

She stood at the window, watching him walk down the steps, then picked up the receiver and dialled Leo's number.

'Hullo.'

His voice astounded her. She had dialled without hope and was unready.

'Leo, is that really you?'

'Carla!' He laughed and the laughter flowed over her like water from a warm shower.

'I thought you'd left or died or something. I've been trying and trying to reach you. Are you all right?'

'Of course. And you?'

194

Diffident victims of a freakish virus, they worried over each other's well-being.

'Really?'

'Yes, yes.'

She told him about Marco, his plane reservations and his urging that she leave for Italy right away.

'Carla, we've got to talk, make some decisions. Can you come here?'

'I think so. I'll try and come right over.' Then: 'I love you,' she told him. 'I'd better ring off. Marco's just gone out for liquor – oh,' she shouted in shock, for she had just turned and seen Marco not two feet from her, staring. He had a wild, strange stare. 'Oh God,' she shouted. 'He's *here*, listening.' She collected some of her wits and produced sensible-sounding words, while wondering if he had heard the others just now. How long had he been there? He looked at her with an appalled, distracted eye. But maybe he was only appalled by the look on her face? 'I've been arranging to have a friend take my dog,' she told Marco. 'You startled me.'

'I came back for my wallet,' Marco said, groping for it in the jacket hanging on a hook behind the bedroom door. He seemed unable to detach his gaze from hers. He *must* have heard something. No. Maybe not. He groped behind him for the wallet, staring at her still. A sunburst of wrinkles surrounded each eye. He was ageing, aged. The last few months must have been hard. 'Marco, darling, it's all right, isn't it?' she asked in a burst of guilt, feeling as though the receiver in her hand were a weapon – then realized that she had not covered it to say this. 'I'll see you as arranged then,' she told it, staring in shock at its perforated ear, then hung up.

'That was Sybil Steele,' she told Marco. 'I told her I was going back to Italy. She'll take the dog.'

Marco kept examining her. 'Why are you crying?' he asked.

'Don't you know?'

'No.'

'Oh God!' She threw herself in the armchair. 'I can't keep this up.'

'What?'

'Don't you know, really?'

195

'Well, you were upset before I went out. But now you look – insane, if you must know, Carla. What is the matter?'

'I want a divorce. Seriously, Marco. Remember,' she told him, 'I told you so weeks ago. On the phone. I meant it. I mean it still.'

Marco's face flinched. He pointed at the telephone. 'Him?'

'He's only the occasion. I don't plan to talk about him. He's not free.'

'Married?'

'Yes.' The lie shut Marco out of her life, restored privacy, protected Leo. High on this triumph, she repeated the singularly effective syllable: 'Yes.' Marco's face showed pain but she must not be moved. Must not. Already, overheard by Leo, she had called Marco 'darling'. 'I'm going out.'

'Carla, for God's sake, you can't just walk out the door. We've got to talk about this. You owe me an explanation. I ...'

'The explanation lies in the last few months. Also there were things in the last fifteen years which there's not much point dwelling on now. Fifteen years is as much as many criminals condemned for life end up serving. I've served my time, Marco.'

A devastated face – but he could produce one at will. Old memories tugged: their youth, the young Marco's grace, gifts he'd given her, shared worries. How could she do this? She could because she must. Let the cut be swift, turning her old companion and love into the enemy he had also always been. Remember his betrayals, bullyings, small stinginesses. All his sins must be to the fore. The unfairness of this smote her and she nearly ran to throw her arms around him. No. See how dangerous he is. Be tough. Be consistent. Say something irrevocable. Provoke the beast in him.

'I'm going out.'

Would he stop her? Triumphant, she waited for he could only do wrong. If he stopped her she would be strengthened in her resolve. He didn't.

To her astonishment she was out the door.

Maurizio, after rushing out the front door, ran some way down the Glen and lurked there to see if his father would follow. When he didn't and he saw the coast was clear, he circled round

196

by back lanes, climbed through the scrubby no-man's-land above the Verdis' garden and, approaching it from behind, reached the pomegranate tree. There was food up there, a stack of funny papers and it was a good place from which to check the house without being seen. He wouldn't go back for several hours. Let them wonder about him. Let them sweat. But he had no money to go any place where you had to pay and besides hoped to keep an eye on the comings and goings next door. He was so full of fury against his parents that it was some time before he realized that the tree house was not empty. Evie was hunched in one corner in a queer little heap. As though someone had thrown her there. She was crying.

'Evie.'

She turned her head away. 'Oh Maurizio, why don't you just go,' she mumbled. 'I wanted to be alone.'

'Well so did I.' Taking offence. Whose tree house was it? In a moment though, Maurizio began to feel mean. 'Listen,' he told the back of her head, 'I'll stay quiet and not bother you. OK? I'll read *Peanuts*. I *would* go only I've had a fight with my father and I've nowhere *to* go.'

She mumbled something which didn't sound like 'No' so must be 'Yes'.

After several pages of *Peanuts*, he sneaked a look at her and noticed raw weals on her legs. Her father must have hit her with a belt or stick. Christ! That guy should be behind bars. If only there were a hot line for kids' complaints: one with clout that would send out a psychiatrist to certify maniacs like Briggs and tell Maurizio's own father to cool it! Maurizio would have rung it right away. If he'd had any hope of them, he'd have rung the police, the NSPCC, anyone who would *help*! Not that any-one would. They waited for you to *die* first, most probably! Maurizio raged. He wished even crummy Cazz were here. But the dumb shit had split. At the first sign of trouble. Before the first sign! The guy must have radar. Still, in a way, he was better than Maurizio's own father who wouldn't as much as *admit* the trouble was there. Evie seemed to have stopped crying.

'Want something to eat?' he whispered.

'OK.'

There was a stack of stuff he had taken from his mother's pantry so as to stop Evie ripping things off at Safeway.

'Cheese?' He offered her parmesan and a hard biscuit. 'It's Italian,' he said and remembered that his father wanted them to leave for Italy in a few days. He wished he could bring himself to run away the way he'd tried to get Evie to do. Run where though? To some crash pad? Some kids managed to live that way for months. But *then* what? They went home and Maurizio's home would be in Italy. His parents would have gone, probably leaving his description with the police. He'd get put into a reform school, be handed over to the Juvenile Authority. And what good would he have done for Evie even if she agreed to come with him? He – he saw this sadly – would only be a drag on her. By herself she'd fit in fine if she wanted to. Well, he figured she'd have to sleep with some guys so they'd give her a place *to* sleep like that kid who was with Cazz that time. Older guys. There was no place for Maurizio in that picture at all. None. In misery, he bit into his cheese.

'How come you had a fight with your Dad?' Evie was talking again.

'What? Oh,' Maurizio shrugged, 'he's one big phony, that's what.'

'Yeah?'

'Yeah.' He remembered he'd talked his father up a lot to Evie, saying how cool he was and wait till my father comes home and so forth. Well, he wasn't telling her what they'd had the fight over. That was for sure. His anger with his father wasn't a bit like the hot blubbery rages he'd got into sometimes last year. It was cold and maybe permanent.

'He's sending Carlomagno back to the pound,' he said. 'Just like that. He doesn't care if they cut him up for experiments. He doesn't care about anything.'

'Was that what you fought about?'

'That. Other things too. What about you?' Maurizio gave a nod at Evie's swollen legs. There was a bruise on her arm as well.

She pulled her short skirt maybe an inch over one of the worst welts. 'Nothing. I don't want to talk about it.'

They chewed some more cheese, then: 'I hate being a kid,' Maurizio said. 'I really can't stand it. Being young.'

198

Evie finished her food, then said: 'I have to go pack.'

'Right now?' Maurizio was disappointed.

'Yeah. You can come if you like. Help me.'

'OK.'

They slid down from their tree.

'When are you leaving?' he asked her.

'Who knows?' She jerked a thumb at the house. 'It's up to him.'

Carlomagno, who had been stretched under the pomegranate tree, loped lazily after Maurizio and Evie as they crossed the stretch of slope separating their two back gardens. Pliable and rubbery as a puppy still, the dog looked the very self of comfortable innocence. Maurizio bent and rubbed his face in the stiff ruff of neck-fur and thought of vivisectors. At this moment he hated his father with a pure, unforgiving rage. Standing up from what was maybe a babyish fit of self-indulgence, he looked downhill and thought for a moment that he had been visited by a vision. Then, holding still to the dog's collar, he darted behind a bush.

'Evie,' he whispered, 'hide. That's my Dad.'

Not thirty yards down the slope, his father was mounting towards the Briggs's front door. What for? To discuss an adoption? Some hope! Maurizio was annoyed with himself for even dreaming that his father would give that a thought. Much more likely was that the bastard – the bastard, he repeated shockingly inside his own head – was on the warpath and looking for him. Maurizio knew a kid whose father had ditched his own family and gone to live with another woman and her children. The son kept a life-size photo of his father in the garage and used it regularly as a dart board. Maurizio could see why he did.

'Let's go hide in your cellar,' he whispered to Evie.

'OK.'

The entrance was out of sight of the verandah onto which Maurizio's father had just stepped. The place was dark and not wired for electricity so Evie struck a match and lit the oil lamp they kept there for their holocaust game. It smelled of rot and mildew and was stuffed with cushions and bedding, a mess of old calendars, packing-cases, broken furniture and a mangle.

Above their heads there was the sound of talk. A chair scraped. What could the two awful fathers be discussing? Them?

'Children,' Maurizio pursued a recent train of thought, 'don't ask to be born. Parents choose to have them, so, if anyone owes anyone anything, it's the parents.' This refuted arguments which had been dinned into his head since he could hear. He'd had it with talk of families pulling together as if in a boat. Evie, Carlomagno – destined for the pound – and himself struck him as equally doomed victims of a selfish, lousy system. A flash of cold foreknowledge – adulthood, he supposed you could call it – made it clear that of the three *he* would fare best and quite likely be happy and reconciled to the return to Italy in a shamefully short time. This discredited the present Maurizio's concern for his fellow victims and made him wish he could have done some noteworthy thing for them while he was still reliably upset.

What he hated most about his father was the way he could win Maurizio round. It was as if Maurizio had no self. Sooner or later – it had happened before – he would cravenly make up the quarrel with both his parents. What choice had he? Dreams of dignity dribbled to nothing – but wouldn't always.

He hoped.

'Oh God!' He bit his hand so that it hurt. 'I'm going up there. I want to hear what they're saying.'

'I'll come too.'

'Well move quietly and leave the dog here. I don't want them to know we're around.'

A grimy window at the side of the house gave a filtered glimpse of the Briggs's living-room. Briggs was sitting at a table and opposite him Maurizio's father restlessly agitated a rocking-chair. Abruptly, Briggs, wiry but pot-bellied like a spider, reached into his shirt pocket and took out a folded sheet of grey, thumbed writing-paper: the letter.

Sliding round the base of the verandah – 'Quiet, Evie, move *quietly*, willya!' – Maurizio climbed onto its deck and stood listening by the screen door.

'... that's what blew my marriage,' Briggs was saying. 'Turned it sour. A thing like that can build up inside you. Get on top of you.'

'Sure,' said Maurizio's father.

200

'After that I didn't have no interest in furthering myself.'

'I can understand that.'

'Funny you should come around. Your wife chewed me out two nights ago, you know. Putting the blame on me – and I was letting her bullshit me, but from what I've heard since ...'

'Mmm?' The rocking-chair squeaked and scraped.

'I dunno,' said Briggs. 'Less said the better maybe? There's a lot of contradiction in what I've been picking up.'

Squeak. Scrape.

'Social worker called Dobrinski was around. Know him at all?'

'Cazz Dobrinski. Sure.'

'Well you ask him if you want to know more. He was kinda hintin' things about the women around here – that would include your wife – being no better than mine, and as regards mine I have a letter here. Was mailed to me from here. Fact is it's the reason I came back. Have a read of this.'

Briggs stood up and tramped across the floor. Maurizio imagined him handing the letter to his father. What was the guy hinting at? What?

'That darned dog musta got into the cellar.' Briggs's voice was suddenly close. Maurizio began to back from the door. Down below, he could hear Carlomagno scratching at the cellar door and yelping. 'Have a read of that,' said Briggs, 'while I go see what's up.'

Suddenly, before Maurizio could dodge, the screen door had been flung open and Briggs was grasping him by the elbow. 'Saw you in the mirror!' he yelled triumphantly as he pulled Maurizio into the room. '*Thought* you was out there listening. Little pitchers, eh? Why so interested, young man? Huh?'

Maurizio's father stood up from the squeaking rocking-chair. 'Maurizio!' He was good at making his voice sound gentle and amazed. Wounded. It was an act designed to make you break down in tears of repentance.

'Someone needs his rear end warmed,' said Briggs whose act lacked finesse. 'Well?' He shook Maurizio a little. 'What have you to say for yourself? Cat got your tongue?'

Maurizio's father held up the piece of grey writing-paper. 'Do you know anything about this?'

201

Maurizio aimed a kick at Briggs's shins, twisted from his grip and rushed out and down the slope. A smell of smoke caught his attention and the shrill, queer yelping of Carlomagno. He rushed on, however, his ears straining for sounds of following feet. There were none. The two fathers, supreme in their power, must have decided not to bother following. He'd have to come back some time they'd reason. Well, maybe it was thinking that way that drove kids to become runaways. He'd seen *them* on the beaches, sleeping under piers, hiding from cops, begging coins from tourists. The beach was a long way though. Where else could he go? To Leo's maybe? It was certainly a lot nearer. For now he was running out his rage, the distress he could feel bursting inside him like an over-ripe fruit, and the sour meaning of what the two men had been saying when they noticed him. Scraps of this hovered in his head like broken print or black ash floating upwards from a fire – *fire*? As his breath started coming shorter and a stitch in his side forced him to slow down, the smell he'd caught on leaving the house began to worry him. Could Carlomagno have knocked over the oil lamp?

Carla stopped at a liquor store on Westwood Boulevard and bought a chilled bottle of Heideseck Brut and two tulip-shaped champagne glasses. It was typical of the city that such things should be readily available to impulsive celebrators. In the grocery section, she picked up a jar of *pâté de foie gras* then. knowing his address by heart, drove for the first time to Leo's. It was a duplex apartment of the sort rented to students and he had reached the door before she had time to ring. Dressed in a blue work-shirt, he looked, she thought, years younger.

They hugged tightly – more like long-lost relatives than lovers.

'I feel as though we'd been through the wars.'

'We have in a way.'

She told him about asking Marco for a divorce. 'He heard me talking to you on the phone.'

'I know. I heard.'

'Did you mind my calling him "darling"?'

'You're married to him. You must have called him that for fifteen years. How could I mind?'

'You might have been jealous.'

Not rising to her flirtatious tone, he said: 'Your past is part of you. I can't be jealous of that.'

His simplicity unnerved her – drew her on but frightened her at the thought that there might soon be no retreat. He's *beautiful*, she saw, amazed by the glow of his face and a sense that he had gone ahead of her into a phase of feeling that was more powerful than she had prepared for. Half deliberately, disappointing herself and – she could see – him, she played for time. Finalities were a threat to the day-to-day which kept one in protective custody.

'Marco,' she teased in a false voice and noted the glow dulling in Leo's face, 'would pretend to be jealous in your position.'

Intimacy, someone – who? – had said, was harder to achieve than passion. Oh, it was Marco who'd said it in the heat of some rowdy debate that had got out of hand. 'Passion,' she recalled his telling a tableful of guests, 'is easy. It just flares up. Intimacy you have to wait for and by then the passion may have fizzled out.' He had tried then to pretend he had been thinking of the cinema and films about tempestuous strangers. Nobody was taken in. Marco himself was too obviously the sort to content himself with quick motel courtships and perfunctory seductions. She had felt embarrassed for him and now, remembering, it was as if he had intruded into the room – as of course he had. Intimacy bound her to him: a knowing tie. Passion was Leo's territory and she had to be leery of it, leery for two since *he* clearly had no notion of the doubts it set up. Matrimony had left her with an emotional limp and here was Leo expecting her to jump from its enclosure like a filly. Frighteningly, she was tempted to try, though hope and recovered innocence were notions as alien to her as they must be native to him who was licensed, after all, to give and receive absolution.

She produced her champagne. 'Shall we have it now?'

'Why not?'

'We may need clear heads – to plan.'

'Oh, we'll manage.' He was easing off the cork.

'Gently,' she said, distrusting him, but he got it off smoothly and filled the glasses.

'To us – to our marriage.'

'Are you sure it's what you want?'

203

'Yes.'

'Aren't you afraid that they – your superiors will say you left the Church for a woman?' This, she had learned, was often a sore point with renegade priests – not 'renegade', ex – no, they disliked that too. Dare she make a joke about this? No. And could she live with a man with whom she couldn't joke? Yes, *yes*. Eagerness for laughter was obviously manic: part of her fever and her fear. 'Oh Leo,' she burst out, 'let's make love. It will calm me down.'

It did. Only afterwards could she admit to herself that she had been suppressing barbaric suspicions of him: deep, semi-formulated fears lest he, being of a different totem, turn out to be carnally alien to her too: wolfish, piscine, hawkish, strange. He was no such thing, but tender and, now, intimate. It was unimportant – no, it was a mark in his favour that he made love unimaginatively and in – yes … the minister's position. His ordinariness – a whiff of male sweat, flesh which was, after all, just flesh in standard good Californian shape for his age – was reassuring and – why not? – titillating. Her delight in him was as complex as – she supposed – his in her was plain. She couldn't ask. The pure were thrilling, being without alloy, but intolerant too. Marrying one of them must surely be a risk?

She remembered a story told to the First Communion class which her father, a good and amiable atheist, had allowed her to attend for the sake of various grandmothers and aunts. It was about a wicked atheist who stole a communion wafer: a simple tale of sacrilege and damnation. Carla, her father's daughter, imagined the thief's combined relief and residual thrill on finding the wafer to be merely bread. Merely and yet not merely, she thought, running her thieving hands over Leo's fit flesh. She delighted in its healthy ordinariness, yet knowledge that to his shocked superiors it was *not* ordinary invested it with a transubstantiating glow which meant that Carla's pleasure came close to eating her cake while having it too.

In the end, having done the act was more important than the act itself. They could relax now and their peace felt binding as though practical difficulties had at least diminished.

'I suspect you're too good for me,' she said, 'too nice.' And poured more champagne. Giddily, swallowing the bubbles

204

before they burst, she let her imagination fizz. Maybe she too could be romantic, though bred to doubts and hedging by a dynasty of Florentine merchants who had been following the canny practice of keeping three sets of account books – to outwit tax-collectors – for several hundred years? Poor Marco! *That* was what he couldn't stand in her: her store of the shrewd, moth-eaten virtues which had been the backbone of the European burgher class until the Industrial Revolution had swept them aside to linger stuffily, though still serving their turn, in such provincial backwaters as Florence. She disliked them herself. They were like the age-freckles people got on the backs of their hands: a deformity. But Leo didn't see them in her. With him, perhaps she could start over? Topping up his glass, she asked about his plans.

He said they were to get a job of no matter what sort and finish graduate school at the same time. 'Then I'll get a better job and be the perfect bourgeois.'

They laughed at this diligent school-leaver's programme.

His family, he added comfortably, would help out. He was lucky. They weren't the sort of relatives who were shocked to bits when a priest left the Church. A lot of men he knew had had *that* to contend with: mothers whose pride was stripped from them when their sons came home in a collar and tie. He thought he and Carla might be able to rent a place in the Glen if she liked. 'Not like yours,' he said, 'more like the Briggs's place.'

That jolted her. He was reminding her – deliberately? – that material things were to be secondary. This was important to him. He must not look like a man rushing to personal comfort or the fleshpots.

'What about Maurizio?' he asked.

'I suppose I'll be divorcing him too,' she said. 'Marco would never let me have him. They might even get on better together without me?' She wondered about this. Hadn't this morning's row been, partially at any rate, sparked by Marco's resentment of *her*? 'Resentment,' she said sadly, 'might draw them together.'

Leo, stroking her jawline with a light, feathery movement, said, 'I'm not going to argue with you about Maurizio. How can I? You must just do the best you can about resolving that. We both must.'

205

'Yes.'

'Change,' he said, after a minute, 'is actually very hard to embrace. Look at the Church: two steps forward and one back. The tug of routine is insidious. *I* say "when in doubt, pick change". You wouldn't even be thinking of it if the status quo hadn't become intolerable.'

'Is that what you told your pastor?'

'Oh, I suppose it was implicit. All I *said* was that I believe in a humanistic Christianity which can accommodate married priests. That went down badly enough. He accused me of going along with a tide of self-indulgent solutions and asked me to leave town if I marry. If I stay where I'm known I can only be an object of scandal. Defections, on a world-wide basis, are running at four thousand a year. I won't leave town. Why should I? I owe them nothing. He said we'd never be happy.'

'Would he prefer me to be your mistress?'

'They've always stood for that,' said Leo. 'They didn't like it but they closed an eye. A woman was a remedy against concupiscence. In herself she didn't really count. It was when they upgraded marriage to a spiritual union as well that clerics started wanting it for themselves. It's part of a questioning process and thence their panic. Once you start relating doctrine to social change then every bit of the old structure is at risk.'

'Does it matter to you that I don't believe any of this?'

'I've been living and working with men whose beliefs were very different to mine. I should be able to live with a good pagan like you.'

'Shall we finish the champagne?'

'Sure.' Up-ending the bottle, he looked at the label: 'Oh, French!'

'What else?'

'I haven't had much experience of drinking champagne.'

'Do you think I'm spoilt?'

'Silly!' He nuzzled her neck. 'I *loved* your bringing champagne.'

She ran her hands down his body. 'What a waste, keeping this for celibacy! All those years.'

'Well, if there was nothing to keep, where would be the point?'

'You accept compliments easily, don't you?'

206

'And don't return them, you mean? I've been swallowing my admiration for fear of sounding like a small-town seducer. You told me that that was how your husband came on.'

She was stricken. 'Was I so mean about him?'

'I shouldn't have remembered.'

He's clumsy, she thought. I'm having an affair with a virgin. She turned the notion round in her mind. When the virgin was male it had no cultural connotations at all.

'Hey, when are you going to move in with me?'

Check. Checkmate? What game were they playing? Had she lost through inattention? Before she'd realized they'd begun? Her move, anyway.

'Am I? I suppose I am? Not till Maurizio leaves though. Marco has a plane reservation for a week's time and has been talking of leaving sooner. Now, of course, he may not.'

'Will he try to change your mind?'

'Yes.'

'Because he needs you?'

'No. He doesn't need me. But he would hate to go back to Italy having lost his wife.'

'But you'll be firm?'

'Oh, I couldn't go back to him now. He'd get his revenge. Slowly.'

'You make him sound horrible.'

'No, just natural.'

'Are you fond of him at all?'

'Oh, Leo, don't torment me! Of course I am!'

'Sorry. Look, I'm sorry. Let's not talk about that. Let's talk about this place. Could you live here for a bit? While we look for something else?'

A test? No. He wouldn't see the place as she did. It was grimy – or seemed so, though perhaps it wasn't. Maybe it was just worn? The shag carpet was of a colour suitable to camouflage just about anything likely to be spilled on it. Walls and lights were dim; easy chairs looked like unevenly stuffed animals suffering from mange. Several objects had been haphazardly mended. She could tell from Leo's expression that, to him, the place was frugal but acceptable.

She wondered whether *she* could get a job? As what? Could

she hire out her housewife's skills? Cook for rich Hollywood people? She had known a French girl who had done that for some months. Her Italian law degree was useless in this country.

She hadn't answered his question and when she went to take a shower found it even harder to do. The bathroom was tacky; the shower didn't drain properly; the jet was weak; the towels flimsy. She tried not to see this shoddiness as emblematic of adultery's defining mess. Why wasn't Leo bothered? His training? His durable youthfulness? Though they were the same calendar age, he still had the tonic and thick-skinned resilience of youth. And then, seeing herself in his steamy mirror, she saw that she too looked young: flushed, plumped and buoyant. Thirty-six wasn't *old!* It wasn't old at all. It was her prime – too old for hesitation, though. For Leo and her it was now or never. She couldn't wait for Maurizio to be fledged. Sorry, darling, she thought, right now it's every woman for herself. Oh, Maurizio, will you be all right? Would he? There was certainly no room for him in this apartment.

'You're worrying about Maurizio.'

'How did you know?'

'I'm getting to know you. Would you like me to talk to him? Put our side of the story in case Marco tries turning him against you. I think he'd listen to me. We get along.'

Her mind swung away from Leo. 'I've got to get back,' she said nervously. 'They had a fight – Marco and Maurizio. It was rather awful. I haven't time to tell you now. Yes, perhaps you should talk to him. Later, when things have come out. Right now I'd better rush. It's after six.'

She was appalled at having left the house for so long – how many hours? Three? No, four. How could she have done it? – and yet she was planning to leave completely.

'Carla!' Leo was holding her. His embrace felt ghostly and irrelevant. 'Are you all right?' he worried. 'You look a little crazy. Are you afraid of Marco – being violent? Are you sure you should go home alone? Let me come with you.'

'*You!*' Her astonishment hurt him. She saw this happen. Suddenly, all over again, she felt old. What would Maurizio think? In his eyes, she was a dispenser of perfect meals, order personified, a matron beyond wantonness and metamorphoses. His fight with his father had been over Evie: a kind of love affair too. In what way was it different from hers? If he was too young, wasn't she perhaps past it? 'Oh God, Leo,' she groaned. 'I may waver. I warn you. You must bear with me.'

'Don't go back then. Stay here. A clean break.'

Could she? Should she? The prospect enticed her: an anarchic picnic. They could buy dinner at a delicatessen and bring it back to eat with more champagne. They could eat in bed, make love again, go dancing, spend a night together . . .

'I can't.'

'Why not? If you're leaving, leave now. Skip the recriminations and the scenes. What good do they do?'

'None. Some. It's because of Maurizio. Marco might take it out on him. They're in the middle of a fight. Leaving a family, Leo, is a lot less abstract than leaving the Church – oh, I didn't mean to be snide.'

'No,' he agreed. 'That's OK. It's probably true. All right. I won't hold it against you. Go home.' In his moment of acquiescence, he looked unfairly humble. 'You're free,' he told her.

She couldn't cope with freedom.

'I can't keep you by force.'

'Oh, you probably *should*!'

'It would solve nothing,' said Leo with a noble and – Carla felt – myopic lack of perception.

Unfair! Unfair! Driving her car too fast and dodging between lanes so as to catch green lights and beat their synchronized delay, she told herself that fifteen years with Marco had deformed her so that now she saw delicacy as weakness whereas, surely, it was strength? What was special about Leo *was* his delicacy. Driving up Sunset, she began to think about going back to him after all. Bargaining with chance, she decided to phone him if she saw a call box and, hopefully slowing, began to scrutinize the leafy dark. But the lawn-lapped family residences which stood sedately back from this part of the boulevard did not cater to dyadic conspirings. There were no public telephones.

Worries nagged at the running Maurizio. His breath was coming in gasps and a stitch in his side, forcing him to slow down, let his mind focus on the smell he'd caught on leaving the house. Smoke. Carlomagno *must* have knocked down the oil lamp, bludgeoning it with his unwieldy rudder of a tail. He was forever sweeping objects off low tables with that agitated, uncontrolled part of himself – and the oil would have spilled. There were dry piles of stuff next to it and the thin frame-house walls would flame like a box of matches. Black floaters danced before his eyes, reddened and signalled to him to go back and warn his father before he was roasted alive. Yet it seemed unlikely that his father would wait for this to happen and Maurizio, now a good mile from home, would never be able to run back at anything like the speed he'd come. Perhaps he should knock on some house door and ask to be let use the phone? It *was* an emergency – but they had noses, hadn't they, his father and Briggs? They'd surely have discovered the trouble by now. Briggs had been heading for the cellar, Carlomagno had been making a racket and Evie knew about the lamp.

Still running, Maurizio had a moment of feeling that he was running from his tamer self and forced the pace. *On*, he bullied himself hopefully. But his throat had begun to pain and his breath to fail and defects in his vision, tearing holes in the scene in front of him, made a new and threatening pattern: fire.

Would his father remember to turn on the sprinklers to save their own house? To damp down the garden and the roof? Sure he would. Sure. 'You're not the head of this house,' he'd told Maurizio this morning. '*I* am.' So let him act like it then! Let him take his chances! The ferocity of this thought curdled it. It was too real. Fires in Southern California could eat up a hillside in minutes. Better go back – if only for the dog. Suppose they didn't release the *dog*? Like a card-player's bluff, Maurizio's rage and desperation shrivelled before the precise likelihood of this. He was pausing, turning and catching his breath when a car drew up beside him.

'Maurizio!' It was his mother.

As he got in, a siren sounded and a fire-truck roared past them followed by a smaller, equally wailing car.

'It's the Briggs's house,' he told her and, surprisingly, she asked no questions but raced after the two red vehicles, ladybird, ladybird flying away home, in pursuit of the wavering bray of the warning signal: *aaahuh aaahuh*, like the distress cry of some wounded beast. *Aaahuh, aahuh!* He'd often lain in bed and heard this same sound swell and fade along the loops of Sunset: a warning prophecy now being fulfilled. The *dog*, he thought in panic, horrified by the reality of the fire-truck. Would they have thought to let him out? Would they be able or bother? Maurizio's father had planned on sending him to the pound and now maybe worse had overtaken him.

A smoke plume, queerly yellow and shaggy like the dog himself, was their first sight of the fire as they rounded the bend. Then they had to drive on past the truck to find parking space in the narrow Glen road. Maurizio vaulted out of the car before it came to a standstill, raced up the slope away from his mother and circled through a neighbour's yard to reach the Briggs's place before anyone could stop him. The air here stung and tingled and the scrub was scratchy and mobile like poised flocks of insects. Furry smoke fell on him and voices were yelling to come back down but meanwhile he had got to within yards of the Briggs's cellar door.

'The dog?' he screamed. 'Did anyone get the dog?'

The heat was burning his throat and he could see that the door, though charred, was unopened. He began to look for something with which to lunge at it, for sparks were falling and he guessed that the knob must be untouchable.

'Get that kid!'

'Hey, son, stand aside. Watch out for falling timber!'

And indeed there was a lurch from the side of the house and a piece of the roof seemed to detach itself and float outwards over his head, missing him by about a yard. Panicked, he began to lose track of where he was or which his direction ought to be for he had lurched foolishly about and the smoke was wound around him like a cloth. Stifling and swaddling, it seemed to knot itself around his head as he teetered through webs and thickets in what must be the right direction since it was downhill; then he stumbled, rolled and felt himself picked up in an agony of soreness and stunned choking. Lights flashed, possibly inside his own head, and his tongue seemed not to belong to him.

'Maurizio!'

'Maurizio!'

His parents' voices yelled his name in a shriek of horrified unison.

Chapter Nine

It was several days later.

Marco told Carla that it was time they had a serious talk with neutral parties present. Not lawyers. Nothing so formal. Just a couple of friends. With this in mind, he had invited Sybil and Terry Steele to drop in for a drink. Soon. In an hour's time to be precise. He hoped Carla wasn't thinking of going out.

'You see,' he said reasonably, 'neither you nor I is in our right mind. We've got no real friends here either. This is a couple who know us – not well, but well enough. I've asked them to come and hold the fort between us. The least you can do is to play along.'

'I think it's ridiculous.'

'It may keep us from fighting or breaking down. Some things have to be said, Carla.'

'What?'

'I'll speak when they're here. I need a formal atmosphere.'

'Am I on trial?'

'Now don't *you* be ridiculous!'

Maurizio was in the UCLA hospital being treated for burns and suffering from shock. His parents had spent the better half of the last few days either visiting him or hanging round waiting to talk to doctors. In between, they had eaten meals in dark restaurants of the sort which serve food at all hours and keep up a fiction that day is night. This added to their disorientation and they conversed like relatives who have scarcely met in years.

'He'll be all right,' they agreed, repeating this vague comfort like a condolence.

'Physically anyway.'

'Yes.'

There had been a brief fear lest Maurizio need plastic surgery. In this world capital of the delicate medical art, a new, identical face could easily be supplied. Fortunately, it now seemed that it need not be. A tiny graft might be necessary, perhaps not even that. Physically, the boy was resilient.

'Oh, mentally too. The young snap out of things.'

'Yes.'

The dog had died and the Briggs's house was a cinder. The family were on their way back to Kansas. Marco had paid Briggs a thousand dollars in exchange for a letter to the effect that this was a gift and Briggs had no legal claim on him. Giving the money without such a quid pro quo would have been dangerous, Marco explained. A man like that would see the situation as one to exploit. Giving more would have the same effect.

'You're in a litigious frame of mind,' Carla noted. 'I doubt if that letter has any legal validity. Still,' she decided, 'the Briggs can use the money. Funny your giving it to them though! A cautious, small-town reaction, don't you think? The sort of impulse you hate in me.'

'Oh,' said Marco. 'It's often myself I see in you. Didn't you know?'

Briggs, he told her, had actually rendered him a service for which he deserved payment. 'Here,' he handed Carla three sheets of paper. 'It's perhaps just as well that you take a look at these before the Steeles come. No need to hang all our dirty linen out in public perhaps?'

'What are they?'

'Read them.'

She did. They were photocopies of letters. *Dear Mr Briggs,* she read. *Do not be surprised to get a letter from a secret friend.*

214

Maurizio's letter. On the same long, legal-sized sheet of paper was a copy of the one from his diary addressed to Cazz: *Listen Mister* ... The other two pages were copies of letters sent to Marco. Obviously, *he* had been poking among Maurizio's things. Among hers too? Well there wasn't much he'd find there. Poor Marco!

He was watching her. 'Read them.'

'I know them – well these two.'

Marco had embarked on a harangue. His mouth was an upside-down crescent, showing only his bottom teeth. 'The boy,' he told her, 'was under acute pressure, neglected by you who, apparently, didn't know what was happening or were too busy with your love affair to care. No.' Marco raised a quenching hand. 'Don't let's start arguing. I just want you to know that on the basis of these letters I have decided that you are quite simply incapable of looking after Maurizio by yourself. So would any legal authority to whom appeal might be made. That's why I'm keeping the originals. You may take the copies. Here. Take them. Get a lawyer's opinion if you choose.' His face was knotted, careful, choleric: just like his son, she saw. Just like Maurizio. 'I am hoping,' said Marco, 'that it won't come to that. I have a proposal to make when the Steeles come, which I hope you may accept. It's a friendly and I think a generous one. You see I want us to stay together. I'm not an unreasonable man – as I think you know. But I want you to be aware of the alternative. If you leave me, Carla, I shall take Maurizio. You will have limited access to him and I shall be obliged to send him to a boarding-school since it is clear that he and I are liable to get dangerously on each other's nerves. I consider that he ought to go to the toughest school available – preferably a military or military-type academy. He's out of control. He'll have to be brought back to reality and discipline before it's too late. Socialized. Naturally, *if* you were on hand, or if I were to know that you were going to be so within a reasonable length of time, we might manage to keep him at home.'

'Blackmail?'

'Not in my view. I have,' said Marco, 'put up with a lot. I am prepared to put up with more – but I won't compromise where Maurizio is concerned. I'm thinking of *him*. He's my only son.

215

He means a lot to me. You can't claim to have been successful lately as a mother, can you?'

The phone rang. Neither of them moved.

Marco waved his hand with a small but ironic movement. 'Surely for you?'

'It might be the hospital.'

'Answer it then.'

She did. It was Leo.

'Carla, is this a bad time?'

'Yes.'

'Well, wait, *please*, I've been out of my mind not hearing anything ... can you just tell me are you all right?'

'Yes.'

'And Maurizio?'

'He's at UCLA Hospital. He's in shock. We think it's mild.'

'I'll ring them then. Just tell me about you. Can't we talk?'

'No.'

'I love you, Carla. Do you keep remembering that?'

'Yes.'

'Do you love me?'

'Yes.'

'That's all right then. Try to phone me later, will you? Must I ring off?'

'Yes.'

She put down the receiver.

Marco smiled. 'I'm not jealous, you know, Carla. You don't have to make up a lie. That was Leo, wasn't it? Father Hausermann?'

'Which Steele did you talk to,' she asked, 'when you were inviting them?'

'Sybil.'

'And she told you ...'

'About your priest? Yes. I tricked her into thinking I knew. Apparently he's blabbed his business around his old parish or else his pastor has. Anyway she knew.'

'Oh she'd have guessed,' said Carla. 'Once she heard he was leaving she'd put one and one together.'

216

'You mean *she* was in love with him?' Marco was quick about things like that. 'The guy gets around.'

'She was but it was unreciprocated. Terry knew. You see, Marco, they're not neutral or disinterested parties.'

'Well, it's too late to put them off.' Marco looked at his watch. 'They'll be here any minute. Anyway, they chose to come.'

'Odd?'

'Yes, actually.'

The two felt drawn together by the mistake, the absurdity, their role as hosts. Marco took and squeezed her hand.

'Carla.'

'Mmm?'

'Nothing.'

'Maybe,' she suggested flippantly, 'the Steeles will break down and fight and you and I can hold the fort?'

They laughed. It was a release, a bark of sad hilarity, a way of breaking the tension of several days and it got briefly out of control. The Steeles, however, could not know this and when Marco opened the door to them – they'd had to ring the bell twice – they looked faintly offended at the sight of their mirthful hosts.

'Have you two been reconciled?' Terry Steele was preparing to look jovial.

'How's Maurizio?' asked Sybil.

'Come in,' sputtered Marco, wiping his eyes. 'It was ...' But he couldn't tell the Steeles at what Carla and he had been laughing, so he said, 'No reconciliation. It's therapy. You laugh so as not to cry.'

Terry Steele marched into the hall. 'Well, the fire didn't affect you,' he remarked. 'I noticed a bit of discolouration on your end gable, some scorched shrubs. You got off lightly. Apart from Maurizio, of course. Hope he's on the mend. Got good news of him, have you? Therapy?' he queried. 'Something new? What's its name? I might use it on my programme.'

'Folk wisdom,' Marco told him.

Terry, dressed perhaps for this mission of mercy, looked priestly. He wore a black turtle-neck sweater of the sort priests had started wearing a decade and a half earlier when they first began to move, crabwise, towards dressing in civvies. Over this he had a charcoal Harris-tweed jacket. Sybil, looking too well turned-out for him, wore a tailored, long-sleeved, visibly 'good' and status-affirming dress. She had lost weight.

'Carla,' she drew Carla into a corner and applied two fragrant, powdery cheeks to hers. 'I've been so worried about you. You know, now, in retrospect,' she murmured, 'I realize that Leo was a flirt. I didn't see it at the time but, in the light of what's happened, there's no doubting it: he led *me* on. After all, I was a settled, sensible woman and so were you. Neither of us would have made advances ourselves. Neither of us would have even thought of the possibility. Not without encouragement.' She paused expectantly.

'I suppose not.'

'Of *course* not! These restless clerics are a menace. They've had no adolescence. They try out their charms. It's a learning process: a natural urge. They have to play around and I suppose one should be indulgent. Well, perhaps both you and I were too indulgent for our own good – but no harm done if things stop in time.' Sybil paused again. 'Has he ...' She drew a quick little breath. 'Has he asked you to marry him?'

'Yes.'

A tremor flicked across Sybil's face. 'Do you know the failure rate in ex-priests' marriages?' she asked. 'It's high. Terry will know the figures.' She turned to attract her husband's attention.

'Don't.' Carla put a hand on Sybil's knee. 'Please. Can we drop the subject?'

'But I thought we'd come to talk about it? That you'd agreed?'

'I didn't. Marco didn't tell me until just now – and *he* didn't know about you and Leo.'

Sybil blushed. 'But that's why I feel so responsible. Why *we* can surely talk frankly – though the thing was very different in my case.'

'Yes.'

'Does Marco know about ... Leo and me now? Did you tell him?'

'Yes.'

'That,' said Sybil with the intuition of bruised pride, 'was what you two were laughing at?'

'No.'

Sybil knew though, but was generous. 'Are you in love with him then?' she commiserated. 'I can see you are. Listen, one does get over it. You remember how I was? I lived two years of hell – all my own making or almost. It's the ambiguity that keeps one dangling – the ambiguity of their situation. And, of course, one can't foreclose on any offer they may make. Supposing Leo ever wanted to go back? You wouldn't want to be an obstacle to that, would you?' Sybil clasped and unclasped her fingers. At the other end of the room, Marco was pouring drinks for himself and Terry Steele. He made no move to offer any to the women. Probably Sybil had agreed to 'have a talk' with Carla. Terry and Marco were facing away from them and apparently chatting intently.

' "They?" ' marvelled Carla in spite of herself – she had not meant to encourage Sybil. 'You say "they" as though they were an alien species.'

'But they *are!*' affirmed Sybil. She sat down on a window-seat. Behind her head Carla could see the part of the hill where the fire had stripped foliage off trees and shrubs. Truncated, whittled forms were blackly angular against the sky. 'They *are!*' Sybil repeated. 'They're like vagrants or the disabled. One's imagination is confused by pity. It's a typical romantic reversal – one ends by thinking that what is loathed is loved. And of course they're *intense*,' she said breathily, 'and *that* ignites sympathy. So does their neediness. But there lies danger. Well-balanced people tend to be integrated into society via our basic social unit: the couple. Terry and I are preparing a series on this for his new station. Had you heard that he's quitting his present job? He is. The sponsors were too commercial and this new project will leave him more scope. He'll be working for an outfit funded by religious organizations and I'm to be his partner: a normal married couple. That's who people want to hear from. Outsiders mostly want in, you know, Carla. Lone people in singles' clubs are Eleanor Rigbys. Priests too. They're going through a very unstable time. Terry's planning a series on celibates and you'd be surprised at what he's turning up. Even within the Church the laity is demonstrably a steadier body of people and should have more control.'

'Are you collecting data? I mean here and now?'

'Carla, you mustn't be bitter. I'm on your side! How could I not be? Remember the state *I* was in?' Sybil's shudder was convincing. For a moment she had the frank but edited look of people who recount harrowing personal experiences on other people's TV shows. Then she recovered control 'Listen,' she said briskly, 'I was temporarily insane; now I'm restored. I'd like to help you, Carla. Sincerely.'

'You don't think that the heart has a sanity of its own? You did,' Carla said brutally, 'think Leo worth loving.'

Sybil's features suffered a barely perceptible spasm. Shadows from the blackened landscape outside gathered in the hollows of her face. As if aware of this, she lifted it abruptly, tilting them out, and smiled.

'I'm not denying that,' she said. 'That's the trouble. I think he's a marvellous person but more complex than you're allowing for. I imagine you've discounted – or just not thought about – the spiritual dimension which was primary in his life until recently? I'm guessing this because you seem to be thinking of marrying him. I suppose *he* has encouraged you to discount it – that he seems to himself. Well, don't you think this odd?'

'Odd?'

'Isn't it possible – forgive me if this upsets you – that he chose someone like you rather than someone like me precisely because you're unconcerned by this dimension? Lots of priests have left the Church and married nuns who left it to marry *them*. Or they've married active members of their parish: women who shared their scruples and with whom they could proceed to slowly resolve and come to terms with their changing beliefs. Leo, instead, has jumped in the deep end: he has proposed marriage to you, a married woman and an atheist, who probably incarnates for him values which are the exact opposite of the ones he's lived by till now. You represent marriage more than a young girl would because you're already married and very … well, domestic. And your lack of religion means that he can forget about it too – for a while. But don't you see, Carla, that it will be a time-bomb in your life together if you marry him.'

'I'm not Mephistopheles. He still practises his religion.'

'But you never *talk* about it, do you?'

'Sometimes. We don't ban it. We don't have regular *discussions* about it, no.'

'Well, a man who's changed his life so radically *should* be having discussions.'

'Maybe he's already had them? You said, after all, that *you* sensed something in him which encouraged you to think he might be available.' Carla felt she had scored a rather neat point. However, it was difficult to resent Sybil's intrusiveness, given what she had done to Sybil – what *had* she done? 'I didn't take him from you,' she reminded them both.

'No,' Sybil acknowledged. 'No, you didn't. Perhaps I, though, in my foolishness, gave you the idea that he might *be* taken.'

'What's so sinister about Leo's choosing me rather than a Catholic? You're implying something which I don't get?'

'Just that a man who leaps in one direction can as easily leap back. Obviously,' Sybil smiled and flung out her hands, 'you can suspect my motives in saying this. Jealousy, you may think. Sour grapes. Maybe you'd be right? How can *I* tell? Even if those were my motives, what I say could be true. Listen: I believe that most of life boils down to a struggle between individual appetites, like yours and mine and Leo's, and the voice of the group whose interests are to preserve order. Leo, at this moment, is an undomiciled refugee from one order who's out to get himself a niche in another.'

'By taking Marco's place?'

'Yes.'

'But if he gets it, if I marry him, then you'll have to accept him. He'll be part of a couple: your basic social unit.'

'The question,' said Sybil, 'is will he accept himself.'

'Well, only he can decide that.'

'Yes.'

'And if there were no doubtful shifts and struggles there would be no need for radio programmes like yours and Terry's. You'd be out of a job. There would just be a heap of stones and a law saying something like "stone all adulterers".'

'Whereas now I get my therapy by advising you?'

'*And* your living! You do all right, Sybil.'

Sybil laughed. She had a wry, ravaged, clever laugh. Lipstick

221

traced the contours of her mouth but had disappeared in the middle. Vivid in vertical, chapped cracks, its surface had been sucked or perhaps bitten. 'Oh,' she agreed, 'we recycle ourselves as best we can. Some centuries ago, you and I, at our age, would, on average, be dead. We'd have married at sixteen, had a child a year, and died of the strain. In a way I *am* a bit dead. I'm numb from my non-experience with Leo. But I'm being as honest with you as I know how to be. I think you'll get a lot more hurt if you marry him.'

'OK,' said Carla. 'I believe you – at least I believe you believe what you say.'

'In that case,' said Sybil, 'it's Marco's turn. He has an offer to make to you.' She turned to the men. 'Marco,' she called.

He twitched, Carla thought, like a gun dog called to attention. Clearly, the men's chat had been a putting in of time like that of walk-on actors in a play. Attendant lords. 'Rhubarb, rhubarb,' they had perhaps been murmuring while waiting for Sybil to prepare the terrain. *Her* revelation of her depression had, Carla felt, made a counter-plea which was more affecting than her official one. Did she realize this? Probably not.

Marco sat boyishly, straddling a chair with its back between his knees and his chin resting on its top rail. This gave him the youthful, vulnerable look of a child in a playpen. This was Marco the Good. His smile was self-deprecating. He ran fingers through his hair. He was wistful and gentle and the Steeles were one hundred per cent on his side.

He thanked them for having come. Then he talked of illusions while staring at a stain on the floor. His voice shook as he remarked that there was no arguing with someone in their grip and that he wasn't using the word to put Carla down but as an old hand who had himself, once too often perhaps, sailed the seas of fantasy, though always returning like Ulysses to his Penelope. It was a shock, said Marco, to find that Penelope had herself heeded a siren voice – because *she* was without immunities, defenceless. Her virtue would be her undoing. She had no cynicism, no realism and neither, from what he'd gathered from Sybil, had this priest. The thought of two such innocents

222

taking off together made one think of the Jumblies putting to sea in a sieve.

Rhubarb, thought Carla angrily, but forced herself to sit and listen. Marco had a right to that. Guilt flooded her and they might have got to her by appealing to *it*. Directly. But Marco spoke only of 'this priest' who might be beset with nostalgia for his function and of Carla as though she were an invalid. It was clear that he and Sybil had had a long talk. Terry Steele said nothing at all. Uncharacteristically silent, he was perhaps taking mental notes like a Clerk of the Court?

'My proposal,' said Marco, 'is that Carla stay here until the end of the summer. I shall continue to support her and what she does meanwhile will be no concern of mine. I want her to take the time to think and make up her mind whether to stay married to me or not. If she chooses to stay with me – as I hope she will – I shall expect her to be in Italy by the end of August. That's five months from now. If she comes we'll say nothing of the past. We all have pasts.' Marco tilted his profile winsomely. He was wooing her and because he was, shame brimmed in her and she was denied the outlet of anger. Her throat ached; her body felt alien and metallic; she had a stiffness in her palate. 'I don't know,' said Marco in controlled and level tones, 'whether we were happily married.' The back of his chair was turning into some sort of official and ceremonial barrier: a bit of courtroom bric-à-brac. His voice hardened. 'Or whether we can expect to be in the future. I'm hot-tempered. I've had money worries. Carla has never concerned herself with these or with the under-pinning of our lives, and it's not cooking, whatever she may think, that keeps the roof over your head. I've been inviting her into the twentieth century for some time. Maybe this new venture will do the trick? Another man? Putting her best foot foremost? It may work. Sex. Novelty. The chance to be a new person. I know the lure. How can I pretend to be shocked? I think . . .'

She didn't hear what he thought. Tears had finally come. Like a thaw, they softened the ramrod inside her; the effort to contain herself collapsed and she gave in with relief to the needs of the body whose hot requirements had got her into this trouble to start with.

223

Her breakdown dissolved the meeting. The Steeles left. Marco poured her a drink and lit a lamp. Standing over it, his face revealed him to her afresh or for the first time. His looks had the virtues of his faults. Drama darkened the scoops of his face. From letting emotion rip – often at her expense – he had developed features as capable of registering the most frantic hurt as a fine, dignified hauteur.

'Do you accept my proposal?'

'Yes.'

'Good. Maurizio is to come to Italy as soon as he can be moved. Paola will look after him.'

'All right.'

'I'll leave tomorrow then.'

'OK.'

It was late June.

Maurizio had been in Italy for two months, Marco for three, and Leo and Carla had been seeing each other daily. They did not live together although he spent most of his nights in the Glen, where a tender new growth had covered all traces of the fire. The shell of the Briggs's house had been removed and the sloping gardens were so vivid with tapestries of coloured birds that the eye searched hopefully for further fabulous incarnations, such as a risen Carlomagno frolicking, live as Lazarus, on freshly sprinkled grass.

They mentioned him sometimes. He was an innocent emissary from a past otherwise best avoided. Planning too was put off. Leo was chary of upsetting Carla, who had been shaken by the events of March: the fire, the dog's death and Maurizio's subsequent depression. In the weeks before his departure, she had had to cope with a lot of tantrums. Now Leo refrained from trying to tie her down or formulating any but the most immediate arrangements. They lived for the day, taking the occasional convalescent jaunt. They'd been to Death Valley to see the desert flower and to Santa Barbara and Ojai and had stayed in Jane's cabin in the Sierras.

Airmail letters bordered in red and green continued to arrive. The ones with a Viareggio postmark were from Maurizio who had probably been chivvied into writing them. They were like letters from a withdrawn, more polite, but much younger child. Marco's were brief and dealt exclusively with money. Paola's were bewildered and restrained.

'Did you find a tenant for the house?' Leo asked lazily. They had been on the beach since morning and were about to leave. Both were the colour of cinnamon.

'Yes,' said Carla and remembered that this meant she would have to phone Marco. The idea panicked her. Hearing his voice. The tenant was a precipitant, the telephone a spy. She nuzzled her face into towel-covered sand. 'Everything's gritty!' she complained.

'Ask him how the divorce proceedings are going,' said Leo, mind-reading. No. If he'd been mind-reading, he'd have known that she and Marco hadn't started divorce proceedings. She hadn't *said* they had either – but what else could Leo suppose? She hadn't told him of Marco's offer, hadn't wanted to discuss the future with him at all.

Her mouth was salty. They had been drinking margaritas from a thermos and licking salt from off each other's skin.

'Ought we to be going?'

'Yes.'

Leo, who had an exam coming up, was planning to spend the evening in his small rabbit-hutch of an apartment preparing for it. Carla, alone in the Glen, would feel her dependence on him more than when he was there. For whom but Leo was she in this town, country or continent? Supposed, by the terms of Marco's pact, to have been thinking, she hadn't thought. Idleness drugged her. She was poised in a trance. When Leo wasn't with her, she kept the radio on and listened to motor shows, money pundits and sports commentaries by enthusiasts whose excitement channelled off her own. A listener-sponsored station had set aside a whole week for begging and she listened for an hour at a time to rhetoric stuck on the groove of a single theme: need. 'We need money. If you're listening then you need us. Send the money and we'll survive. You know you need us and we need you, so ...' It was like a lover's plea – lunatic, repetitive, voluntarily oblivious of every reality outside that imagined symbiosis. It mocked and relieved the itch in her own head.

Marco, by letting her off the hook of immediate decision, had turned her affair with Leo into something provisional and carnal. By setting her free, he had deprived her of her function. Not a wife, not a mother, who was she? From a distance, he magnetized her mind.

'Ask him when the divorce will be final,' said Leo.

How had she got into this morass? Had she actually lied to him? She raised the thermos and poured out the last drops of cocktail. 'Want it?'

'No. I've got to work.'

'I'll ring you this evening,' she said. 'We'll talk.'

Back in the Glen, the sun had gone down and its afterlight, trapped in fleshy foliage, webbed the place in dim reflections. Cazz and Jane were drinking on their terrace under a large, multi-coloured sunshade.

'Come and join us,' Jane shouted.

'Thanks, no. I've got to phone Italy. It's getting late over there.'

Four o'clock here, she calculated, climbing her steps with the basket of beach things. Midnight there. Marco would be home from wherever he'd dined. She imagined cooling streets dampened by the water truck, stacked chairs, a smell of dusty potted bay and privet hedges expanding in this moment of freshness, the subdued slither of late traffic, the painted faces of streetwalkers.

The bedroom telephone was smooth under her hand and streamlined as a snake. Dangerous instrument of knowledge. She couldn't talk about the tenant, then just put down the phone. Marco would expect – rightly – some indication of which way she was preparing to move. He had given her till August, but surely she wasn't going to wait until the last day to make up her mind?

Quickly, as though the thing might bite, she put the receiver down.

Then, slowly, she picked it up again.

'Leo.'

'Hullo.'

'Working?'

'Unh.'

226

'I just wanted to hear your voice.'

'That's OK. We can talk a bit.'

'Listen,' she said in a rush and must have squirmed, for sand fell from under her clothes, 'I'm not divorcing Marco. I'm going back to him. I wasn't sure before so I didn't – couldn't let you know.'

There was a silence on the phone.

'Leo?'

'I heard. Have you told *him*?'

'No. I had to tell you first.'

'But you mean it? You're sure?'

'Would you rather we talked some other time – after your exam?'

'No. Tell me now. Get it over with. What decided you? I guess I should have guessed. There was something ...' His voice trailed off. 'Feverish. Recently. I kept thinking it was because of the past: old things, Maurizio, remorse and stuff. But I knew things weren't right.

'Will you be all right? Your exam? Maybe I should have waited?'

'I'm very controlled. I'll manage. Just tell me whether this is final. I can't take any more changes.'

'It is.'

'Oh God, Carla ... I'm not going to argue. By now you must know what you want. Obviously, I didn't measure up. In some way.' There was a proud, hurt, implicit question.

'It's not that,' she tried to reassure him. 'Leo, I'll miss you dreadfully. I'll miss – I'll have killed – a whole part of me that only came alive with you.'

'So *why*?' It was a croak, a groan, a deep, animal emission of distress.

'Oh Leo, I haven't reached the why. I've told you too soon perhaps? Before I've worked things out. I just *know* – I've been waiting to know instinctively, in an intuitive way, the way things come to one, to *me*, first. And now I do. But only in that way.' Outside her window, the Glen greenery had turned grey. Cazz and Jane's terrace floated above it like a boat. They had lit a Mexican lantern which Jane had bought in Olvera street. They were getting on well together recently, were very close.

227

'Try,' Leo commanded. 'Find out. Maybe you're mistaken?'

'No.'

'Well then, off the top of your head: what are the reasons?'

'That you don't need me.'

'I *do*.'

'No. You're self-sufficient. I don't think you need anyone really. You enjoy me and I enjoy you. You're marvellous to be *with* but that's not the same thing. I think you've probably never got close enough to anyone to need them and so you won't know what I'm talking about – but I promise you, you're very remote. If you'd needed me you'd have been less forbearing. You'd have pressured me.'

'Like Marco? But Carla ...'

'I know. I *know*. You were being sensitive – but, Leo, you're sensitive because you don't really care. It's your religious training, I suppose. I'm not being critical, but you wanted to know and maybe, now that I think of it, I should get to the reasons if only so that you won't think me a heartless bitch. I'm not, Leo, really, I'm not. I've been puzzled by you. I've been waiting, staying very quiet like an animal on the watch, for you to get close to me, to show yourself a bit – and you never did. You probably can't. You can't help it. You're invulnerable, strong, fenced in. You believing Christians have an enormous ego, massive pride. I imagine it comes from the notion that your first duty is to save your own soul – that's breathtaking egoism, after all, and yet you learn it as a duty, a maxim and foundation-stone to your moral system. As I say, there's a paradox, because your invulnerability makes you able to appear passive and humble and forbearing – and all the time, inside, you're utterly sure of yourselves.'

'Is that so bad?'

'It's probably very good for the thing you were trained for – getting on with a parishful of people, easing your way to power. It's no good at all for a relationship with one person. You never get close.'

'What do you mean by "close". Tell me. I'll learn.'

'Oh, Leo ...' She laughed, sighed, stopped herself from wanting to cry. 'I feel idiotic saying all this.'

'Say it.'

'Look, there isn't a manual on "How to Get Close" – oh, maybe Terry Steele has one. I don't know. Here in California ... But, look, another man would have started raging at me and you say "Tell me. I'll learn".'

'I will. I want to.'

'Well, we've never had a fight. I've provoked you and you never rise – I know, you'll say you didn't want to fight. You wanted to learn what I wanted and give it to me – but giving doesn't bring people close. Fighting and wounding are what do.' Carla was thinking of Maurizio's angry, puffy, childish lips and adult eyes which had turned fiercely from her when they'd said good-bye at the airport. Close? Distant? She dreamed of him almost every night. 'You know,' she remembered, 'the way children sometimes scratch their arms to make them bleed then mingle their blood as a pact of friendship? That's the thing that happens in fighting and mutual wounding. A flowing together takes place. It's not just rational. It's more intimate, almost tangible. I can't explain it in words. Lots of life evades words, Leo, but you live by them.'

'Christians understand wounds – they're the symbol of salvation ...'

'Christ's wounds? I know. You take day-to-day realities and blow them up into myths and think so big that you can't see small things any more. But life is made up of small things, Leo. I suppose in the light of eternity they look trivial, but ...'

'I'm not living by the light of eternity – not with you.' Leo's voice was angrier than she'd ever heard it. 'Look, to hell with my exam, I'm coming round right now to talk some sense to you and ...'

'I'm sorry.' She was shocked at herself. 'I've ruined your working evening.'

'You have. I'm coming round to have a fight with you.'

'Oh, Leo,' she was caught between tears and laughter. 'It's too *late*.'

'I'm coming.'

'Leo, what difference would it make? We'd make love – and then what? You're my lover. I need a husband. I'm an ordinary, secular person. I like keeping things together – we have to do that, you know, those of us who believe only in the temporal world. We have to make the best of it and do the best for it. That's *our* morality and I've been ratting on it, thinking I'd find a new reality with you. I haven't. Maybe it's not your fault but mine? Maybe the only reality I can have is my family? I want to go back and prop it up – Marco and Paola and the others. I want to make pasta and give dinner parties and contribute to order. You're a wrecker, Leo. You left your parish and you'd probably end by leaving me. Why not? You've got all eternity to think about. This world is Plato's cave to you – you juggle shadows. I juggle realities. I've only got now. It makes a difference. I didn't think it did, but it does. I'd end by driving you mad and making you leave me because you bring out the worst in me. You said I was feverish, well . . .'

'Why are you suddenly saying all this?'

'Any first time is sudden. I've been suppressing it.'

'I'm going to hang up and come.'

'Don't. I'm going to phone Marco. Then it will be too late.'

'I'm coming,' said Leo and hung up.

Carla too hung up and gave a horrified little laugh. He was programmed, she thought. She'd pressed the 'fight' button and now he'd come round in a fighting mood ready to simulate humanity. Poor, lovable Leo! He could do anything. He just never knew when to do it. Had no instinct. They'd trained it out of him. Sadly, she picked up the receiver and dialled zero.

'Hullo, operator?' She gave Marco's number and waited. It would be the small hours in Italy now and he would be cantankerous at being woken up. Her pulse quickened. Had Marco, her old intimate, foreseen all this? A Lucifer whose instrument was the snaky telephone in her hand, he had left his familiar behind in this pretty Eden to work for him. She cupped it to her ear and heard, harsh and imperious and vigorous as a dog-trainer's bark, the familiar voice shout: '*Pronto? Pronto. Pronto – Carla?*'

93 94 95
|| || |

NO RENEWALS!

PLEASE RETURN BOOK AND REQUEST
AGAIN.